PRAISE FOR THE MACE BAUER MYSTERY SERIES

Mama Does Time

"Who knew that a who-dun-it would not only keep you guessing—but have you laughing! Deborah Sharp is the new Edna Buchanan."   —Hoda Kotb, NBC's *Today* show co-anchor

"Native Floridian Deborah Sharp's acute comic timing and detailed perceptions of old Florida sparkle in her lively debut . . . highly entertaining."   —Oline H. Cogdill,
South Florida Sun-Sentinel

"[A] humorous, touching reflection on familial love and politics."
—*Mystery Scene*

"A fast-paced start to a new series with fun characters."
—MysteryReader.com

"With a strong, funny heroine, colorful characters, and a look at a part of Florida the tourists rarely see, Deborah Sharp has an engaging new series."   —Elaine Viets, author of *Clubbed to Death*, a Dead-End Job Mystery

"*Mama Does Time* has it all—murder, mystery and a brand-new take on Florida's particular version of mayhem."
—Bob Morris, fourth-generation Floridian and Edgar-nominated author of the Zack Chasteen Mystery series

Mama Rides Shotgun

"An amusingly wild ride through parts of Florida tourists rarely visit."   —*Kirkus Reviews*

"[Sharp's] descriptions of a part of Florida most of us know little about add to the appeal of this entertaining mystery."   —*Booklist*

"Sharp delivers a wide swath of humor and a keen sense of Florida's history and present."   —Oline H. Cogdill,
South Florida Sun-Sentinel

MAMA gets TRASHED

A Mace Bauer
MYSTERY

MAMA gets TRASHED

Deborah Sharp

MIDNIGHT INK
WOODBURY, MINNESOTA

FIRST EDITION
First Printing, 2013

Book design and format by Donna Burch
Cover design by Lisa Novak
Cover illustration by Gail Armstrong/Illustration Ltd.
Editing by Connie Hill

Midnight Ink, an imprint of Llewellyn Worldwide Ltd.

Library of Congress Cataloging-in-Publication Data

Sharp, Deborah, 1954–
  Mama gets trashed : a Mace Bauer mystery / by Deborah Sharp. — First Edition.
      pages   cm   (A Mace Bauer mystery; #5)
   ISBN 978-0-7387-3615-0
1. Bauer, Mace (Fictitious character)—Fiction. 2. Mothers and daughters—Fiction. 3. Florida—Fiction. I. Title.
   PS3619.H35645M366 2013
   813'.6—dc23   2013012989

Midnight Ink
Llewellyn Worldwide Ltd.
2143 Wooddale Drive
Woodbury, MN 55125-2989
www.midnightinkbooks.com

Printed in the United States of America

9484

DEDICATION

With love to Kathleen Robelen—
my sweet, Southern, second mama

ACKNOWLEDGMENTS

I owe a huge debt to my readers, especially those who've stayed with the Mace Bauer Mysteries from the start. No one can predict where life will lead. You've made this part of the journey a total blast. Special thanks to Elaine Naiman, whose charitable donation earned her a character name; and to the Alabama ladies of the Mama Posse: Dab, Muffin, Beth, and Lucie. Y'all know what you did!

As with all my books, I had help from myriad sources. Early readers of *Mama Gets Trashed* included Karen Feldman, Victoria Allman, and my fabulous sister, Charlene Bogolub. My agent, Whitney Lee, also applied her talents to improving the manuscript. I'm grateful for all their suggestions.

Paul Laska, a law enforcement consultant, offered advice on bombs and explosions. Several sources helped me understand the ins and outs of garbage trucks. Vince Ruano, the former city manager of Bushnell, Florida, spent some time with me on the phone. David Peters and Jeff Coleman, of the Stuart, Florida, public works department, gave me an up-close gander. Any errors are mine, and should not reflect on their expertise or knowledge.

I'm grateful to my editor, Terri Bischoff, and the talented staff at Midnight Ink. Lisa Novak designs great covers; Connie Hill edits like a dream; Bethany Onsgard helps spread the word. Thanks also to Alisha Bjorklund, for making "Trashed" sound enticing.

The world's greatest husband, Kerry Sanders, and the world's greatest mama, Marion Sharp, have my eternal gratitude for their love and inspiration. And Okeechobee, Florida, the real-life model for fictional Himmarshee, always holds a special place in my heart.

Finally, I'm indebted to book-sellers and librarians, who do so much for readers and for authors like me. Where would I be without you?

ONE

I TOED ASIDE A pink take-out bag from the Pork Pit. Barbecue sauce stained the cuff on my jeans. A soggy onion ring clung like a barnacle to the leather laces of my work boots. Flies buzzed. Mountains of household trash rose around me. Brushing at a sweat droplet that rolled from my forehead down my nose, I glared at Mama.

How had I let her drag me along on this search expedition to the Himmarshee dump on the hottest day of the year?

"Tell me again how you tossed out your wedding ring with the garbage?"

"I already explained all that, Mace. It was an accident."

She sounded more annoyed at me than she had a right to, since I was the one doing most of the looking under a scorching sun. She stood in the shade cast by my Jeep, fanning herself with a paper cutout of a largemouth bass, a freebie from Gotcha Bait & Tackle near Lake Okeechobee.

"In other words," I said, "you were careless because you were trashed."

"Trashed?"

"Right. Tipsy. Blotto. Drunk."

Mama pulled herself up to her full height of 4 foot 11 inches, smoothed her perfectly coiffed platinum hair, and regarded me regally. Well, as regal as someone standing in a pile of moldy cantaloupe rinds and coffee grounds can be. "I was not drunk. I'd only had a tiny glass of pink wine. Barely a thimble-full, really."

I stepped on a squishy disposable diaper. Used, of course. A rat ran over the toe of my boot. I decided to continue our discussion, but keep my eyes on the ground.

"That's not what Marty said. She said you just about finished the whole fiesta-sized box yourself. You barely left her enough wine for half a glass."

"Marty's wrong."

"Right. My trustworthy little sister is a liar."

"She's not lying; exaggerating, maybe. Anyhoo, I'd taken off my ring to scour the stovetop. I must have swept it off the counter into the trashcan with the used paper towels. We'll never have to worry about the same thing happening with that new ring of yours, since you never scour anything."

I took pity on her and didn't press it, figuring she felt bad enough about losing the enormous diamond wedding ring Husband No. 5 had recently given her. Amazingly, Salvatore "Big Sal" Provenza from Da Bronx was turning into a keeper. No such luck, apparently, with his ring. I kept quiet, working my way through another pile of rubbish. The silence stretched out, without Mama saying a word either. That was unusual enough that it made me look up to check on her.

She was tapping away at her smart phone. I heard the whoosh sound, signaling she'd just sent a message.

"You've gotta be kidding me!"

"What?" She raised her face from the phone, all blue-eyed innocence.

"Is my busting my sweaty butt to help you find your stupid ring keeping you from some more important business on that telephone?"

"Oh, this?" She lifted the small electronic beast in her hand. "I was returning an email from your sister Maddie. She's in crisis."

Mama closed the gap between us, and shoved the phone toward me. "Look at this picture. See the yellow dress? That's what she's supposed to wear to Kenny's party next week. You know I absolutely cannot let Maddie wear that dress, Mace."

"Why? Is it against the law to wear yellow for your husband's forty-fifth birthday?"

"Don't sass me, girl. You're not too old for me to grab a switch." She leveled a look that could still scare me a bit, even though I'm thirty-four years old and tower over her by almost a foot. "Yellow turns Maddie's skin tone as green as my wrist got after Husband No. 3 bought me that watch from the man with the card table in New York City."

I shielded the phone's screen from the sun and examined the dress. It was smiley-face yellow. I thought it looked cheerful. Mama ran the Color Me Gorgeous franchise at Hair Today Dyed Tomorrow beauty parlor, so she considered herself an expert in what shades of clothing did and did not match which skin tones. I had

3

less fashion sense than the guys at the feed store, so I didn't really see the problem.

"Maddie and her yellow dress is hardly a crisis, Mama. I'll give you a crisis. If we don't recover your ring, and Sal finds out you lost it even before he's had the chance to pay it off because you got blitzed on too much sweet pink wine—"

"—Say no more, Mace." She took back the phone, and slipped it into the pocket of her orange-sherbet-colored pantsuit. "I'll take that corner over there by the fence. I see a bunch of white paper towels and some empty cans of that dog food Teensy likes. Maybe that'll be the trash from my house."

Picking up a broken broom, Mama began using it to delicately poke at garbage piles. I had to smile at the look on her face when she lifted the broom handle to examine what was stuck to the end and a banana peel dropped down her blouse. I was about to say something smart-alecky, when a sparkle of light shining between a bunch of spoiled beets and a flat bike tire caught my eye.

I walked over to get a closer look. A fishy smell about knocked me out. A week's worth of leftovers from Jimbob's Seafood Shack moldered. Sure enough, though, I saw the unmistakable glint of a diamond.

"I found it," I yelled, only to hear Mama's excited shout at the same moment.

"I've got it!" she cried from across the dump. "I found my ring."

She was waving, and the sun reflected off the big rock returned to her hand. If Mama had found *her* diamond, what exactly had I found? Kicking aside some crab shells and rotten shrimp, I lifted the bike tire. Up came a stained sheet tangled in some snapped-off spokes. Underneath was the body of a scantily clad woman, with one hand flung out. Against the deathly pallor of her wrist, a diamond bracelet glittered.

TWO

A LACE-UP BODICE OF black leather barely contained the upper half of the young woman's body. On the bottom, she wore a short leather skirt, also in black, with fishnet stockings. Dark hair fanned out across a bare shoulder. What looked like a dog collar encircled her neck, black leather with silver spikes and a ring for a leash. On her left foot was a five-inch stiletto heel; the shoe's mate was missing. Pale pink polish on her toenails gleamed through the wide mesh of the fishnet. The demure color, such a contrast to the revealing leather, made her seem especially vulnerable. Aside from the missing high heel, the rest of her clothing looked intact, if scanty.

"Do you know her?" I asked Mama.

She shook her head, eyes riveted on the body. Considering the heat, the girl couldn't have been dumped too long ago.

"Me neither. I'd say she's in her twenties, maybe thirty. Younger than me."

Mama nodded. To my surprise, tears pooled in her eyes. I put a hand on her shoulder. "Don't cry. You know this isn't the first time we've found a body, unfortunately. We can say a prayer for her, if you want. Either way, this poor gal is past caring."

Mama plucked a sherbet-hued handkerchief from her pocket. "I can't help it, Mace. Seeing her dumped here like household garbage just breaks my heart. I think of how I'd feel if harm like this ever came to you or your sisters. She was somebody's daughter."

Now I felt the sting of tears, too. Mama grabbed my hand. We recited the verses of Psalm 23, Mama filling in where I faltered: *The Lord is my shepherd, I shall not want...*

When we finished, I raised my head and looked around the dump. I added a silent prayer that God would receive the soul of the dead girl into heaven. If she did get the chance to sit beside Him, I hoped she wouldn't remember what had brought her to such an end on earth.

I had the urge to cover her again with the bed sheet. But I'd already called the police, and I knew we should disturb things around the body as little as possible. We retreated a short distance away to wait. We both pressed close to my Jeep, seeking the small amount of shade the vehicle provided.

The morning was young, but the sun was already demonstrating its hot hold on middle Florida. Even at eight a.m., it was sweltering. Mama had made me promise I'd swing by before work at Himmarshee Park to bring her to the dump. Now, all I could think of was how many places I'd rather be. She consulted her mirrored compact, dabbing with the handkerchief at her mascara. It was melting from the heat and her earlier tears. I squinted past her toward the open gate.

"Here comes a car. That's got to be Carlos," I said.

Mama licked the tips of two fingers and spit-patted my unruly bangs. "Your hair's a mess, Mace. It looks like a bunch of raccoons crawled in there and threw a party."

I ducked out of her reach. She offered me her mirror, and got a scowl in return.

"Mama, this is a murder scene. I doubt whether a little hair frizz is going to be the paramount issue on my boyfriend's mind."

"He's not just your boyfriend anymore; he's your fiancé. You better get used to saying the word."

Out came her Apricot Ice lipstick. While Mama attended to her face, I watched Carlos Martinez climb from the driver's side of his unmarked car. A homicide detective with the Himmarshee Police Department, he was also my fiancé. I was still having a bit of trouble getting my head around that description. Not the homicide part. I was used to that, since Mama and I had managed to encounter him at an unusually high number of crime scenes over the last couple of years. It was that word, "fiancé," that threw me.

It had only been a couple of months since he popped the question. Before that, we'd traveled a rocky road, romantically speaking. We might be officially engaged, but I still kept expecting us to plunge into a relationship pothole or run ourselves off the pavement into a ditch at any moment.

"Yoo-hoo, Carlos!" Mama sounded like we were at the malt shop and she was saving him a seat. "We're over here, honey!"

"Shhh! I'm the one who called him to come out here, so he knows where we are. He sees us," I whispered. "And don't forget there's a body lying over there just a few yards away."

"Well, I know that, Mace! I prayed over that gal just like you did. But just because she's gone to meet her Maker is no reason for me to be rude to my future son-in-law."

Carlos walked toward us, the sun casting a golden glow on his face. Despite the serious circumstances, I felt the same tingle I always got at the sight of this gorgeous man. With his black hair and eyes, his jaw set in grim determination, he looked like a Spanish conquistador charging into battle. He might be dodging garbage piles instead of galloping over the plains on an Andalusian steed, but he still looked mighty fine doing it.

He waved, and allowed us a fleeting smile. "You two are in the bad place at the bad time again, aren't you?"

Born in Cuba, moved up to Himmarshee from Miami, Carlos sometimes got his English vernacular mixed up.

"Absolutely. Wrong place; wrong time." I pointed to where we'd discovered the body. "She's over there. Earlier, Mama found a broken broom handle. We stuck it in a trash pile to mark where the girl is."

"And you're sure you don't recognize her?"

We both shook our heads.

"She's not from Himmarshee," I said. "She's wearing some kind of sexy, black-leather getup. I can tell you I've never seen anything like it on sale at the Home on the Range Feed Store and Clothing Emporium."

He raised his eyebrows. "You should know better than to make snap judgments, Mace. You'd be surprised what people are like behind closed doors; even people in little bitty towns like Himmarshee."

"Well," Mama said, "I think it's safe to say she wasn't a church-goer at Abundant Forgiveness Love & Charity Chapel. Not wearing an outfit like that."

"One thing's for sure," I said. "She ran out of Love."

Carlos gazed around the dump, his nose wrinkling at the stench of garbage and worse. "She ran out of Charity, too."

Mama said, "When Mace called you, did she mention the girl's diamond bracelet?"

He looked at me. I gave him an apologetic shrug. "I forgot," I said. "I work at a nature park and trap nuisance critters on the side. It's not like I'm a professional detective."

"I'll remind you of that fact when you go stepping your size-ten shoes all over my investigation. Speaking of the case…" His sentence trailed off as he started toward the dead girl. He spoke over his shoulder. "The medical examiner and the crime scene van will be here soon. You two should go. Someone will contact you later to give official statements."

Mama stopped him, tugging on his arm. "I just wanted to tell you one more thing. That girl might have been short on Love and Charity, but that leather bustier she's wearing doesn't leave much to the imagination. Between what she's showing up top, and that string of jewels on her wrist, your murder victim had Abundance to spare."

THREE

CHARLENE PUT A PLATE of steaming biscuits on the breakfast table at Gladys' Diner. It was the day after Mama and I found the girl at the dump. I helped myself to two of the flaky morsels as Charlene moved around the table, filling our coffee cups from a glass carafe.

When she got to my big sister, Maddie covered the rim of her cup with her hand. I'd never known her to turn down fresh, hot coffee before. Or little else, for that matter.

"Are you sick?"

Maddie touched her stomach. "Woke up with a little something."

"It's probably just nerves over the big party next week."

Mama had just started in with Maddie about the yellow dress, when the cowbells clanged on the door of the diner. Our little sister, Marty, pushed through, with the *Himmarshee Times* in one hand. Mama stood up and snatched the paper away, even before Marty had a chance to sit down.

"Let me see! Is there anything on that murdered girl?"

"Don't know, Mama. I didn't even have a moment to glance at it before someone ripped it forcibly from me."

Marty had been the reliably sweet sister since the three of us were girls, but she was speaking her mind more and more these days. It was partly because she had more responsibility at her library job, but I thought it was mainly Maddie rubbing off on her. Mama seemed not to notice Marty's snarky tone. Picking up on subtle criticism wasn't her strong suit.

She took her seat again, and spread the purloined paper on the table. "Yes! Here it is: 'Murdered Woman was New Resident.'"

Maddie and I angled closer, each reading over one of Mama's shoulders. Marty moved behind her, peering over the top of her head. "Ohmigod." She barely breathed the words as she gripped the back of Mama's chair.

"What?" Maddie and I asked at once. Our sister's fair skin had paled to alabaster. She clutched a hand to her throat.

"Th … tha … that picture," Marty stammered, pointing at the article's photo of a serious-looking young woman with long dark hair and intelligent eyes. It appeared to be a reproduction of a picture on a driver's license or employee badge.

"Did you know her?" Mama turned in her chair to look at Marty.

"She works with me at the library. I mean, worked."

"Oh, honey!" Mama patted gently at Marty's arm. "Were you close?"

Marty lowered herself into a seat at the table. "Not really. She's only been with us for a few months. But we just sat together at lunch last week. It's so weird to think she's dead."

"What did you have?" Maddie asked.

Mama, Marty, and I looked at her like she'd stepped off a space-ship from Planet Clueless.

"Is that relevant?" I said.

"Probably not." Maddie shrugged. "I just wondered."

"Veggie pizza," Marty said.

"This says her name was Camilla Law. She was originally from England, but she's been in the United States for several years," Mama read from the paper.

"That explains her accent," Marty said. "A lot of people just thought she was snobby."

"Maybe she came from money. That would fit with the diamond bracelet," I said.

"What diamond bracelet?" Marty asked.

"She was wearing one when we found her," I said. "You'd never seen her wear it at work?"

Marty shook her head. "I'd have remembered that."

Mama tapped the article to get our attention. "It doesn't mention the bracelet. It goes into a few details about the black leather and fishnets, but nothing about that strange dog collar." She continued scanning the story. "Your fiancé is quoted, Mace."

"Let me guess," I said. "He told the reporter the murder is under investigation, and the authorities will pursue all possible leads."

Mama grinned. "Very close. He didn't say the word 'murder.' He called it 'the circumstances of the victim's death.'"

"Oh, it's murder," I said, taking a sip of my coffee. "People don't die of natural causes while they're out walking in the city dump wearing leather sex clothes."

Mama tapped at the paper again. "Oh, y'all… listen to what our brand new mayor, Big Bill Graf, had to say. 'The risqué clothing this young woman was wearing in no way reflects community morals in Himmarshee. We're all about family values here.'"

"What a tool." Maddie stuck a teaspoon into my coffee and stole a swallow. "Needs more sugar, Mace."

I moved the cup out of her reach.

"Sounds like he's blaming the victim," Marty said.

Maddie said, "So a leather … what was it called again?"

"Bustier," Mama provided.

"Right. A leather bustier is a sin, but murder is okay?" Maddie clucked her tongue. "A total tool."

"Shh," I said, nodding toward a semi-private alcove at the back of the room. "Our illustrious mayor happens to be right over there, holding court."

A towering man, hence the nickname, Big Bill Graf had a barrel chest and a bright red face. He seemed to come from nowhere, pumping money unheard of in Himmarshee into radio advertising and yard signs. He'd won the mayoral race just a few months before.

We all quieted down, to see if we could listen in. Big Bill's booming voice carried across the crowded restaurant.

"Like I told the *Himmarshee Times*…" His voice swelled with importance, as if he were recounting a personal conversation with the *Washington Post*. "Sexual deviance isn't on our civic agenda. And I told that reporter his article better not infer that it is."

"I think he means 'imply,'" said Maddie, the school principal.

Marty shushed her.

"We must look at how that young woman's behavior implicated her murder," the mayor continued.

"Does he mean 'was implicated in her murder?'" Marty whispered.

I shrugged. "Maybe he means 'precipitated her murder.'"

"Why do people try to use big words when small ones will do just as well?" Mama asked.

"Especially when they use them wrong." Maddie dipped a clean teaspoon into Mama's coffee for a taste. "Too much cream."

"Why don't you just order a cup?" Marty asked.

"My stomach's upset," Maddie answered.

"Well don't send your germs my way," Marty said.

I still watched His Honor, even though a loud table in between us had drowned out his words. Several rapt hangers-on crowded around his table, devouring every sentence. A poodle-permed woman who looked familiar gazed at him with adoring eyes.

"Who's the big gal with the golf course tan and the red poodle pouf?" I asked. "She could use an emergency visit to Hair Today Dyed Tomorrow."

"My goodness, Mace, you've got to get out of the woods and start paying attention to civic news. That's Mrs. Mayor, Beatrice Graf," Mama whispered behind her hand. "She's already become a Newcomers' Club muckety-muck. I know it's not very Christian of me, but I think she's as big a blowhard as her husband."

"Then she's a pretty big blowhard," I said. "He's got a lot of nerve lecturing on how and why that girl came to be tossed in the dump. It's pure character assassination. Nobody knows anything for sure yet."

Just then, Beatrice Graf dropped a hand on her husband's shoulder. He stopped talking so fast, it was like she'd hit a switch. She smiled at his audience, the ingratiating smile of a political wife. Suddenly, the chatterboxes at the loud table in between us grew quiet as Charlene stopped to take their order. The cultured voice of the mayor's wife carried across the room.

"I think at the end of the day, we'll find that young woman was engaged in something sinful, and every one of you knows what the Bible says: *the wages of sin is death.*"

Our table was hushed as each of us digested Mrs. Mayor's words.

"My stars and garters," Mama finally said. "That was certainly harsh."

FOUR

The cowbells clanged. Henry Bauer, Esq., paused at the door to Gladys' Diner. Eyes searching the Saturday morning crowd, he acknowledged Mayor Graf with a tight smile and dutiful wave. Then he made a beeline to our table, probably because he smelled our second plate of biscuits.

"Mornin', cousin." Maddie gave Henry a cloying smile. "Keep your thieving paws off our food."

Henry, belly straining the waistband of his weekend-casual khakis, returned her greeting. "No smart food thief would choose a table where you're sitting, Maddie. All the food is usually gone."

Mama looked up from her smart phone for a moment to pass him the platter of biscuits. "Ignore your cousin, honey. You're still a growing boy." She went back to typing.

"Growing and growing," Maddie mumbled under her breath.

"Sticks and stones, Maddie." Henry slathered butter and honey on the biscuit, polishing off the first half in one bite. "That's good enough to make your tongue slap your eyeballs."

"Want me to call Charlene over to take your order?" I asked.

"Nah. I've already eaten. I just like to tick Maddie off." Henry popped the second half in his mouth, chewed, and then opened up to reveal to Maddie the gloppy mess inside.

She leaned over to punch him in the shoulder; he balled up a napkin and tossed it at her.

"Very mature, you two!" Marty said. "Henry, is that the way you conduct yourself in the courtroom?"

"I would if I ever got a judge like Maddie."

Henry was actually a successful attorney, the best in Himmarshee. Of course, there were only four lawyers in town, and one of them was in his mid-nineties and lived at the adult-care facility, so our cousin didn't have a lot of competition.

I heard the whoosh of Mama's phone sending her message, probably an inspirational story she was forwarding to unsuspecting recipients in cyberspace. She left her virtual world to rejoin real life. "Be nice, sweetheart." She patted Henry's hand. "Maddie's not feeling well this morning."

He cocked his head, eyes showing authentic concern. Maddie, with a stomach like a steel-hulled freighter, was hardly ever sick. "Everything okay, cousin?"

She waved away his worry. "It's that blasted forty-fifth birthday party for Kenny. He's getting on my last nerve, y'all. I'm going to a lot of trouble, and he's fighting me every step of the way. He acts like he doesn't even want a party."

"Forty-five?" Henry said. "That explains it. I know y'all won't believe me, but women aren't the only ones who get sensitive about their age. Maybe Kenny doesn't want to be reminded he's getting older."

"That's just plain stupid." Maddie made an X in a spot of water left by her glass. "Getting older is a fact of life. It happens to everybody."

Marty's hand shook a bit as she put down her coffee cup. In a quiet voice, she said, "It won't happen for Camilla. She was murdered, and dumped like yesterday's trash. She was only twenty-nine."

The table went quiet: no chewing, even. Petty bickering and Kenny's party seemed too silly as subjects when a young woman had lost her life. Mama turned off her phone, sliding it off the table and into her purse.

"What's the courthouse crowd saying, Henry?" My question broke the silence.

"Nobody knows much yet. She'd been strangled. The dump likely wasn't the murder scene. She was dropped there."

Mama tsk-tsked. "What's happening to little Himmarshee?"

"We're all going to have to move to escape our spiraling crime rate. Maybe we should relocate to Miamuh." Henry used the "Old Florida" pronunciation for the wicked city four hours south.

Marty traced the picture of Camilla in the newspaper on the table. "I wonder if she knew her killer?"

"Well, she was all dolled up for something," Henry said.

"Maybe the killer dressed her that way," Maddie said.

"It'd be a challenge to dress someone else in an outfit that tight. I think she dressed herself, like for a special date," Mama said.

We all stared at her. "What kind of dates have you been on?" I asked.

A blush reached clear to the dyed roots of her platinum hair. "Oh, not me, y'all! I don't have any personal knowledge. I do watch TV, though."

I leaned in close and lowered my voice to a whisper. "Mama did seem to know a lot about the details of that leather top Camilla was wearing."

"It's called a bustier. Everybody knows that, Mace."

Before we could correct her on that assumption, Mama closed the newspaper, creasing the fold with finality. "I am certain about one thing: I'd prefer it if that poor girl knew her killer."

"Why?" Marty asked. "It makes the whole thing even sadder if it was someone she thought she could trust."

"Well, if it was a stranger, then we've got us a big problem here in little Himmarshee," Mama said. "If the killer didn't even know the librarian, and had no particular reason to murder her, there's no telling who in town could be next."

FIVE

"SON OF A BEEHIVE!" Mama dug her fingers into my Jeep's dashboard, her Apricot-Iced nails leaving small scrapes. "You nearly ran into the back of that stock trailer, Mace. You came so close, I could see the fear of death in a couple of those heifers' eyes."

I passed the trailer, giving a wave to the cowboy-hatted driver. Once I pulled back in my lane, I eased off a bit on the gas.

"I suppose you'd rather we poked along behind it, enjoying the aroma of two dozen head of cattle and untold pounds of manure. Besides, I missed the trailer by a mile."

"You better get your eyes checked, honey. You're not as young as you used to be."

I glanced into the rear-view mirror at my sister Marty. "Are you hearing this abuse? Doesn't Mama have a lot of nerve criticizing my driving, seeing as how I'm her default chauffeur every time that turquoise bomber of hers is in the shop?"

Marty lowered her eyes and pressed her lips together. No answer.

"What? Now, you're piling on, too?"

"You could slow down a little, Mace." My sister's tone was measured. "You also made a right without even stopping as we were coming out of the parking lot at the diner."

"*Et tu*, Marty? Anyways, that's a stupid place for a stop sign." I turned on my blinker and pulled toward the shoulder. "I suppose I could stop and let both of you out here. I mean if my driving is so terrifying, and all. It's just three or four miles to the library."

Mama smoothed her hair. Marty cleared her throat. "We appreciate the ride. We're not criticizing, Mace."

"I am," Mama said. "Even so, Marty and I are not walking anywhere. Have you had a look at my shoes?"

She propped a foot up on the dash. It was clad in a yellow slingback sandal with a three-inch heel. The shoes matched the rest of her outfit, from the chiffon scarf tied jauntily at her neck, to the daffodils embroidered on the lapels and cuffs of her lemon-sherbet-colored pantsuit. Mama won the point. No way was I going to let her out to traipse along the roadside looking like a walking slice of banana cream pie. Everyone knew I was her daughter.

Defeated, I pulled back onto State Road 98. Marty had asked for a ride to the library, where she was going to fill in for the murdered woman's shift. Mama was tagging along.

She tried to make up with small talk as we passed the various business establishments in Himmarshee. At Juan's Auto Repair and Taco Shop, she said, "Juan thinks he can have my Bonneville done by the middle of next week."

I sat in stony silence.

Undeterred, Mama pointed out the window. "Looks like they're having a sale at Fran's Fancy Frocks and Duds. Do you have something to wear for Kenny's party yet, Mace?"

I grunted a *yes*.

"In that case, maybe you should start thinking about a wedding dress."

I rolled my eyes.

The sign for Pete's Pawn Shop loomed into view, showing a road-kill armadillo with a word balloon over its head: *Don't Wait Too Late to Visit Pete's*.

"D'Vora from Hair Today Dyed Tomorrow said her loser husband went to Pete's and tried to pawn her mama's good china. Pete's wife told him to take a hike."

I shrugged an *I don't care*. Marty chimed in from the back seat, "I like D'Vora. What is it about good women who stay with bad men?"

Finally, something I *was* interested in talking about: "Mama, you want to tackle that question? Having had five husbands certainly qualifies you as an expert."

She waved a hand. "Only a couple of them were bad, and only No. 2 was really bad. I'd say I wasn't in my right mind after your daddy died. I should have given myself time to grieve, but I thought it would be good for you young girls to have a man in the house."

Mama was silent a moment, her eyes taking on a faraway look. She gave her head a little shake. "Number 2 was an awful mistake on my part; and an awful time, for all of us."

I felt a bit guilty about poking a painful place out of pure spite.

"How were you supposed to know he was a drunk and a con man who'd steal from all the relatives?" I said.

"There's the library." Marty's voice rescued me just before I said I was sorry.

"Now," Mama said, "be sure you don't turn in front of that red truck up ahead and give that poor driver a heart attack. And try not to kill any pedestrians once you get in the parking lot." Her advice had such a snide ring, I was glad I hadn't apologized.

———

We walked through the library doors, air conditioning enfolding us like wintry arms. Marty's boss, Kresta King, hurried out from a glass-enclosed office behind the circulation desk. The welcoming smile she usually wore was gone. Up close, I could see her face was drawn and tense under her cap of curly brown hair.

"Thanks for coming in. Isn't it awful about Camilla?" She put a hand on Marty's shoulder, her voice funeral-home quiet. "We found a sister in Atlanta listed as an emergency contact in her personnel file. The police have already contacted her, and she's on her way south."

"Thank goodness you didn't have to make that call," Marty said.

Kresta's eyes widened. "Oh, that would have been horrible. I'm not sure I could have done it."

As much a community center as library, Marty's workplace was usually a swirl of activity. Today, it seemed hushed. Staffers moved about slowly, cautiously, as if a thick fog blanketed the banks of computers and shelves of books. The workers, and a few customers, looked shell-shocked. I turned to Kresta. "Was Camilla popular? Did she have lots of friends here?"

"Not really." She shook her head. "Some of our patrons had even complained that she was short with them. I just think it's sinking in how she died, and where she was found. She sat right at that desk." Pointing to the reference section, she gave a little shudder. "It makes the world seem a very dangerous place. I've never known anyone who was murdered."

"We have." Mama linked elbows with Marty and me, pulling each of us close. "But you still don't get used to it."

An image of Camilla, garbage-strewn, diamond bracelet on her wrist, flashed through my mind. "No," I said. "You don't get used to it."

"That must have been hard, finding the body." Kresta leaned toward us, perhaps anticipating what Mama and I would say. I didn't want to go there.

"I was wondering, did you ever notice Camilla wearing a bracelet at work?" I asked.

She cocked her head; bit a thumbnail as she thought. "You know, I really couldn't say."

Mama added, "It was a diamond bracelet."

Her mouth formed an O. "Well, that's different. I definitely would have noticed a diamond bracelet. Not too many of those in Himmarshee."

I heard the doors sweep open behind us, letting in a blast of furnace-like heat from outside. Towering over two women from the Chamber of Commerce, Beatrice Graf marched in. She carried a basket with a black ribbon, and her jaws flapped a mile a minute. "It's the right thing to do," she said, as the women on each side nodded like bobble-headed dolls. "We want to make sure the family knows Himmarshee is a caring community. Mr. Mayor and I always say you'll find your heart in Himmarshee."

Mama curled her lip. "She didn't sound so big-hearted when she was carving up that poor girl's reputation at Gladys' Diner."

Marty gave Mama a quick pinch as Mrs. Mayor approached. Her face under that red perm was as tanned as a leather saddle bag. She was dressed in a white pencil skirt that would have been too short on a woman two sizes smaller. Her red-and-white polka dot blouse showed an alarming expanse of sun-freckled cleavage.

"Excuse me," she flashed a chemically bleached smile at Kresta, ignoring the rest of us completely. "Aren't you one of the help here?"

Kresta's smile was unenthusiastic. "I'm the branch manager. What can I do for you, Mrs. Graf?"

"The mayor and I were out of town when that young librarian was murdered. Such a scandal to return to! I want you to make sure her family receives this token of our sympathy."

She held out the basket. I peered inside. There was an offer for a tanning session, some coupons from the Pork Pit, and a discount booklet for the Dairy Queen. I also saw a bass fishing lure and a couple of purple combs from Hair Today Dyed Tomorrow. Stamped on a coffee mug was Himmarshee's civic motto, shockingly inappropriate under the circumstances: *Your Journey Ends Here.*

"How, er ... nice," Kresta said.

"It's the least we can do," said Mrs. Mayor.

"It sure is," Mama agreed, side-stepping to escape Marty's pinch.

As she handed off the basket, the threesome turned as if one, and headed toward the door. Beatrice wiggled her fingers over her shoulder at us. "Toodle-loo, ladies."

The doors opened with a whoosh of hot air, and they were gone.

Kresta held up the basket. "What am I supposed to do with this?"

"Throw it in the trash?" Mama suggested.

"I doubt the first thing the grieving sister will want to do is drop a line in Lake Okeechobee or rush to the Queen for a butterscotch-dipped cone," I said.

"Be nice, you two. She's making an effort." Marty's gaze followed Beatrice outside. She hiked up her painted-on skirt and climbed into a black SUV. It was in a handicapped spot.

"She just wants to be liked, as do most people," Marty said.

"Most people except you know who." Mama pointed at me with her chin.

"That doesn't make her a bad person, Mace."

We'd see about that, I thought.

SIX

Frowning, Maddie wrinkled her nose as soon as she walked in the door. "What is that awful smell?"

I sniffed. Hair Today Dyed Tomorrow smelled just like it always smelled, like a fruit roll-up dipped in ammonia. "I don't know what you're talking about, sister. It smells normal. But why don't you raise your voice a bit? I don't think the customers under the hair dryers were able to hear you."

Maddie waggled her fingers at Betty Taylor, the salon owner. "Sorry. I woke up with the queasies this morning. My stomach's not right."

"Did you tie one on last night, Maddie?" Betty grinned.

Everyone in Himmarshee knew my sister was a teetotaler. Mama never poked fun at Maddie's abstemious nature, figuring it left more sweet pink wine for her.

"Maybe she was worried about coming here today to see what kind of hair torture you have in mind for her for the big birthday party," I said.

Betty shook her purple comb at me. "We should be thinking about how to do *your* hair if you ever commit to a wedding date. When is hell going to freeze over, by the way?"

"Marriage is a sore subject with Mace," Maddie said. "She feels like everybody's rushing her. We've told her Carlos won't wait forever, like some old man in the mall holding her purse."

"Carlos has never held my purse," I said.

"You know what I mean."

"I don't understand you, Mace." Betty handed Maddie a stack of hairstyle books. "Most women would jump like a duck on a June bug on a proposal from that good-looking man. Then again, most women enjoy a trip to the beauty parlor, too." She waved her comb, taking in the shop's walls, sinks, and chairs, all in a vivid purple. "You're a little unusual in hating to have your hair done. Course, anyone with eyes could tell that by that snarl-fest you call hair. God gave you a gift, honey. Why treat it like a curse?"

She advanced on me, holding her comb like a bayonet. I ducked out of reach.

"Mace is a little unusual in a lot of ways," Maddie said. "But I have to be nice. I talked her into coming to give me hairdo advice. I'm sure she'd rather be out communing with the bugs and the trees in the heat at Himmarshee Park."

I looked at my watch. "Speaking of the park, I have to be there in an hour to take care of my animals. Could we lay off me and get started on all those fascinating styles for your hair?"

Betty took another long look at my hair. Thick and black, it was filled with knots because I was pretty sure I'd forgotten to brush it that morning. Shaking her head, she went to ring up a customer, leaving us with the style books at a small table where Mama does her color-by-season charts. A little sign on the tabletop said *Color Me Gorgeous.*

"She's right, you know. I'd kill for hair like yours." Maddie lifted a handful of her own locks. With the humidity, her hair hung in tight coils, like a bright-red scouring pad. "You'd only have to make a minimal effort, Mace, and you could have a glossy, sophisticated look."

"I'm sure the critters in our wildlife rehab at Himmarshee Park would be wowed."

I plopped the first book on the table. "Now," I said, "let's find you something that'll knock Kenny's socks off."

Maddie, head bent, stared intently at the book. "That might take some doing," she said softly.

"What do you mean?"

She raised her gaze to mine. "It's the weirdest thing I've ever seen. Normally, my husband loves a party. And cake and ice cream? He's in heaven. But Kenny's lost weight recently, and he's distracted all the time. I feel like I barely know him anymore."

"Midlife crisis." Betty, returning from the register, leaned in to add her opinion. She had the heard-it-all tone of a woman who'd spent her life in a beauty parlor. "It's Kenny's time. He'll probably be buying a go-fast sports car next."

I snorted. "Not Kenny. No way, no how. That man's had his feet solidly on the ground since he was in short pants. He's so straight, he sells *insurance.*"

D'Vora, once Betty's trainee, now a licensed stylist, pursed her lips as she clipped the bangs of a teenager next to us. Was that look due to her concentrating on the cut? Or, was she making a non-verbal comment on male midlife crises?

"What's your take, D'Vora?"

She stopped snipping and started fidgeting. She brushed back a lock of her own hair; fingered the purple appliqué butterflies on her uniform top. Finally, she spoke. "Maybe Kenny is tired of being a grown-up all the time."

"D'Vora, honey, look people in the eye when you're talking to them. You look shifty if you don't," Betty said.

The young stylist's eyes darted toward me, but she carefully avoided looking at Maddie. I wondered for a moment if D'Vora had ever been sent to the principal's office at Himmarshee Middle School. Maybe Maddie's scary principal routine had given her post-traumatic stress.

"Maybe that midlife thing hits especially hard for a man who's always been mature and responsible," D'Vora said.

Betty fogged her customer's 'do with hairspray. The woman let out a strangled cough. "Well, then, we won't have to worry about that no-account skunk you live with having a midlife crisis." She looked into the mirror at D'Vora, who ignored the jab.

"I'm just sayin,' maybe there's a reason when men go off the rails." She lifted the scissors again, and resumed cutting the teen-ager's hair.

I looked at Maddie. My sister was uncharacteristically quiet, perhaps weighing D'Vora words. "What?" I asked. "You cannot possibly doubt Kenny after all these years. He's the perfect husband."

The shop's front door slammed shut, bells jangling cheerily. "Who's the perfect husband?" Mama asked as she walked in.

"Nobody!" D'Vora's customary shyness was replaced with uncommon authority. "There's absolutely nobody who's perfect."

As if her boldness surprised even her, the young stylist shifted her gaze back to the floor. Mama, meanwhile, launched into a story about the inappropriateness of the mourner's basket the mayor's wife delivered to the library.

"We should have offered a complimentary shampoo, Betty. Now, that's something that would be useful. Nobody needs a bassbug fishing fly from Gotcha Bait & Tackle when they've just lost a loved one."

As Mama went on, describing the rest of the contents, my eyes were on D'Vora. No one else seemed to notice her scissors had gone still. She still focused her eyes on the floor, the teenager in the chair seemingly forgotten. She sneaked a look at Maddie, who by now was leafing through the picture book.

I was just about to ask D'Vora what was the matter, when Mama's sharp tone snapped me back to attention. "Did you hear me, Mace?"

"Yes, you said the basket was extremely tacky and not at all right for the occasion. Who wants a coffee cup that says *Himmarshee: Your Journey Ends Here* when their sister has just been murdered? And, you added, the mayor's wife needs to do something about those painted-on eyebrows. Plus, her skirt was far too tight for a woman of her age."

"I'm not even talking about the mayor's wife anymore, Mace. I just said Sal texted me."

"Sal texts you all the time. You two are worse than a couple of silly teenagers." I nodded to the young girl in D'Vora's chair. "No offense."

"None taken," she said.

D'Vora stood still, wringing her hands.

"You and Maddie need to take a look at what he sent. It's really cute."

As Mama thrust the phone at us, I noticed D'Vora place her scissors on the counter and head for the front of the shop. Mama poked me in the wrist with the phone, trying to get me to take it. I glanced down, noting some LOLs, a heart symbol, and an OMG.

"Like I said, teenagers."

By the time I looked up, D'Vora had yanked open the front door, bells clanging. Then she walked out of the shop, leaving her abandoned customer in the chair, staring after her.

Now what, I wondered, was that all about?

SEVEN

I INHALED THE SMELL of the swamp. Black muck, tannic water, and the woodsy scent of cypress trees. A gator lolled on the bank of Himmarshee Creek, his body half-hidden in fire flag and duck potato plants. A squirrel sat high on a branch in a laurel oak tree, scolding me as I traversed the path below. With a wild flapping of black-tipped wings, two wood storks rose from a still pool of dark water beside the boardwalk that led to the office of Himmarshee Park.

It felt like home.

Through the office's large glass windows, I saw my boss, Rhonda, on the telephone. It was a familiar sight. As park supervisor, she handled most of the managerial tasks. That suited me fine. I wasn't cut out to be anybody's boss. And I'd wither up and die if I had to spend as much time in the office as Rhonda did, even with the nice view from our big windows.

Inside, I caught her eye and waved as I dropped my purse onto my desk, next to the dried-out shell of a gopher tortoise. Rhonda made the yak-yak sign at the phone, and mimed a big yawn. My boss was a stunner, even with her mouth gaping open. A former New York model who returned home to take care of her ailing mother, she looked like she could step back onto the runway at any moment. She was the only parks employee I knew who rocked the ugly, olive drab uniforms we had to wear.

"Right, that sounds like a perfect action plan." She was wrapping up on the phone. "Send me a memo with the talking points. I'll take it up at the budget meeting."

There were any number of phrases in that sentence I hoped never to have to utter. Not for the first time, I gave silent thanks for Rhonda's efficiency and people skills. She handled schedules, budgets, and meetings with our higher-ups; I did nature discussions and cared for the critters that wound up in our makeshift zoo and rehab center.

The coffee machine in the corner gurgled. The freshly brewed scent of Colombian roast told me Rhonda had just made a pot. I helped myself. Returning with my cup, I cleared a spot on my desk between a stuffed swallow-tailed kite and a package of brochures on Florida's poisonous snakes.

The moment she hung up, Rhonda turned to me. Compassion warmed her brown eyes. "I heard about the librarian. How horrible!"

"Yeah, it's going to be tough for her sister. She's been notified to come down as Camilla's next-of-kin."

Her eyes searched my face. "How are you?"

"Me? I'm fine. I'm not the one somebody strangled and left at the dump."

"But, Mace, it has to take a toll. This is the fifth body you've found."

"Fourth. Mama was on her own when she discovered that first murder victim in the trunk of her convertible at the Dairy Queen."

"I remember. That was when Carlos tossed your mama in the slammer."

"Occasionally I wonder why we worked so hard to get her out." Rhonda tsked me.

"Seriously, though, that seemed like the start of a string of bad things happening in little Himmarshee," I said.

"Well, at least one good thing happened." Rhonda's face, the color of rich mahogany, glowed with a smile. "How is your hunky detective anyway? Still as steamy hot as a cup of *café Cubano*? You better grab that man while the grabbing is good. He's asked you to marry him; he's not going to wait forever, you know."

Just as I was about to gripe about how oddly obsessed everyone was with my love life, my desk phone rang. Saved by the bell.

"Speak of the devil," I said, when I heard Carlos on the line.

"Speaking well of me, I hope," he said. "Tell Rhonda hello."

When I did, she made a noisy smack-smack sound and blew a big kiss toward the phone. Carlos chuckled. "I love that girl!"

"Hey!"

"Not like I love you, *niña*."

"Uh-huh," I said, stealing a glance at Rhonda. "Anything new on the murder?"

"Can't a guy call his girl without being grilled about work?"

"Just curious," I said.

"We're looking into her background. Nothing I'm prepared to talk about." His end of the phone was quiet for a moment. "I do, you know. Love you."

Rhonda was busy re-stacking the stacks of paperwork on her desk, but I could see her head cocked my way, her right ear tuned in to my conversation.

"Uh-huh," I finally answered. "Back at ya."

He laughed. "I pour out my heart. I get 'back at ya.' You can do better than that."

I swiveled my desk chair so my back was to my boss, ducked my head into my chest and mumbled into the phone, "Love you, too. I'll see you tonight."

As I put the phone down, I could feel Rhonda's eyes on the back of my head. I turned, and she didn't even try to pretend she hadn't been eavesdropping. A big, silly smile was pasted on her lips. The more she grinned, the more I felt a blush spreading up my neck and onto my cheeks.

"What?" I demanded.

"Nothing," she said.

"Have your say, boss. Everyone else has."

To my surprise she started humming. Then she started singing. "Mace and Carlos sitting in a tree, K I S S—I N G ...'

I flashed on third-grade and the jungle gym. I'd climbed past all the boys to the top. Danny Blue screwed up his courage to follow me and steal a kiss. The other little girls watched from the ground, chiming in to sing that same song.

"Seriously? How old are you again, boss?"

"Sorry, I couldn't resist. You're so close-mouthed and private about everything. You make an easy target. Didn't your mama teach you that people who hate to be teased are the people everybody loves to tease?"

I relented, and returned Rhonda's grin. If the bulls-eye fits, may as well wear it.

"So, have you lovebirds set a date? When's the wedding?"

"That's a popular question," I said. "There's no rush."

"There is if you want children." Rhonda's voice lost its teasing tone. "You're not getting any younger."

"Thanks for the reminder."

"I'm serious."

"We've only been engaged a few months. We've got plenty of time."

"That's what people always say, until they run out of time."

———

"Who's hungry?"

Claws skittered. Wood shavings rustled. Pepé Le Pew put a paw to his food dish, banging it against the floor of his enclosure. "Whoa, Pepé my man! Didn't anyone ever tell you patience is a virtue?"

The skunk was a permanent resident. His moronic former owner had him de-scented, and then left him to fend for himself in the wild without his only natural means of defense. I'd been called out to capture him by a newcomer who objected to having her garden parties crashed by a skunk. If you asked me, some of her over-perfumed guests smelled much worse than Pepé.

I would have rather released him into the woods. Without his scent, though, the skunk was safer with the other injured, abused, or unwanted critters we kept at Himmarshee Park.

Once the inside inhabitants were taken care of, I went outside to the pond to feed Ollie.

A cool rush of air hit me in the face, blowing my hair off my neck. Suddenly, the leaves high in the trees started shaking. The sky had blackened. Big, angry-looking clouds scudded over the park, blowing toward us from Lake Okeechobee to our south. The temperature dropped by at least ten degrees. The sudden chill raised goose bumps on my sweaty flesh.

"Storm's coming, Ollie."

The gator swam toward me, powerful tail propelling him through the water. His jaws gaped, as he regarded me with his one good eye. Lightning flashed, zigzagging across the dark sky. Maybe it was the threatening weather, or the lightning reflecting off those acres of teeth, but something made me think of the close call Mama and I had survived with Ollie, at this very pond.

I stepped back from the wall. Turned to look behind me. Dark shadows filled the woods. The gnarled branches of old oaks seemed to reach toward me, like the grasping fingers of malevolent giants. A shiver started at my neck and traced a trail all the way down my spine.

I held out my hand. The barest tremble betrayed an uncommon onset of nerves. "Look at me, Ollie. Spooked by a little foul weather."

I went to the wall again; found the gator still awaiting his supper. "I wonder if it's starting to get to me, how everybody's always asking me when I'm getting married? I'm not ready right now, but I'll tell you a secret."

I thought I saw an interested look in Ollie's eye. Maybe he was anticipating the secret. More likely, it was the thawed raw chickens

I had in the bucket at my feet. I looked around to see if anyone lurked nearby, close enough to hear me revealing my deepest feelings to a one-eyed, three-legged alligator. He'd come out on the losing end in a fight with another male over territory.

"I really do love this man, Ollie. I'm happy." I dangled the first chicken over the wall. The reptile's jaws gaped wide. "I can hardly believe it myself. Nothing's going to happen to screw up this relationship."

I tossed the plucked bird. Ollie's mouth slammed shut with a resounding crack. I thought of the awesome force of a gator's jaws, more than twice as powerful as the mightiest lion. The water churned, and I shuddered a bit. Silently, I uttered a prayer I'd said more than once before at Ollie's pond. *Thank you, God, for saving Mama and me from such a gruesome fate.*

EIGHT

THE PORCH LIGHT SHONE at Maddie's house. I raced through the rain to her front door. The potted geraniums she always hand-watered and plied with fertilizer to force cheerful red blooms were wilting on the front porch. That was as odd as the phone call I'd gotten from her on my way home from work.

"Could you stop by tonight?" Maddie had asked.

It ran through my mind I'd be looking at more pictures of hairstyles. Maybe I'd have to watch my sister try on that yellow dress while she asked if it made her butt look big. "I don't know, Maddie. I'm awful tired, and it's raining buckets."

As if to emphasize my point, the rain picked up, pounding the top of my Jeep. I turned the wipers up a notch and rubbed at the foggy window. It was almost dark, and I could barely see five feet in front of me. The rain fell in sheets. The wind gusts came close to blowing me over the highway's center line.

"Please?" Her voice was pleading, and so soft I could barely hear her. Very un-Maddie-like. When I hesitated before answering, I heard a strangled sound come over the phone.

"Are you *crying*?"

"N-n-n- nooo …" Maddie took a couple of hiccupping breaths. "Y-y-y-yesss."

My tough-as-nails older sister, capable of silencing an entire auditorium of middle-school students with just her scary principal glare, CRYING? I yanked my steering wheel to the left and made a U-turn.

"I'm on my way, sister. Hold on."

Now, Maddie held open her front door. She handed me a bath towel to dry off the rain. I knew things were bad when she failed to mention like she always did that I should wipe the mud off my boots. Her red hair was matted. Her eyes were puffy and swollen.

"What's wrong?" I asked.

"Follow me." Maddie led the way down a hallway to her laundry room. The top on a bright pink hamper was open. She pointed. "Look in there."

I peeked in. I saw a couple of dish towels, a tablecloth with barbecue stains, and a man's silky, long-sleeved shirt in a vivid orange-and-maroon print. "Do you have a houseguest visiting from Palm Beach?"

"It's Kenny's."

I'm sure my face betrayed my shock. Kenny's style, if you could call it that, was jeans, T-shirts, and NASCAR caps. I'd never seen him in a shirt without a logo promoting farm equipment, his insurance company, or a monster truck show.

Maddie plucked out the shirt, holding it gingerly between a thumb and forefinger. "Smell."

"I'd rather not."

She waved it under my nose, and raised her brows at me. When I didn't answer, she made another pass with the shirt. That time, I got it. Despite the damp scent of rain on my uniform, mixed with the dusty grain smell of the animal chow I'd spilled on myself earlier, I detected the cloying, floral scent of a woman's perfume.

My mind immediately went back to Mama, and Husband No. 2. She'd found a red shirt of his, reeking with My Sin. Mama didn't say a word. She just doused the whole thing with bleach. Number Two found his fancy shirt neatly folded and put back in the drawer, the red fabric turned into ugly splotches of pink and white.

"There's got to be an explanation," I said.

Maddie balled up the shirt and tossed it back in the hamper. "There is: He's cheating."

"I mean another explanation."

"Before Mama finally wised up to No. 2, how many times did we see her find some evidence, and then overlook it?"

"Lots of times."

"Well, I'm not going to be that blind, Mace." She glared at the shirt. "I should have known even before I smelled the perfume. The man has never in his life managed to hit the dirty clothes hamper."

"What are you going to do? Confront him?"

"Not yet." Maddie shook her head. "I want to get all the facts first, just like I do when the kids act up at school. Before I say a word, I always know exactly what's been done, who did it, and what punishment they'll get."

I couldn't help but think that despite Maddie's bluster, marital betrayal is a lot more complicated than shooting spitballs at Himmarshee Middle School.

———

Maddie traced at a stray drop of herbal tea on her kitchen table. A steaming cup of chamomile sat untouched in front of her. I sipped at my lemonade. I would have preferred a beer, but my sister refused to have alcohol in her house. Mama's Husband No. 2 had been a heavy drinker in addition to a con man and serial cheater. As the oldest of us three girls, Maddie was likely more aware of the emotional fallout from that poisonous combination of character flaws.

"What about the party?" I asked her.

"We're going ahead with it. I don't have a choice. The VFW hall is rented. The invites are out. C'ndee already bought most of the food for Saturday night. Kenny's birthday cake is already paid for, too. I asked them to inscribe it 'To the World's Best Husband.'"

Maddie, seemingly exhausted, went quiet. She stared at her stainless steel refrigerator. Normally as shiny as a silver dollar, it was marred with greasy fingerprints. If Maddie were herself, she'd have been after it with a roll of paper towels and a bottle of spray cleaner. Instead, her eyes got teary again. I felt the sting, too, from sympathy and disbelief.

"Maybe Kenny's using drugs or something," I said. "There's got to be a reason." She shook her head. "It's sex, pure and simple. Not only is that shirt of his a peacock-looking thing, it's a full size smaller than what he wore a couple months ago. I should have known something was up when he started getting in shape."

Maddie sniffled. "Bastard!" She plucked a napkin from a holder on the table and blotted roughly at her eyes. "Don't mention a word of this to Mama."

"Lord, no!" I said.

"I want to show you something else."

I followed Maddie down the hallway to their bedroom. Pictures of her with Kenny and their daughter, Pam, hung along the walls. She jerked open the closet door and removed a hideous yellow-and-peach-colored golf outfit. The cap was a plaid tam-o'-shanter, complete with a yellow pom-pom.

"That looks like something from the Sal Provenza resort-wear collection," I said.

"I know, except my idiot husband paid for it with our money." Maddie dropped it on the bed in disgust.

"Will you investigate for me, Mace? Find out who he's running around with?"

"Oh, Maddie..."

I let my words trail off. I was reluctant to delve into something so personal. The last thing I wanted to do was hurt Maddie with what I was afraid I'd find out about her husband.

She put a hand on my arm. "You know how to get to the bottom of things, sister. Besides, I just don't think I can face it alone, whatever he's up to."

She wiped a tear from her cheek. "Will you, Mace? Please?"

"It's probably just a big misunderstanding."

"I don't think so. It's not just the perfume-stink and the fancy clothes. He bought a set of golf clubs. Got them second-hand off

Craig's List, but still. And, last weekend, when I wanted to go to the Pork Pit, Kenny said we should try that new bar and grill that serves wine by the golf course. He called the Pork Pit a 'cholesterol nightmare.'"

"That doesn't sound like the Kenny I know," I said. "I didn't think he could pronounce cholesterol."

"That's exactly my point." Maddie blew her nose. "Please?"

How could I say no?

NINE

LIGHTS SHONE ON THE ornate sign for Himmarshee Links Country Club. The mechanical arm at the guardhouse rose, allowing my Jeep to roll right through the entrance. The geniuses who ran the place milked their members to build the guardhouse, but then cheaped out when it came to hiring someone to actually work the gate as security.

What did they hope to guard against with that gate and little house? With all the alligators that populated the water hazards, it seemed like at least one threat was already inside the perimeter of the golf course community. I kept the skull of one such critter as a key receptacle on my coffee table at home. The gator had been deemed a nuisance after it became a bit too comfortable sharing space with golfers. My cousin, a state-licensed trapper, enlisted me to help him wrestle it from a pond near the eighteenth hole.

Turning into the parking lot, I remembered something else about the golf course. I'd met the pro once, a strapping young guy with sexy blue eyes and a full head of sun-kissed curls. Josh? Jason?

He'd come on pretty strong. Even though I was an engaged woman, I pondered for a moment on whether he'd remember me.

Inside, I didn't have to wait long for the answer to that question. The hunky pro stood next to the hostess stand in the club's dining room. He put his hand over his heart and spoke to me, even before I could state my business.

"Better call heaven. I think they're missing an angel." His voice was a deep purr; a smile crinkled the darkly tanned skin near his eyes.

"Really?" the hostess raised her eyebrows at him. "You think that'll work for you?"

He looked wounded. "Even beautiful women like to hear they're beautiful."

The hostess took me in with a practiced glance: No makeup, rain-dampened work clothes, the grainy scent of animal chow no doubt still wafting off me. She didn't appear to agree I was heaven's missing angel.

"How have you been?" I asked the pro.

His face was a blank.

So much for my stunningly memorable beauty. "We met here a couple of years ago. I came in asking questions after a body had been discovered in my Mama's convertible?"

A dim light lit in his eyes. Forty-watt smart. "Oh yeah, questions. I remember now. Your mother's married to Big Sal, right?"

"She is indeed," I said.

So he remembered Mama, but had only the foggiest memory of meeting me. I shoved aside my bruised ego and re-introduced myself. His name was Jason, not Josh. I asked if he had a few minutes to talk, told him I'd buy the drinks. The hostess shot eye darts at me the whole time. Jason guided me to a table at the far edge of the dining room, near the bar. The 19th Hole. Cute.

"Do you know Kenny Wilson?' I asked, once we were seated.

He cocked his head, appearing to think about it. "Not by name. What's his handicap?"

A cheating heart, I wanted to say, but I knew Jason was probably talking about golf. "I have no idea."

"What's he look like?"

"Forties, overweight, though not as much as he used to be. One of his golf outfits has yellow and peach in it."

"That doesn't narrow it down much."

Stroking his chin, Jason turned toward the bar. Behind it, a woman who looked to be in her mid-thirties reached up to put away wine glasses in the wooden racks over her head. Each time she stretched, the hem of her blouse rose in the back to reveal a tramp stamp. The tattoo snaked its way south from the waistband of her hip-hugger skirt, down past the curve of her butt.

"Hey, Angel," Jason called to her. "Can you come over here for a few minutes? And bring us a couple of…" His eyebrow rose in a question.

"Just a Coke," I said. "I've got a long drive home."

"A couple of Cokes, please."

When the barmaid turned to us, I got a better look. Pretty, in a hard way: Heavy makeup, skirt too short, blouse too tight, showing plenty of cleavage. She set up a cocktail tray with two cans of soda and two glasses of ice. Brushing a strand of bright blonde hair from her eyes, she approached the table.

"Angela Fox, this is…" The blank look flitted onto Jason's face again.

49

"Mace Bauer," I completed the introduction for him.

"Sorry," he said. "Your beauty must have shorted out a few of my brain cells."

I didn't doubt Jason was short a few million cells, but I suspected something other than my beauty was to blame.

"Mace is some kind of investigator," he added for Angel's benefit.

"Not exactly," I said.

Her brow furrowed. "Are you looking into that woman who was found murdered at the dump?"

"Why? Do you know something about that?"

"No," Jason butted in quickly. "Angel's just curious. Everybody's talking about it."

"Actually, I'm looking into something personal," I said.

She placed the sodas on the table, tucked the tray under an arm, and reached out to shake my hand. "Angel's short for Angela, but nobody calls me that."

Her grip was pleasantly firm. I never trusted a woman whose hand plopped into mine like a gutted black crappie. "What can I do for you, Mace? I can't take much time away from the bar."

"Have a seat for a few minutes." Jason poured one of the Cokes; half a can in his glass and half in mine. "It's really slow before dinner."

She glanced around the almost empty room, and then stared pointedly at the empty chair. Jason jumped up to pull it out.

"That's a good boy," Angel said.

He beamed, like the classroom screw-up who'd just managed to impress the teacher.

When she'd settled herself, she looked me in the eyes. Hers were sharp, assessing. I couldn't quite place her accent, but it definitely wasn't local. Up north, somewhere. I got right to the point, asking her about Kenny.

"Sure, I've seen him around. Nice guy; sells insurance. He doesn't seem like much of a golfer, though." She turned to Jason. "You know him. He uses a set of beat-up Callaways. He's got a big pickup with mud flaps and a No. 3 for Dale Earnhardt on the rear window."

Jason looked through some sliding glass doors to the lighted parking lot beyond. The grilles of a couple of Lexuses and a Mini Cooper pointed toward the clubhouse. Kenny's Ford F-350 would stick out in that lot like a fat man at an organic restaurant.

"Oh, yeah: Ken," he finally said. "He's got a terrible left hook."

Not knowing a hook from a slice, I brought the conversation back to my purpose. "Do you know who he plays golf with out here? My sister's married to him, and she suspects somebody he's been hanging around with owes him a lot of money he doesn't want to tell her about."

I'd learned most people are more comfortable poking their noses into problems about money than love.

"I really dig the way you talk," Angel blurted out. Under lashes thick with mascara, her eyes were wide and interested. "That little ol' country gal accent is so adorable."

I think I was still in diapers the last time someone called me adorable. It's not a word usually applied to a woman who stomps around in work boots wrestling nuisance critters.

"Thanks," I said. "But back to Kenny…"

She lowered her voice to a seductive purr: "You know, I've always wanted to taste something country fresh."

"Down, girl!" Jason slapped playfully at her wrist.

The glare she gave him did not seem playful. With a contrite look, he stood and shoved his offending hand into a pocket. "I need to get back to the pro shop. Watch out for Angel, Mace. She's a devil."

I had no doubt he was right. "Wait a minute," I said as he walked away. "What about Kenny?"

"Can't tell you much." He spoke over his shoulder. "He usually just picks up a game when somebody's short a player. Sometimes, he fills in for a threesome with our potty-mouthed mayor."

The mayor? I was so surprised, I choked on my Coke. An errant swallow started a coughing fit, which didn't subside until Jason was back at the cash register in the pro shop. Angel handed me a napkin.

"Do you know anything about that?" I finally managed to ask.

"The mayor?"

I nodded, the napkin pressed to my lips.

"Tosses his clubs and swears like a sailor whenever he makes a bad shot, which is a lot."

"I meant about him and Kenny."

She shrugged. "Neither of them is a very good player, so they're evenly matched. It's just a round of golf. It's not like they're best friends. At least I don't think they are. I barely know your brother-in-law."

My mind refused to form an image of Kenny golfing with Himmarshee's mayor. Then again, I hadn't been able to picture him cheating on my sister or wearing that plaid tam-o'-shanter cap, either.

"The mayor's wife comes out here a lot, too," Angel said. "Her book group meets right over there." She nodded at a round table for ten in the center of the dining room. Couples were beginning to filter in for dinner.

"She runs the group?" I asked.

Angel raised her brows. "Have you met Mrs. In-Charge?"

"'Nuff said."

"She's always spouting off about some 'important' book, tossing around a lot of big words like character arc and narrative tension. I don't understand half of what she says. Of course, that could be because…" She cocked back her head and made the hand motion for drinking.

"She's a boozer?" I asked.

"Big time. And the more she drinks, the more she likes to hear herself talk." Angel took a swallow of Coke from the glass Jason left. "I'm not much for reading anyway. My dad always used to say street smarts are better than book smarts."

"They aren't mutually exclusive. Reading's not just a way to learn about things, it's a great way to escape reality. Get into an imaginary world."

"I don't need to escape. How about you, Mace? Do you like to try new things? Escape your usual world?" Her voice had gone all low again. She reached across the table and stroked my wrist.

I pulled away and held up my hand to display the ring Carlos gave me. "I'm engaged."

"That's all right. Maybe your fiancé would like to come out here and play, too?"

I suspected she wasn't talking about golf. Ducking her question, I looked at my watch. Those sharp eyes of hers didn't miss the gesture. She pushed back her chair and stood.

"My shift's over. The dinner crew is coming on, and I'm going home. Sorry I couldn't be more help."

Her apology sounded more reflexive than genuine. I dug in my pocket; found a damp ten-dollar bill. I put it on her tray. "Keep the change."

Her face lit up. No smirk or seduction now. It was the first truly happy smile I'd seen from her. Money was clearly a strong motivator for Angel Fox.

TEN

After I left the bar, I roamed around a bit, waiting to see if Kenny would wander in to the country club. I perused some golf-related art: a bronze sculpture of two old-timey looking players, bags slung over their shoulders; framed posters of greens and fairways at legendary courses; portraits of famous golfers from Ben Hogan to Bubba Watson.

I checked out the driving range, and then made a pit stop in the ladies' locker room. Its plush carpet was Kelly green, patterned with miniature golf balls and clubs. The place was immaculate. I didn't detect a whiff of sweat. It smelled sweet, like vanilla candles and maraschino cherries. The sink countertop offered an array of folded hand towels, fancy body lotion, and complimentary combs. I popped one into my purse, preparation for the next morning I left the house without remembering to brush my hair.

Outside, I caught up with a few phone calls. I confirmed with Mama that I'd see her for church in the morning; and then checked on Maddie. Kenny still hadn't come home. According to my wristwatch, I'd been killing time for at least forty-five minutes. If Kenny planned to show later, I'd have to miss him. Carlos and I had dinner plans.

On the way to my car in the parking lot, I glanced in through oversized windows and saw the dinner crowd. The women were tanned and tight, wearing lots of makeup and jewelry. The men slapped backs and downed dark whiskey from rocks glasses. Angel was still behind the bar. When she saw me staring, she ducked her head, and got busy polishing a brandy snifter.

I kept walking. So her shift wasn't over after all. Big deal. She wasn't the first worker dependent on tips to tell a customer a convenient lie. I decided to turn and give her a friendly wave, signaling no hard feelings. When I did, I saw she'd lifted her face to watch me leave. Her eyes were slits; her expression was arctic.

For some reason, an image of the gator my cousin and I had wrestled out of the golf course pond flitted into my mind. I wondered whether another of the big reptiles had moved in to take his place. At least in the wild, you know which animals are predators and which are prey. Unlike people, they don't have the capacity to conceal their true nature.

———

Carlos's phone rang. He answered, listened for a bit, and then eyed me warily.

"I need to take this outside," he said to the caller. Tucking the phone protectively to his chest, he turned from me and walked out the kitchen to the back door. I heard it shut. A few moments later, there came an indistinct murmur from the farthest corner of his apartment's courtyard.

Jeez. A girl eavesdropped a few times, and he never let her forget it.

Surveying the table, I spooned up the last flecks of a custardy *flan* from a dessert bowl. Those flecks and crumbs from a loaf of Cuban bread were all that remained of the yummy supper he'd had waiting when I arrived. Bowls of thick garbanzo bean soup, fried plantains, and a cup of *café con leche*. I was so stuffed I felt like a hot water bottle filled to bursting. I trundled off my kitchen chair and into the living room, intent upon collapsing on the couch.

A framed, vintage travel poster of Cuba held a place of honor on the main room's wall. A hefty cigar rested in an ashtray; a treat Carlos allowed himself a couple of times a week. Photos of family members were displayed on a small table next to the couch: His grandfather, on horseback at the cattle ranch the family owned before Fidel Castro took power. Carlos's older brother, who died in a tragic accident when the two were just boys. His parents, standing on an airport tarmac facing an uncertain future as Cuban exiles. His beloved grandmother, cooking *picadillo* in Carlos's Miami kitchen.

There were photos of Carlos in police uniform in Miami, but no pictures of his late wife. That loss may still have been too painful for him to remember.

The door slammed shut. I heard the hollow thud of his shoes hitting the tiled floor in the hallway. By the time he made it to the living room, I was stretched out on the couch with my feet on a pillow and the button at the waist of my work pants undone.

"Comfortable?" he asked with a grin.

"Like a pig in slop." I shifted a bit on the couch and patted the space beside me. "Was that call about the girl we found dead at the dump?"

He groaned.

"What? I'm just wondering if you've had any breaks in the case."

"You mean have I solved it yet? This is only the second day."

"I'm not criticizing, Carlos. I'm just wondering if you've found out any more about how she got there. You managed to identify her pretty quickly."

"Her purse with the wallet still in it was under the body. Can we talk about something else?"

"So between that and the bracelet, we know it wasn't robbery."

"Mace!"

"Okay, okay." I picked up the remote. "You want to watch TV?"

He shook his head. "Is there any *flan* left?"

"Uhmm … sorry."

"I'll forgive you for eating my share of the dessert if you get off your butt and help me clean up." He patted my stomach. "Maybe it'll burn off some of those extra calories you scarfed down."

I waggled my eyebrows at him. "I know another way to burn calories. And it's a lot more fun."

I tugged at his belt. He nestled closer and kissed me.

"Well, I guess cleaning the kitchen can wait," he said, his dark eyes smoldering.

Later, Carlos handed me a water glass. I dried it, and put it away in the kitchen cabinet. His glasses were arranged neatly by size, like Little Leaguers in a team picture. The first time I was at his apartment, I was impressed that he had a full set of dinnerware and glasses made of actual glass. The guys I'd been used to dating had nothing in their cabinets but oversized plastic cups from McDonald's and a motley assortment of foam beer huggies. You don't show up as a shirtless suspect on *Cops* without drinking a lot of beer.

He handed me a clean plate, the last one. The drain in the sink made a sucking sound as the dishwater disappeared. "Want some more coffee?"

"Naw, I need to get some sleep. I promised Mama I'd take her to church in the morning, and she gets really upset when I snore in the pew."

"Will you see your sisters afterwards?"

Carlos knew they wouldn't be in church, since Marty was a practicing Buddhist, and Maddie found Mama's religion a bit too heart-on-your-sleeve-Christian. She preferred the more restrained worship at the Methodist church. Thinking about Maddie made me worry again about what Kenny was up to.

"Mace?"

I realized I was still standing there next to the sink, holding the wet plate. It dripped onto the tail of the white dress shirt Carlos had loaned me to wear to bed. After we made love, we'd showered and changed into nightclothes.

I swiped the dish towel across the dinner plate, and placed it in the cabinet on the top of a same-sized stack of china.

"I think I will have a bit more coffee," I said, holding up my thumb and forefinger, an inch or two apart. "*Un poco café*, with lots of *leche*."

Once I had my milky coffee, we sat at the table. The spoon clinked softly as I stirred, staring at a calendar on the refrigerator. It was only six days until Kenny's party.

"Is everything okay, *niña*? You seem distracted."

Carlos looked across the table, his eyes warm with kindness and concern. I'd seen every kind of emotion in those eyes: dark with anger; burning with desire; narrowed in suspicion. But for some reason, it was the kindness that really did me in. I'm sure Kenny must have looked at Maddie that way a million times. It made me feel like crying.

Instead, I blew on the *café con leche* to cool it. "I've got some bad news about Maddie's husband, Kenny."

"Is he sick?"

"Yeah, sick of being married. He's cheating on her."

"No way!"

"Yep. She's asked me to nose around and see what I can find out about who he's running around with." I sipped at the coffee. "It's a secret, Carlos. You can't tell anyone. And for God's sake, don't say anything to Mama."

He added another spoonful of sugar to his espresso-sized cup, a *cafecito*. "I'm a detective. I'm used to keeping secrets."

I smiled at him. "You can say that again!"

We drank, sitting comfortably together in the kitchen. The clock ticked on the wall. A drip of water fell from the faucet. I've never been one to fill in a silence with chatter. Fortunately, Carlos was the same way. I thought about what he said about keeping secrets.

"What do you suppose was the murder victim's secret?" I finally asked.

He shook his head, lips pressed tightly together above the rim of his cup.

"I mean, a librarian? Dressed up like that? Who'd imagine it?"

"Who indeed?" He sipped his coffee.

"It's not like I'm interested in the case. I didn't even know the woman. I'm just curious how she wound up like she did. Dressed like that? Strangled?"

When Carlos didn't answer, I lifted the top off the sugar bowl and peered inside. It needed more sugar. No surprise. He was as big of a sweet freak as I was.

"And now," I continued, "with Kenny cheating? It just makes me wonder the kinds of things people hide; even people you see every day."

Carlos put his cup down. "Everybody is hiding something, *niña*."

"I'm not. What you see is what you get with me."

He gave a short laugh. "Really? You may think of yourself as no-nonsense and straightforward, but you're a bundle of hidden motives and contradictions."

"I am not!" I said, insulted.

"Are too."

"For example?"

He brushed a bit of hair from my face; caressed my cheek. "Just look at how long it took you to admit you wanted to be with me."

"Ha! I think I made it pretty clear I wanted to be with you, almost from the first minute I saw you. Well, as soon as you let Mama out of jail, anyway."

"I'm not talking about sex."

"Really? That's too bad."

He smiled—that slow, sultry smile that always knocked me off balance. "Well, we can talk about sex." Holding gently to my wrist, he raised my left hand. The light over the kitchen table caught the diamond on the engagement ring. "But only if you admit first you played games and kept secrets before you accepted this."

I was silent, watching the ring as it sparkled and gleamed. The sight, a symbol of our commitment, still gave me a thrill. But now it was tinged with another emotion, some niggling fear that burrowed like a tick into my happiness.

It was Kenny's fault for hurting my sister. For betraying her love. I'd always looked up to the two of them as a perfect couple, everything a long and happy marriage should be. If he could cheat on Maddie, anything could go wrong with any couple. Even Carlos and me.

"Mace?" He released my wrist. "You were going to confess?"

The question in his voice brought me back to the kitchen table, to the present. To the future, with Carlos.

"Okay, I admit it. I wasn't entirely upfront about my feelings for you. I'm not even sure I was telling the truth to myself."

"Now, that's what I like to hear, you admitting to having a bundle of secrets!"

His kiss was slow; sweet. When we drew apart, he traced the line of my lips with his finger. He continued, following a well-traveled trail down my chin, along my neck and down, down, to the buttons of the shirt I'd borrowed. I melted. He moaned.

"And now…" His fingers were performing magic beneath the cotton fabric of the shirt. "Now, I think we can talk about sex."

Threading my fingers into his thick hair, I pulled his face to my breasts.

"Talk?" I said. "That's all? You know, we wouldn't want anyone to accuse us of being all talk and no action."

With that, we got down to action.

ELEVEN

MORNING SUNLIGHT STREAMED THROUGH the window in Carlos's kitchen. He whistled, scrambling eggs on the stove. I handed him the bowl of cheddar cheese I'd grated. Carefully, he extracted small pinches and sprinkled it over the eggs so that no section got more or less than any other section. I grinned at him.

"It's not surgery, Carlos. I usually just toss it all in there. It gets scrambled up anyway."

"Anything worth doing is worth doing correctly."

"Right."

"Exactly. That's what I said."

"No, the saying is..."

Right, correctly. What difference did it make? Maybe the idiom was off a tad, but the meaning was clear. I lined up little slices of cherry tomatoes across the eggs, as neat as columns of numbers. I was rewarded with a knowing smile from Carlos.

"Now you're getting the hang of it."

I set the table and then took a seat while he popped bread from the toaster and plated our breakfast. When he placed the eggs in front of me with a waiter's flourish, I got a warm feeling in my stomach. I don't think it was just hunger, either. I felt taken care of. Content.

"I could get used to this."

"Careful, Mace. I might take that to mean you want us to move in together."

Suddenly, the warm feeling in my gut tightened into a knot. It was too soon. I wasn't ready. We'd only been engaged two months. Who knew whether it would last between us? When Maddie and Kenny wed, hadn't she thought her marriage would last forever? *Until death do us part.*

The familiar words from the wedding vows made me think of the murdered woman, Camilla. No doubt she was not ready for death to take her. I saw her lifeless body in my mind's eye, discarded and left to decay in the dump. I stared at my untouched food.

"Is something wrong? Your eggs are getting cold," Carlos said.

"It looks great." I took a couple of bites, pushed the food around my plate. "I guess I'm not as hungry as I thought I was. Maybe I ate too much garbanzo bean soup last night."

"Not to mention more than your share of *flan.*"

Outside the window, a cloud passed over the sun. The kitchen fell into shadow. What was wrong with me? I had a good man, who'd just cooked my Sunday morning breakfast. So why was I obsessing about a murdered woman? Why was I feeling trapped?

"Look at the time," I said, glancing at the kitchen clock. "I've got to get home to change into church clothes."

"So soon? You've barely eaten a thing."

I scooped the eggs onto my toast and made a sandwich. "I'll finish it on the drive home."

"We've got to talk, Mace."

Thankfully, his cell phone rang at that moment, saving me from having to explain my mood change. How could I do that when I didn't understand it myself? He grabbed his phone from the kitchen counter and checked the caller ID.

"I should take this."

I'll call you. I mouthed the words, hand-signaling a phone to my ear.

He answered his cell, and then burst into rapid-fire Spanish. I couldn't *comprendo* a word. Even as he spoke to the caller, he held up a wait-a-minute finger to me. His puzzled frown followed me as I walked toward the door.

———

The music minister at Mama's church hit the first chords on his portable piano. "What a Friend We Have in Jesus." I hoped that was true, because I felt a bit short on the friend front that morning. I was playing games with a man who loved me. I'd already insulted both Mama and Sal. And I'd slipped up and called the pastor by the wrong name.

Even the little boy in the pew beside me pinched me on the thigh when I slid in and gave his head a friendly pat. It wasn't shaping up as my best Sunday morning ever.

We were still standing outside on the sidewalk before services at Abundant Forgiveness Love & Charity Chapel when Mama started sniping about my fashion missteps.

"Is that the only clean blouse you had in your closet, Mace?" She picked some lint off my wrinkled collar. "You know what I always say about black fabric: It picks up everything but men and money. Not to mention, it's more appropriate for a funeral than for Sunday worship."

I took in her watermelon-colored pantsuit, accessorized with dangly earrings and bangle bracelets in the same shade of reddish-pink as her scarf. And Mama was calling me out on my wardrobe choices? I lifted her fingers off my collar.

"My blouse is navy blue."

"Uh-huh." Mama dug around in her purse, and then held out her tube of Apricot Ice. "Here you go, honey. This won't make up for that nest of knots in your hair ... did you even brush it this morning? But it will perk up your complexion a bit. I wish you'd listen to me when I tell you that those drab shades aren't your best choice. You should be wearing the vibrant colors from Color Me Gorgeous's winter palette. "

"My complexion is fine." I started to run a hand through my hair. When my fingers snagged in snarls, I realized she was right. "Speaking of color, you've got Apricot Ice smeared all over your incisors. I guess your eyes aren't what they used to be."

She whipped out her mirrored compact; rubbed a finger over her teeth. "My eyes are fine, sweetheart. They're sure good enough to see you got up on the wrong side of the bed today."

Sal draped a massive, bear-sized paw over each of our shoulders. I squirmed to get away, but he just drew Mama and me closer. "What's the problem with my two favorite girls? I want youse two to stop all this fighting. How's about a kiss to make up?"

"Jeez, Sal, you smell like a humidor." I waved a hand in front of my nose. "Didn't you tell Mama you were giving up cigars?"

His smile faltered, and his grip loosened on my shoulder. He flashed a guilty look at Mama, who was now regarding him through narrowed eyes. Good. Once they got going at each other, I was off the hook. As the minister approached to bid us hello, I had a momentary stab of conscience over stirring up trouble. I think I was breaking that commandment to honor thy father and mother. Or, in my case, thy mother and fourth stepfather. And there we were, right outside God's house—even if it was a storefront in a strip mall next to the Pork Pit barbecue joint.

"Good morning, Mace." The minister took my hand. "What a pleasure to see you after such a long time."

"It hasn't been all that long, Reverend Idella."

Sal smirked. Mama poked me in the side.

"It's Delilah, dear." She gave my fingers a gentle squeeze before she moved on to greet the next, likely more faithful, member of her flock.

Now, the hymns had been sung. Next to me, the pinching kid was punching his little brother. The Rev. *Delilah* was preaching her sermon. She'd chosen to focus on the murdered librarian, since that was all anybody in town was talking about.

"I've heard, like all of you have, about how that poor girl was dressed. Don't gossip about her; don't be quick to judge. Remember what Jesus said: '*He that is without sin among you, let him cast the first stone...*'"

She counseled the congregation not to fear the evil on the loose in Himmarshee that would drive a person to murder: " '*Don't let your heart be troubled,'* " she said, quoting from the Book of John. *"You believe in God…"*

But even if God is watching over us, that's no reason to be stupid, Delilah warned. "If you see something that doesn't seem right, something that makes you suspicious, let the police know. We need to pull together as a community and make sure the person who committed this sin is not free to kill again."

Amen to that.

When the service ended, the worshippers gathered for food and fellowship in a second storefront the church had taken over next door. The little chapel was growing. After that trouble with Delilah's ex-husband, who had been the previous minister, she was proving to be a popular attraction. At first, crowds came to the church solely because of the scandal, not to mention the murder. But memories fade. Now the congregation was one-hundred percent behind Delilah, and the female perspective she brought to the pulpit.

The tables nearly sagged with plates of goodies. There was a country ham, with flaky biscuits for mini sandwiches. Cold side dishes, prepared with copious amounts of mayonnaise, included coleslaw, macaroni, and potato salad. Pies and layer cakes competed for space with homemade candy, like pecan divinity and chocolate-marshmallow fudge. The members of Abundant Forgiveness definitely took their abundance seriously. Nobody had a hope of counting calories here.

Loading up my plate, I saw D'Vora, from the beauty parlor, alone against the wall. She'd foregone any food at all, watching the crowd as she sipped a soft drink from a plastic bottle. I grabbed the chair next to hers.

"Fancy meeting you here," I said.

She nodded hello, giving me a forced smile. So, even D'Vora was mad at me?

"Was it something I said?"

"Sorry, Mace." She balanced the plastic bottle on the seat between her knees. "I'm not myself this morning."

"Late night?"

She shook her head.

"Trouble with Darryl?"

"No more than usual."

Sal wandered up. "Why do gorgeous girls always gather together? Youse two are like pretty bluebirds in a garden."

I think I must have preened a little, but D'Vora just stared at her soda bottle.

"She's not herself this morning," I explained to Sal.

"Probably the murder." He took a cigar from his top pocket, caressed it like a precious jewel, and put it back. "That's got everybody on edge. It's a hell of a thing. People are trying to make sense of it, and having trouble doing it. What do you suppose happened to her, Mace?"

"Beats me. It's too strange to even contemplate."

When Sal began talking about the murder, D'Vora had shifted her focus to the nutritional information on the soft drink's paper label. She picked at the paper until the glue gave, and then peeled off the label in tiny strips. She was as intent on the task as a heart surgeon performing a bypass.

My eyes met Sal's over D'Vora's head, and I nodded slightly toward her. He shrugged a little, perhaps a sign he'd also noticed that the normally gossipy beautician was strangely uninterested.

The big man took a seat on D'Vora's other side, lowering his body gingerly into one of the flimsy folding chairs. His voice, usually a Bronx blare, was surprisingly soft and gentle. "Sweetheart, is there something you want to talk about?"

He lifted her chin. Was Sal looking for evidence on her face that Darryl might have hit her? We all knew he liked his beer, hated work, and was as immature as a junior high school boy, but I'd never heard the slightest hint he was abusive.

She smiled at Sal, and shook her head. "Nothing's wrong, y'all. I'm just not feeling great this morning."

Uh-oh. Morning sickness? A bawling infant was the last thing D'Vora and the chronically unemployed Darryl needed in that crowded trailer with those three Rottweiler dogs.

"D'Vora, you're not…" I put my hands over my own belly.

"Lord, no! I'm already taking care of one baby who refuses to grow up."

"You're sure you're okay?" Sal aimed his interrogator eyes at her. She nodded, her gaze drifting back to the label she was shredding.

"I hope you're feeling better in time for Kenny's big party. It's gonna be a blast," he said. "Are you taking Darryl?"

The plastic bottle tumbled off D'Vora's lap, bouncing on the tiled floor. The last few swallows of the drink spayed out all over my dressiest flip-flops. My toes would be soda-sticky the rest of the morning.

"Sorry, Mace," she mumbled. She bent to retrieve the dropped bottle, and her church program slid from the chair to the floor. She was trying to pick up that, when her shoulder purse fell off her arm. Sal scooped up the bottle, and I handed her the program and her purse.

"What in the world is wrong with you, D'Vora?" I asked.

"I told you I'm fine!" Her tone was sharp. "Quit hounding me. If I had anything to say to you, don't you think I would have said it?"

Clutching her church program and purse to her chest, she stormed out the door.

TWELVE

"Mace, honey, close your mouth. You're gonna catch flies."

I was staring slack-jawed out the church-front window. I'd called to D'Vora as she left, but she ignored me, which was becoming a pattern. She was already at the curb, hoisting herself into the passenger seat of Darryl's big truck. Gunning the engine, he darted into traffic on State Road 70, causing a Hawaiian-shirted tourist in a rental vehicle to screech to a stop. Cars swerved. Horns honked. Darryl flicked a cigarette butt out the window, lifted a beer from the cup holder in the console, and made an illegal U-turn across a double yellow line.

Where was a cop when you needed one?

"Mace!"

I turned. "I heard you the first time, Mama. Catch Flies. Close Mouth."

"See? I told you. No respect!" She spoke to one of her fellow church ladies, who tsked-tsked at me in motherly empathy. "We were trying to get your opinion on whether the soprano in the choir and the music minister would make a nice couple."

"I suppose so, Mama. Not that it's any of my business." I glanced out the window again. The truck was gone, and Darryl and D'Vora with it.

"She hasn't been the same since her husband passed away, poor thing. But it's been a year. I think it's time, and Phyllis agrees. Don't you think so?"

Both Mama and her pal Phyllis raised their brows, awaiting my answer.

"Everybody's different, Mama. You can't put a stopwatch on grief." My focus shifted to the music minister, a middle-aged man with a slight paunch and a quick smile, despite an overbite. Someone standing next to him at the food table said something and his laugh boomed across the room.

"He's got a heart as big as that laugh," Mama said. "Too bad about those buck teeth, though. He could gnaw an ear of corn through a picket fence, bless his heart."

I watched as he scanned the rows of seats until he found the soprano. She studied an open hymn book in her lap. As if she could feel his gaze, she raised her face. Tucking a lock of hair behind an ear, she rewarded him with a radiant smile.

Darned if Mama wasn't right about the two of them becoming a couple. She might have been unlucky in love, but Mama's sense about other people's relationships was uncanny. Of course, I'd rather chew glass than admit that to her.

She jabbed her elbow at her friend Phyllis. "Look at those two. I'm telling you, a musical romance is abloom."

She nodded, satisfied, and then turned her attention from the soprano to me. "Now, speaking of couples…"

Before I had a chance to escape, she said to Phyllis, "Have you heard Mace is engaged?"

I showed her my ring. Her oohs and aahs brought a couple of other church members over to our little group.

"When's the date?" one asked, picking up my hand to turn the ring this way and that.

"There's no hurry," I answered, extracting myself from her grasp.

"Oh, yes there is," said another woman, as she too grabbed at my hand. "You're not getting any younger."

"That's certainly true," Mama said.

Et tu?

"The bigger issue, though, is whether my daughter will stop this back-and-forth with her wonderful fiancé, Carlos. Now, y'all know Mace's rocky history…"

"You do realize, Mama, I'm standing right here? Maybe your friends would like to hear a story about someone who drank too much pink wine and managed to misplace her own fancy ring?"

She gave me a long look, and then continued. With an eager chorus chiming in, she narrated the highs and lows of my notorious love life. Mainly the lows.

"Remember when Mace spotted an ex-boyfriend on *Cops*, on TV? What was he in trouble for again, honey?"

When I didn't answer, one of the church ladies chimed in. "Wasn't that the mo-ron who robbed the Booze 'n' Breeze, only to have his old truck break down when he pulled out of the drive-thru to make his getaway?"

"Yep," another of the women said. "The sheriff's deputies caught him when he ran off and jumped in a canal. Mo-ron forgot he couldn't swim. And all of it caught by the TV camera, too."

I tuned out, and began to think about what Mama said about me going back and forth with Carlos. There was more truth in her accusation than I wanted to admit. What was my problem, anyway? With my thumb, I spun the engagement ring on my finger. I still wasn't used to the heft of it on my hand, or the way the diamond on top poked into my pinky when the ring slipped off-center.

"How 'bout that rodeo cowboy?" I vaguely heard one of the women say. "Didn't he leave Mace way back when for the home-coming queen?"

"He gambled something awful, I heard. Good-looking guy, though," another one of Mama's friends added.

"Honey, the bad ones always are." Phyllis chuckled.

I was half-listening, half-watching the music minister as he took a seat next to the soprano and handed her a coffee. I'd learned long ago it wasn't worth interjecting when Mama and her church pals got going on a topic, even if this one happened to center on me.

"Wasn't there a little something she had going with Lawton Bramble's boy, too?" someone asked.

"That was the awful year we did the horseback ride on the Flor-ida Cracker Trail. Even Carlos had to understand Mace wasn't in her right mind when she started messing around with Trey Bramble. That's what happens when somebody's trying to kill you."

"Rosalee, you mean trying to kill *you*, right?" one of the women said.

"Well, both of us, the way it turned out."

"Awful sad about what happened to Lawton, though." All the women nodded at the redhead who spoke. "Just proves you can be as rich as Croesus in cattle and still wind up dead, face first in a vat of cow-hunter chili."

Their momentary silence was broken when Phyllis gasped, her eyes as wide as collection plates: "Speaking of murder, what if one of Mace's exes had something to do with that poor girl at the dump?"

"Don't be ridiculous!" Mama slapped Phyllis's arm. "None of my daughter's loser boyfriends ever committed anything more than petty crimes. Plus, now she's engaged to a police detective, one of the good guys."

A newcomer to the conversation turned my hand to peer at my ring. I feared a stress fracture at the wrist from the repetitive motion.

"Murder is a nasty business, y'all." Mama clucked her tongue. "Now, about Mace's love life…"

Someone interrupted her, drawing talk back to the deadly fate of the unlucky Camilla. A gruesome homicide with sexual overtones would always trump rocky romance. Mama realized she'd lost her audience.

She hooked an elbow through mine and pulled me aside. "Honey, I just want to make sure you're not going to jack around that man of yours again. He won't take it another time."

I sighed. "Carlos is the one, Mama. I'm certain." I held up my hand. "I've got the ring to prove it. It's settled."

The engagement ring really was lovely. Not so the skin around my wrist, which was starting to redden from all the church ladies tugging at my hand.

Mama looked dubious. She eyed the assembled crowd, stopping when she located a knot of church folk gathered by the coffeepot.

"Maybe you should have a backup in case things go wrong. A Plan B Man."

My eyes followed hers, which were focused on the choir's geeky baritone. I snorted. "That man is fifty years old if he's a day. And he still lives with his mama. Plus, he rides a three-wheeled bicycle to work, bagging groceries at the supermarket."

I waved my ring under her nose. "I am a happily engaged woman, Mama. I don't need a Plan B."

She batted away my hand. "There are plenty of rings on fingers out there. Plenty of bad marriages, too. That ring doesn't mean a thing if you—or your husband—end up with a broken heart."

I thought about Mama's aptitude for understanding romance. Did she sense something about me I myself didn't know? Maybe having witnessed *her* series of marital train wrecks spoiled me for commitment. I saw Maddie's tear-streaked face in my mind. I couldn't help thinking about Kenny; about their twenty-plus years of marriage, now endangered. Carlos and I weren't even married yet. Things could go bad. Maybe I did need a backup plan.

For some reason, an image of the gorgeous golf pro flitted behind my eyes. That was immediately followed by a rush of guilt. I don't know why. It wasn't like I planned to do anything with the guy. I was just thinking. Harmless daydreaming. It wasn't like I was considering making Jason—or was it Josh?—my Plan B Man.

Was I?

THIRTEEN

My mouth watered. The aroma of meat on the grill drifted through the dining room at the golf course. They don't call Himmarshee County the buckle in Florida's beef belt for nothing. Speaking of which, my own belt might need a new hole if I managed to finish the still-sizzling slab of steak in front of me.

"Hand me that steak sauce, would you Mace?" Sal pointed his fork at the house brand bottle on the table.

"Try it before you douse it. You can't beat the taste of a fine cut of meat, simply prepared." Sawing off a hunk from my own Porterhouse, I held it up for Sal's inspection. "Nothing but meat, a nice marbling of fat, and some salt and pepper."

He plucked it off my steak knife and popped it into his mouth. "Mmm-hmm," he said, chewing.

"What'd I tell you?" I grinned. "Carnivore nirvana-vor!"

My sister Marty, likely the only vegetarian in a twenty-five-mile radius, speared a cucumber from her salad. She chomped on the celery stalk garnishing her virgin Bloody Mary. "You'd both be a lot healthier if you'd cut back on the meat, and bulk up on your greens."

Catching the waiter's eye, Sal tapped the rim of his empty glass to signal he wanted a second martini. "Do olives count as greens, Marty?"

She shook a finger at him. "Not when they're soaked in gin."

Mama looked at her watch and frowned. "It's one o'clock. I thought Maddie would be here by now."

I'd been so distracted—studying the menu, selecting my steak, lecturing Sal on the virtues of un-sauced meat—I'd forgotten to mention my big sister wouldn't be joining us.

"I talked to Maddie on my cell on the way here, Mama. She can't make it."

"Why not?" she asked.

The truth was Maddie was too upset over this mess with Kenny to enjoy the family's company, not even with the added bonus of dessert. But I wasn't about to reveal that.

"She's not feeling well," I said.

"What's wrong with her?" Marty asked.

Mama snatched a French fry from my plate, leaving her own healthy serving of rice untouched. I thrust my steak knife at her in warning.

"She's just a little under the weather," I answered Marty.

"How so?" Mama asked.

Now, even Sal had put down his fork and was awaiting my update. Nothing gets my family interested like evasiveness. I glanced around at the nearby tables and lowered my voice to a whisper.

"She has her period, okay?"

Reddening, Sal changed the subject. "Hey, I think I see the mayor and his wife coming in. You know them, don't you Mace?"

Mama interrupted before I could answer him. "I gave Maddie some special raspberry and chamomile to make Time of the Month tea. That should help her cramps. Isn't she using it, Mace?"

"I'm not sure, Mama. I'm not in charge of monitoring Maddie's herbal tea intake."

Mama slipped her cell phone from her purse. "I'm going to call her right now. I have to make sure she remembers to drink that tea."

"No, don't!" I said, more sharply than I intended.

All three of them stared at me. "I just meant don't bother her. She said on the phone she was going to fill a hot water bottle and take a nap. She's probably asleep right now."

"I remember my own periods." Mama happily shifted the focus to herself.

Sal tugged uncomfortably at his collar. She continued.

"Cramps so bad it felt like somebody crushed my uterus in a vise. An unnaturally heavy flow, too. I mean, I'd go through a package of tampons…"

"Here comes the mayor," Sal blurted, jumping up from our table.

"Oh, joy," Mama muttered as Marty giggled.

Sal, looking relieved, stretched out his big paw for a shake. "How are you today, Mayor Graf? And Mrs. Graf, too, of course. Join us!"

"Maybe for a minute or two," said the mayor.

Sal pulled out a chair for the mayor's wife, and all of us shifted around to make room. From the flinch on Sal's face after he took his seat, I could tell Mama had aimed a swift kick at him under the table.

"Now, Sally, these two probably have all sorts of important people to see." She offered a saccharine-sweet smile to Himmarshee's power couple. "Don't let us keep you."

Beatrice Graf settled into her chair, tugging at a short skirt of fuchsia satin. Her blouse, in the same shade of bright pink, clashed mightily with the permanent curls of her pomegranate-hued hair. A sprinkling of rhinestones glittered along her plunging neckline, like stars dotting a vast, bosomy galaxy.

"I'm never too busy to chat with my constituents. After all, you put me in office."

The mayor flashed a campaign poster grin—all white teeth, dark suit, and insincerity. I knew Mama had voted for his opponent. I admired her restraint, for a couple of seconds anyway.

"Actually," she said, "I supported the other candidate. He's a native Himmarsheean, and I've known him since I taught him in Sunday school, way back when. He's a good man, and would have made a fine mayor. No offense."

The mayor waved a hand, a diamond winking from his pinky ring. "None taken."

"Speaking of Sunday school, where do y'all worship?" Mama asked.

A look passed between the mayor and his wife. "Actually, we haven't found a permanent church home," Beatrice Graf said.

Mama cocked her head at Big Bill. "So you got a seat at the Chamber of Commerce, secured a political office, and joined the country club, but you haven't had time to find a church?"

"We're still looking for a good fit," the mayor said.

Beatrice began gathering up her purse. "We really must go, Bill. We've been out of town," she explained to us, "and social obligations really pile up."

A confused look crossed the mayor's face. "We haven't been out of—"

"—Of course we were! Your memory is getting terrible, Bill. Now, I said we have to go."

She shot to her feet. Mama put a hand on her arm.

"Just one more thing," she said. "I don't believe I've seen you 'looking' at Abundant Forgiveness Love & Charity Chapel. That's my church."

Mama rustled around in her purse, extracting Juicy Fruit gum, a broken blueberry-colored earring, and a crumpled receipt from Fran's Fancy Frocks and Duds. Finally, she pulled out a program from the morning's church service. "We'd love to have you stop by."

Beatrice snatched the program, folded it without a glance, and stuffed it into her own bag, a rhinestone-studded number in silver leather. I'd lay money that's where it would stay. In a week or so, she'd toss it out with candy wrappers, hair from her brush, and other garbage she mined from the bottom of that spacious satchel.

Beatrice and Big Bill gave lip service to religion. But between the mayor's filthy language when he missed a putt, and the way his wife filleted the murder victim's character without even knowing her, I'd venture a guess they weren't the worshipful type.

With Mama's invitation still hanging in the strained silence, a friendly visit to our table by the club's barmaid came as a welcome interruption. Nodding at me in recognition, Angel dropped her strong hands on Sal's shoulders. She massaged playfully, like a manager looking after a prizefighter.

"How's the martini, Sal? Loosening up those tight muscles, I hope. I made it dry as dust, just the way you like them."

Mama sat up straighter in her seat; Mayor and Mrs. Graf forgotten. She narrowed her eyes at Angel, whose bright blonde bangs were bouncing adorably onto her forehead. "I don't believe we've had the pleasure. I'm Rosalee, Sal's wife."

"Of course! He talks about you all the time. You're just as pretty as Sal said." She offered her hand. "I tend bar in the 19th Hole. I'm Angel, by the way."

Mama, mollified by the compliment, smoothed at her perfectly coiffed hair. She waited just a beat, and then took the barmaid's hand.

From across the table, Beatrice Graf cleared her throat. "Angel, the mayor and I are absolutely parched. We need some drinks, dear."

The tone of her voice was an odd mix of imperiousness and wheedling.

"I don't do table service," Angel said flatly. "I'll send over a waiter."

Seemingly chastened, Beatrice cast her eyes to the tablecloth, and began examining the silverware.

"Don't worry about it, Angel." The mayor's voice was chipper. He stood up to join his wife. "We'll find a seat in the bar."

He dropped a friendly hand on Angel's shoulder. With a frigid look, she shrugged it off and left our table. The mayor immediately went after her. After an awkward moment, his wife followed him.

"That was weird," Marty said, voice low. "What's the deal between those three?"

I shrugged, eager to get back to my steak. Mama speared another French fry from my plate. She made a face when she took a bite.

"It's colder than a heart on Wall Street," she said, depositing the half-eaten fry back on my plate. "What kind of people sit down and monopolize the dinner table right after your food is served?"

"You're the one who kept them around, interrogating them about church," I said.

"Sal was the one who took time away from dinner to flirt with that barmaid," she countered.

"I wasn't flirting, Rosalee. It's called being friendly."

"You may not think so, but she was definitely flirting with you." Mama dabbed her napkin in my water glass and scrubbed at a spot of ketchup on Sal's lapel.

"I was drinking that water, Mama." I slid the glass out of her reach. "Besides, Angel fools around with all her customers like that to boost her tips. She doesn't care about Sal."

"Thanks," he said, looking wounded.

"Are you dissing my husband, Mace?"

"Who wants dessert?" Marty said, employing the one sure-fire suggestion that would make us stop sniping and start eating again.

"I do!" all of us answered at once.

Sal signaled for the waiter, and we put in our dessert requests. As I sat, waiting for my Key lime pie and plotting how to keep Mama's fork out of my plate, I spotted Jason making his way across the dining room. A dozen pair of female eyes followed the golf pro's progress. I had to admit, he had a confident, sexy stride to match his sexy smile.

When he saw me, he cut a straight line to our table. He shook Sal's hand, asked him how he was hitting, and then turned his attention my way.

"Hello, gorgeous." He leaned and planted a kiss on my cheek.

Mumbling a greeting, I brushed my finger over the spot he'd kissed. It felt warm.

"I've been wondering when I'd see you again." He looked into my eyes. "I've thought about you a lot."

Mama coughed. Marty bit her lip. Sal tapped the table nervously.

"Jason, this is my mother and my sister." I gave him their names. He nodded hello, but barely seemed to register them. He didn't even do a double-take when I introduced Marty, whose doll-like beauty captivated most men.

His eyes held mine. "Do you think I could call you? I've thought about some of the things we talked about."

I felt a shiver of dread. He must know something about Kenny, but this was definitely the wrong time and place for him to bring it up. I fished a business card from the nature park out of my pocket and quickly concocted a cover story. "Give me a call tomorrow. If you've got a gator in the pond again, I can definitely help."

He looked confused, but palmed the card anyway. I suspected Jason spent a good amount of time not completely understanding what people were saying.

He bent to kiss my cheek again, his lips lingering just a bit longer this time.

"Goodbye, gorgeous."

No one said a word as Jason walked away. The waiter approached, with our dessert plates and coffee crowding a tray. Mama leaned close and grabbed my wrist, so hard it hurt. She whispered in my ear, her breath a hot blast.

"You know what they say about playing with fire, Mace. Somebody's bound to get burned."

FOURTEEN

MARTY TOOK A SHARP breath. Step faltering, she clutched my hand.

"It's like seeing a ghost." Her voice was hushed. "She's the image of Camilla."

From Mama's living room, we could see our dinner guest through the glass panels of the front door. Illuminated by the front porch light, the sister of the murder victim hesitated. She looked like she was trying to decide whether to ring the bell, or turn and run.

Mama was in the shower. She'd insisted Sal go out and leave us women alone to meet Camilla's sister. He'd taken Teensy, so the frantic-barking, early-warning system was absent. The young woman had crept so quietly across the porch, her presence took Marty and me by surprise.

The doorbell rang. I gave Marty a little push across the living room.

"Buck up, sister. You invited her over because she can use some support. Now, answer the door so we can be supportive."

Squaring her shoulders, Marty welcomed Prudence Law into Mama's home.

She did indeed look just like the newspaper picture of her slain sister. Her features were small and serious; her hair was long and dark. A fringe of bangs framed enormous eyes. Tonight they were puffy and red, and filled with sadness.

My sister clasped Prudence's hand in both of hers, and pulled her across the threshold. "I'm Marty, and this is Mace. I worked with Camilla at the library. We are so terribly sorry for your loss."

Nodding in agreement, I stood by feeling useless. Marty and Mama were more skilled at giving comfort. I was relieved to hear the clack of Mama's kitten-heeled sandals as she bustled from the bathroom hallway to the living room. She must have hurried to finish dressing. Her hair was damp, and she wore only one of the lemon-sherbet colored earrings that matched her pantsuit and shoes. A yellow scarf at her neck was slightly askew.

"Oh, honey… C'mere and let me give you a hug." She enveloped Prudence in a baby-powder-scented squeeze.

Stiffening slightly, our visitor seemed taken aback. I'd always heard the English were standoffish. Mama's hold didn't loosen. Soon, Prudence surrendered. She lowered her head to rest on Mama's shoulder.

"What an awful, awful thing." Murmuring, Mama stroked the young woman's back. "Don't worry. We're going to find out how this happened to your sister, aren't we Mace?"

When I didn't answer, she peeked around Prudence's head and scowled at me.

"The police are doing everything they can." I refused to let Mama bully me into making an empty promise to Prudence about something that didn't involve me or my family. "I just know they'll get you some answers soon."

———

"You're missing an earring." Maddie deposited several take-out containers from the Pork Pit on the kitchen counter, and then pointed to Mama's right ear.

Mama examined her reflection in a silver toaster. "Well, you girls might have mentioned that before Maddie got here. Plus, my scarf looks like a monkey escaped from the zoo and came to my house to practice his knot-tying skills."

Removing her scarf, she shook out the wrinkles from the lopsided bow.

Marty peered down the hallway to make sure Prudence was still in the bathroom, and then hissed at Mama: "We were a little distracted!"

I brought Maddie up to speed. "We were busy trying to comfort the loved one of a murder victim. But I can see how providing fashion commentary for Mama should have taken precedence."

"Don't sass me, girl." Mama slapped my wrist with the sherbet-colored scarf. "You are not too big for me to go out to the tree and cut a switch."

"Ooooooh!" I held out my hands and shook them. "I'm trembling."

Mama turned her back on me and re-tied her scarf. She started searching through her cabinets for serving platters for the meat and big bowls for the side orders.

"I don't know why we can't just eat out of the take-out boxes. You're making extra work with all those dishes to wash," I said.

"Well, why don't I just dump out everything right on the table? We can eat off that. Who needs plates anyway?" Mama rapped her knuckles on the tabletop. "Heck, who needs a table? Maybe we should put dog bowls on the floor, and get down there and eat with Teensy. That way we wouldn't have to wash any silverware, either."

"Since when does Teensy eat from a dog bowl? Every time I'm here, you're feeding that ridiculous mutt by hand."

I looked at my sisters. Marty gave me a conspiratorial wink. Maddie didn't seem to be paying attention. She'd pulled one of the white plastic containers aside. "No Sauce" was scrawled across the top with a heavy black marker. "The plain chicken breast is mine." She pointed to the box. "My stomach's still not feeling right."

Mama's brow immediately furrowed, but Marty shushed us all with a whisper. "Here comes Prudence! Try to behave, would you? And let's use the plates *and* the silver. We don't want to reinforce her worst stereotypes about Southerners."

"Agreed." Mama put a finger to her own lips, kissed it, and then placed it gently over my big mouth. "No sniping tonight, honey. Best behavior."

"I second that," said Maddie. She poured herself a glass of soda water. When she sipped, a loud burp escaped.

"What did I just say?" Mama scolded. "Manners, Maddie!"

Prudence's face was flushed, and a bit damp. She'd been in the bathroom for quite a while. Had she been crying? I thought of how I'd feel if one of my sisters died. A natural death would be bad enough. But to know Marty or Maddie had suffered at the hands of some sex maniac? I don't think I could stand that.

Mama finished dishing up the food. Marty was laying out plates. Maddie followed with silverware and a folded napkin for each place setting.

"What would you like to drink?" I asked Prudence. "We have sweet iced tea, wine, beer, or soda."

"Maybe I should stick to soda. I should have my wits about me, in case the police call with news."

She looked with longing at a box of sweet pink wine Mama had just hefted out of the refrigerator. Not waiting for Prudence to amend her order, Mama said, "One little glass isn't going to hurt you, honey. You can dilute it with a bit of fizzy water or lemon-lime soda, if you'd like."

Relief flashed across Prudence's face. "No, the wine alone will do quite nicely."

Mama handed over the glass, filled to the rim. Prudence didn't protest that it was too much, or that she didn't usually partake. She steadied the glass in both hands, raised it to her mouth, and took a huge swallow. Marty, Mama, and I exchanged a glance. Maddie didn't seem to notice.

As Mama and Marty finished pouring their drinks, I watched Maddie. She smoothed her napkin, tucking it under her plate. Then she straightened her fork, which she'd already placed at a precise angle. She pulled her smart phone from her pocket, and checked for messages. With a small shake of her head, she put it away.

This was the longest I'd ever seen my sister last without filching a bite or two of food before a meal began.

"Let's eat," Mama said, as she sat. She reached across the table and the four of us joined hands. Prudence, who'd begun unfolding her napkin, looked wary.

"We normally say a blessing, honey." Mama nodded for Maddie and me to include her in the circle. "Do you mind?"

Her face reddened. "Of course not. Please, do go ahead."

Mama thanked the Lord for the food she was about to serve. Hopefully, He didn't subtract points for the fact she hadn't actually cooked it. She thanked him for bringing her girls together, and for showing Prudence the path to her home. Then she finished up.

"Please God, watch over this dear girl. Help her overcome her sorrow. Please guide the authorities in their efforts to find out what happened to her sister, Camilla. And, if you should wish it, please make Mace do what she ought to and use her skills to find the murderer."

I aimed a sharp kick at Mama's shin. Too late. Prudence dropped our hands and lifted her face. She stared at me, those big eyes filled with questions.

"What does your mother mean? Can you find out what happened to Camilla? Can you find out who killed my sister?"

In the silence that followed, I heard Maddie take another sip of soda water. Marty's foot tapped nervously. The Elvis Presley clock on the wall made a brushing sound as the singer's famous pelvis swung back and forth. Mama's smile was as innocent as a baby's.

Finally, Marty spoke. "Mace is an amateur detective."

"She's solved several murders—with my help, of course." Mama patted her hair.

"I'm not sure the cops would put it that way." I was thinking of one particular cop. "They might say I've stuck my nose into some cases where it didn't belong."

"She's being modest." Marty offered our guest the platter with the chicken and ribs. Prudence took a serving of each, dousing them with barbecue sauce. "Mace has a different way of looking at the world—"

"You can say that again." After interrupting, Maddie added nothing more.

I missed her jibes, the normal Maddie behavior. This Maddie? Quiet? Worried? Hurting? This wasn't normal. I wanted normal back.

Our little sister also seemed to be waiting—in vain—for Maddie to toss a zinger. "Anyway," Marty finally continued, "Mace notices things other people don't. She usually arrives at a conclusion of who might have done the crimes before the police do."

"Crimes, plural?" Prudence tackled her chicken leg with knife and fork.

"My family is exaggerating. I've gotten lucky a couple of times."

"Four," Mama said.

A bite of drumstick paused midway to Prudence's mouth. "How common *are* killings in Himmarshee?"

"The last few years have been unusually murderous," I said.

"How fascinating. I'd love to talk to you some more about your methods. What kinds of things do you look for? What clues tell you someone might be capable of murder?"

She hoisted her empty wine glass, eyebrows raised in a question. Marty refilled it. It appeared Prudence had stopped worrying about how sober she'd be if the police should call.

"Why don't you tell us something about your sister?" Marty smoothly changed the subject from Himmarshee's recent history of homicides. "Were you identical twins?"

Prudence took a swallow of wine. Her eyes welled with tears. Marty looked stricken.

"Oh, I'm so sorry. I didn't mean to bring you pain."

"It isn't your fault, Marty. I'm feeling a bit guilty. I'm angry at myself that a petty argument led us to become estranged."

"What was the fight about?"

Now, *that* was the Maddie I knew: To the point. Short on sensitivity. Prudence frowned at Maddie's blunt question.

"It was just something between sisters. Our bond as twins wasn't broken; merely frayed." She pressed her lips together, gaining composure. "If you don't mind, I'd rather not talk about that. I'd rather remember how close we once were: like peas in a pod, everyone said. We even spoke our own secret language as children."

"That's not uncommon with twins, I've heard," Mama said.

"My sister was always so clever. Far smarter than I . . ."

Prudence worked on the rib she'd taken, slicing off a bite of meat from the bone. Ribs were usually eaten with the hands, chicken drumsticks, too. But none of us pointed that out. She poured on more sauce; sawed off another piece. "My, that's quite good!"

"Anyway," she finished that rib and continued, "that's why I can't understand . . ." Her words tapered off as she helped herself to a couple of spoonfuls of potato salad.

"What?" Mama prodded.

"Well, that outfit," Prudence said. "That was not the outfit of a smart girl; a girl who was top of her class."

I came to her sister's defense. "Now, we don't know how or why she was wearing those clothes—"

"I do," Prudence said. "I know a bit about these kinds of things. Leather wear and a fetish collar, complete with metal O ring; being submissive. It's sick is what it is. I thought it was something Camilla had put behind her."

"Maybe that clothing wasn't her choice," Marty said.

"Sad to say, it probably was. She took risks, romantically speaking." Her voice went cold. "*Sexually* speaking. I did not approve. For such a clever girl, Camilla could be quite stupid."

What seemed like raw hatred flickered in her eyes, but the look was gone so quickly I wasn't even sure I saw it. A strained silence settled over the table. Prudence stared at her plate. When she finally looked up, her expression was pleasant. Neutral. She gestured at the meat platter.

"Do you suppose I could have another one of those ribs, and some more of that sweet red sauce?"

Until then, I hadn't noticed she'd blotted up every bit of her barbecue sauce with a piece of cornbread. Camilla Law's grieving twin seemed to have an unusually hearty appetite.

FIFTEEN

A HIGH-PITCHED SOUND PENETRATED Mama's front door—like a dentist's drill crossed with a power saw.

"Mama, if you don't make Teensy stop that hideous barking, I'm going to skin him alive and make a couch pillow out of his coat."

Maddie must have been feeling better. She was back to slinging zingers.

"He's just happy to be home, honey. By the way, if you ever harm one hair on my dog's head, I'll—"

"—Give her a medal?" I finished the sentence.

I heard the key turn in the door. The little dog skittered across the tiled entryway, bounded through the living room, and burst into the kitchen. He ignored everything but his mission: To reunite with his mistress. Teensy rounded a kitchen chair, performed an aerial launch over my outstretched legs, and leaped onto Mama's lap.

"Just look at my precious little boy." She held the Pomeranian aloft, waving a paw at Maddie and me. "How could you girls even joke about hurting him?"

"I wasn't joking," Maddie said.

Dinner was done, but we still lingered at the kitchen table. Pleading exhaustion, Prudence had left as soon as she finished her dessert. Considering how much she'd drank, it was a good thing Marty offered to drive Prudence in her rental car to her motel. I was glad she was the sister keeping her company.

Sal's Bronx boom echoed from the living room. "Could you believe that scrawny mope? Offering to arm wrestle me?"

I heard Carlos's more subdued tone. "It's the typical barroom correlation between number of beers and lack of sound judgment."

Even the timbre of his voice gave me a little shiver of desire. Mama was right. If I was smart, I wouldn't do anything to burn what we had together.

"We're in here, Sally." Turning in her chair, Mama quickly surveyed her reflection in the countertop toaster. She Apricot Iced. Then, she offered the lipstick to me. In vain, of course.

"Well, at least wipe the barbecue sauce off your face," she hissed.

"Carlos likes barbecue sauce."

Maddie laughed, and the sound warmed my heart.

I handed Mama a banana from the fruit bowl on the table. "Quick, take the peel off this and drop it down your blouse."

She cocked her head in a question.

"I told Maddie how good that rotten banana looked on you when we were digging through the dump for your ring."

"Shhh!" She craned her neck to look toward the living room. "Don't remind Sal. He's none too happy his ring nearly got trashed."

The ceramic ducks on Mama's display shelves shook as Sal's heavy footsteps led the way to the kitchen. "There's my gorgeous gal!"

Gawgeous, he said. "Am I the luckiest husband in the world, or what?"

Mama jumped up for a hug. Sal gave her a long, wet-sounding kiss. Trapped in the center of their tight embrace, Teensy squirmed to get free. Sal placed the dog on the floor and went in for a second smooch, this one even more passionate.

"Get a room, would you?" Maddie said.

Carlos squeezed around Sal to put a hand on my shoulder. When I lifted my face for a more personal greeting, he pointed a finger toward my chin. "You've got something orangey-red all over there."

Mama's smile was victorious as she handed me a damp napkin.

I wiped the remnants of dinner off my face while the two men got settled at the table. Teensy hopped onto Sal's lap, and was soon snoring atop the spacious expanse of the big man's stomach. Carlos asked, "How'd it go with the victim's sister?"

"Prudence," I said. "And the dead girl's name was Camilla."

"I'm working the case. I know their names."

"So why don't you use them?"

"Carlos don't mean nothing by it, Mace. Sometimes cops depersonalize the people involved in crimes—both the victims and the perps. It makes the job easier. Right, partner?"

Carlos's only answer was a curt nod.

"Well," I said, "we just spent a couple of hours with Prudence. It seems to me the death of her sister was quite personal."

Carlos glowered at me. "I think I know that better than most."

I felt a sharp jab on the top of my foot. Mama should have stomped even harder with that kitten heel. I deserved it, for pointing out that murder is personal to a man who lost his wife in a vicious homicide.

Maddie rescued me. "Prudence told us she and Camilla were estranged."

Carlos lifted an eyebrow. "How estranged?" I could almost hear the wheels and gears grinding in his detective's brain.

We caught him up with what she'd said—how their twin bond was strained but not torn, and how she didn't want to elaborate on exactly why. "Did anyone else notice that mean look on her face when she talked about how Camilla was dressed?" I asked.

I was met with blank stares from Mama and my sisters. "I did think it was strange she wanted to grill Mace about solving murders," Marty said.

"Prudence had the tough task today of officially identifying her sister's body," Carlos said. "She took it pretty hard."

"Has the medical examiner determined how Camilla died?" I asked.

Carlos exchanged a look with Sal. "It'll all be in the newspaper tomorrow."

"My cousin Henry already told us what he'd discovered from his sources at the courthouse," I said. "She was strangled, right?"

Another curt nod.

Sal gently petted the sleeping dog. "Strangulation often has sexual overtones."

Flashing back to the racy getup Camilla wore, I fought the urge to say, *Gee Sal, ya think?*

Mama stood up and began clearing the table. "I'm putting a moratorium tonight on any more talk about murder, *or* sex."

"Sex, too?" Sal grinned at her. "I hope that doesn't mean you're sending me to sleep on the couch. We haven't been married long enough for that."

Mama snapped a dish towel at him. "Stop it, you!"

Teensy awoke with a bark.

"We have leftovers," Mama said. "Are you two hungry?"

Sal licked his lips. "Starving—"

"—We already ate," Carlos said at the same time.

All of us laughed, except Maddie. The look on her face was serious. "Everything in this world seems to come down to sex one way or the other, doesn't it? Wanting it. Getting it. Doing the wrong thing because of it."

Sal cocked his head at my sister. Strait-laced Maddie voluntarily bringing up *S-E-X*? Carlos and Mama aimed puzzled frowns her way, too. I was the only one at the table with any idea why Maddie's mind was on sex.

The quizzical stares didn't seem to register with Maddie. Frowning, she took out her phone again. Her face darkened as she began typing out a message, thumbs striking the keypad like angry pistons.

SIXTEEN

"JUST ME. I'M BACK."

Marty's voice from the front porch kick-started Teensy's engines again. The dog darted to the door. In addition to shattering eardrums with his piercing barks, he seemed intent on protecting the home and the helpless humans inside. To wit: One hardened police detective from the mean streets of Miami; a three-hundred-plus-pound tough guy from Da Bronx; a principal whose raised eyebrow could silence a cafeteria full of middle-schoolers; an outdoorswoman and sometime alligator trapper; and a four-foot-eleven-inch dynamo whose dainty feminine stature belied an iron will.

"Teensy! Quiet!" Sal's shout was so loud it made waves of the sweet pink wine inside Mama's vibrating glass. It stopped the barks in mid-yap. Teensy let out one final protest whine.

"Good dog! Everybody's safe." Marty scooped up the Pomeranian and brought him to the kitchen. Her face glowed a bit from hiking a mile or so back from the hotel in the warm evening. "You are SUCH a brave boy."

Wagging his whole body, Teensy dog-kissed Marty's face from chin to forehead.

"Gross," I said.

"Don't encourage him," Maddie added.

"Don't listen to your sisters, Marty." Mama chucked Teensy under the chin. "Only truly mean and awful people don't like dogs."

"Oh, I like dogs, Mama. I just don't like *that* dog." I pointed at the offending animal wiggling in Marty's arms.

"He's not so bad." Carlos reached out a hand to pat Teensy. Letting out a yip, the dog bit him on the thumb.

¡*Dios mío*, that hurt!" He narrowed his eyes. "Little bastard."

When Sal and I laughed, both Mama and Carlos scowled at us.

"Why don't we all move into the living room?" said Marty, making peace. "Teensy can stay here and defend the kitchen against any further intruders."

Grabbing a bottle of soda water, Maddie followed the men out of the kitchen. Mama twisted the spigot on the box of wine, adding a half-glass more for Marty and her. I took three beers from the 'fridge for Sal, Carlos, and me.

"Uh-oh, Mama's having more wine," Marty said. "Somebody keep an eye on her ring."

Meeting Marty's jibe with a frown, Mama spooned up some premium dog food for Teensy. When he skittered over to his bowl, she slid a doggie gate across the kitchen entryway and made her exit. Loud enough for us to hear her in the living room, she said, "It's a shame the only one of my babies who never criticizes me has to stay in the kitchen."

I grabbed a seat next to Carlos on Mama's peach-colored sofa. When I offered him one of the beers, he winced as he grabbed the bottle.

"Let me look." I lifted his right hand, and examined the thumb. "The skin's barely broken."

"It still hurts."

"Give me a minute," I said.

In the bathroom, I rustled up some cotton balls and alcohol. I stepped over the doggie gate to get ice and a clean dishtowel from the kitchen. Teensy, scarfing his supper, barely noticed.

When I returned bearing my Nancy Nurse supplies, Carlos looked embarrassed and pleased at the same time. There is not a man alive who doesn't like being fussed over—no matter how *muy* macho he is, or how hardened from a career of chasing scary criminals. If I'd learned nothing else from Mama's lessons about womanly wiles, I had at least learned that.

Plus, I liked to be in charge in a medical emergency, so it was win-win for me.

I swabbed the wound—more of a scratch, really. "Does that sting?"

"Not too bad."

I put my mouth close and blew on his thumb, just like Mama used to do for us when we were children.

"That tickles," Carlos said.

"If you're a good boy, maybe Mace will give you a lick off her lollipop." Sal leered at us from his recliner.

"That sounds pretty good." Carlos smiled suggestively. "There's nothing like a sweet, juicy lollipop. I like the cherry ones best."

Marty laughed. I'm pretty sure I blushed.

"Has every couple in this family regressed to acting like hormonal teenagers?" Maddie said. "Get a room, you two."

"Don't be such a sourpuss, Maddie," Mama said. "You're really off your oats, girl. Your 'monthly visitor' still giving you trouble?"

Sal cleared his throat. Carlos got interested in reading the label of his Budweiser bottle. "Have you gone crazy?" Maddie stared at Mama.

Before Maddie inadvertently revealed I'd lied with that cover story about menstrual troubles, I said, "Nope, Mama's not crazy. Just a little inappropriate, due to all that pink wine she's consumed. Let's talk about something else, why don't we?"

"Fine with me," Mama said. "Let's see if we can figure out what Maddie should wear to Kenny's party. I'm still opposed to that yellow dress, honey." She took a magazine off the coffee table and started leafing through the sticky-noted pages. "Now, I've marked pictures of dresses in shades that would be much more flattering with your complexion."

Sal heaved himself to his feet. "Fashion? That's my cue to go to the den and catch some sports on TV." Carlos wasted no time following the big man's lead.

As soon as they were gone, Maddie exploded: "The yellow dress is fine. I have no damned intention of changing it, Mama. And I'll thank you to keep your big nose out of my business."

I'm not sure which shocked Mama most. Was it pious Maddie using a curse word? Or was it her inaccurate characterization of Mama's cute-as-a-button nose?

In a teasing tone, Marty said, "C'mon, Maddie. Mama's nose isn't *that* big."

Maddie turned her wrath on our little sister: "I am *not* in the mood for your appeasements. Not every insult can be forgiven, Marty. Not every slight can be patched over with a lame joke."

Marty looked like she'd been slapped. I tried to step in. "Okay, everybody, tempers are a little short tonight."

"There's nothing wrong with my temper." Mama glared at Maddie. "She's the one who's not acting like herself. You better shape up, girl. You don't want to ruin your husband's birthday party."

"This is not about Kenny! Can't there ever be a single thing that's about me?"

If I didn't know about the current problems between Maddie and her husband, I'd have laughed out loud. In their marriage, Maddie had *always* had the upper hand. Kenny was worshipful, always trying extra hard to please her. Their relationship was always 80 percent about Maddie; 20 percent about Kenny. Until now.

"Mama's right," Marty said. "There's nothing festive about this mood of yours. You better get yourself into that yellow dress and a celebrating mood by Saturday."

Maddie was quiet; staring at her hands in her lap. I prayed she wasn't going to cry. That would change things in an instant. If the other two ever witnessed Maddie in the state I'd seen, they would not rest until they knew what was wrong. And then they'd try to fix it.

"Lay off her, would you?" I said. "Can't a gal have a bad night without her family jumping all over her?"

Marty gave me a suspicious glance. "Why are you sticking up for Maddie? Seeing you two as allies is as likely as seeing the snake lie down with the pig."

Before Mama could pile on, Maddie got up and collected her purse from the table by the front door. Without a parting word, she walked out. The slam of the door shattered the stunned silence in the living room.

Of course, that started up Teensy again. If he hadn't been causing such a ruckus, yapping and trying to breach the doggie barrier, I'd have asked Marty whether she pictured me as the serpent or the hog. Either way, I wasn't flattered.

———

Carlos and I sat on Mama's front porch swing. It was just us, holding hands. Our silence was comfortable; companionable. Jasmine scented the warm air. A half-moon glowed above, outlining the clouds in silver. Crickets chirped. A barely-there breeze rustled through a magnolia tree. In the distance, a car with squeaky brakes stopped at the traffic light on State Road 70.

Mercifully, Teensy had settled down. Either he'd fallen back to sleep in the kitchen, or he'd choked to death on a second helping of his canine cuisine. Whatever, the quiet time alone with Carlos was a welcome change.

Mama and Marty tried unsuccessfully to get me to speculate on Maddie's wordless departure. Marty left shortly after, saying she had to wake up early for work. Sal and Mama had decided to turn in, too.

Suddenly, a low moan sounded in the night. Both Carlos and I straightened on the swing, instantly alert. Was someone in pain? Did they need help? I stood and went to the railing. Leaning over, I peered into the yard. Bushes and trees cast dark, shadowy shapes. I couldn't tell if anything out there was moving.

There was the moan again. And then a sigh. And then a high-pitched, feminine giggle.

Ohmigod, how embarrassing. "We can hear you, Mama!"

The commotion was coming from the open window of the master bedroom, on the far side of the house.

Mama's voice floated onto the perfumed air: "Shhhh! I think I heard something, Sally."

"You heard *me*! I'm trying to tell you to keep it down. Carlos and I can hear everything out here."

"Mace?"

"Yes!" I rolled my eyes at Carlos.

"I thought all y'all went home."

"Well, Carlos and I didn't. And we know what you're up to inside. You should stop. Now."

The sound of muffled laughter and snickering made its way from the side of the house. Then came frantic whispering, and more giggling.

"Oh, for God's sake," I said. "Stop acting like adolescents. Get a room!"

"We *have* one," Sal called out. "If youse two would give us some privacy, maybe we could get around to using it."

"Yeah," Mama added. "Why don't you take your own advice, Mace?"

Great. Hearing the two of them wasn't bad enough? Now, my own mother was advising me to spirit away my fiancé and get some sex on?

Carlos grinned at me; a sly, sultry smile that made me want to melt into a puddle on the porch. He fished his keys from his pocket.

"Did you hear me, Mace?" Mama called. "Why don't you and Carlos 'Get a room?'"

He dangled the car keys in front of my eyes.

I didn't bother to answer Mama. I pulled Carlos off the porch and steered him onto the path that led to his car. His car with that nice, *roomy* back seat.

SEVENTEEN

THE ROAD HOME WAS dark, but I was still aglow. Nothing lifts your spirits like some back seat love-making while parked in a cow pasture. Climbing out of Carlos's car and stepping on a cow patty didn't even dampen my mood. Smooshing a second one, though, was a bit of a bummer. But more for Carlos than me.

"¡*Dios mío*, you stink!" he said, with typical male sensitivity. "Good thing you followed me in your Jeep. There's no way I'd let you back into my car."

I high-kicked my leg outside, bringing one of the crap-clodded boots close to his face. He started the car and rolled up the window, leaving a tiny slit at the top to talk to me. "No kidding; that's disgusting. I'll wait here in my manure-free zone to make sure your engine starts."

"Oh, that's nice: I show you a good time, and you toss me out like used kitty litter."

He blew me a couple of kisses through the window. That was probably less an authentic gesture of love and affection than a chance to cover his nose with his hand.

Now, I was tooling home with the windows rolled down in my Jeep, trying to air out my stinky boots. It wasn't working.

I looked at the ring on my hand, and grinned. I never thought I'd be engaged to such a city boy. Carlos's family may have kept cattle a couple of generations back in Cuba, but he was much more Miami these days than Camaguey. Imagine being so put off by the smell of a little manure. Then again, it *was* pretty fresh manure. I leaned my face out the window, grateful to the local grower who had decided to plant orange groves. The fragrant blossoms on several hundred acres of trees in the distance were sending out some much-needed aroma assistance.

When my sisters and I were kids, we used to complain about the biological byproduct of the cattle on our ranch. Daddy would always laugh and say, *That's the smell of money, girls.*

That was before his cow-calf operation started hemorrhaging cash; before the stress of losing our ranch led to his fatal heart attack. By then, the manure didn't smell like money anymore. It just smelled like shit.

I shook my head to clear away sad memories. Mama's always big on handing out advice, most of which I never take. But there's one bit of her counsel that's always stuck with me: *Don't look back, Mace. What's passed is past, and you can't change it. Focus on making the best of what lies ahead.*

I was pretty happy about what seemed to lie ahead for Carlos and me. Come to think of it, I wasn't exactly unhappy about what had just passed between us. Given the potential for embarrassment if caught, we'd decided against doing anything X-rated in his parked car in front of Mama's house. I'd shuddered at the thought of her coming out to rap at the window while Carlos and I were ... occupied. Getting it on in a deserted pasture was as much revisiting my misspent youth as I was willing to do.

The highway home cut right through the center of Florida's interior—citrus and cattle country. Agriculture was still managing to hold on in the region, despite encroaching development—like the new golf course community on Himmarshee's southern edge. Under the light of the moon, I took in the shapes and sounds that defined my slice of Florida. Sabal palms, tall and thin with a top like a Q-tip, dotted a flat landscape. Bushier cypress trees were silhouetted in the distance, like dark sentries guarding the watery perimeter of Starvation Slough. A cow lowed. A night heron squawked as he hunted in the wetlands nearby. The eyes of a small critter, maybe a raccoon or opossum, reflected my headlights from the undergrowth along the shoulder. I slowed, just in time to avoid hitting the possum that ambled onto the road.

As I drove out of the orange grove, the citrus scent began to give way to the smell of garbage. The turnoff to the city dump was just ahead. An image of Camilla's lifeless body popped into my mind. Silently, I repeated a prayer for her soul. Mostly, I hoped she hadn't suffered too much before she died.

The glare of bright lights in my rear-view mirror startled me from thoughts about the murdered woman. It was unusual to see another car on this stretch of road, this late at night. It looked like the vehicle was tearing up the pavement, too. Within moments, it was right on my rear. Before I knew it, a powerful, American-sounding engine was revving behind me. The car drew closer. High beams flashed. A horn honked. Big and black, with tinted windows, the vehicle came closer still.

I murmured into my mirror, "What do you want me to do, asshole? Levitate out of the way to spare you the monumental effort of passing me?"

I stuck my left arm out the Jeep's window, waving at Mr. Hurry Up to go around me. He could easily pass. There was nothing in the oncoming lane between here and Wachula. Finally, he got tired of riding my bumper. Gunning it, he blew by me in a blur, and I saw it was a sedan. Between the dark windows and high speed, I didn't get a good look at the driver. It could have been *Mrs.* Hurry Up, for all I saw.

My headlights caught a Florida plate and a red-white-and-blue bumper sticker. But the sedan pulled ahead and disappeared before I could read what it said. I repressed the urge to honk my horn and flip him the bird. Florida's drivers are notoriously prone to road rage. You never know what might set off somebody's crazy fuse, even in little Himmarshee.

As the big car's taillights became miniature red dots, I wondered where he was headed in such a rush. My mind wasn't completely on my driving, or what happened next would never have happened. An alligator—eight or nine feet, at least—had heaved itself out of the reedy wetlands and onto the pavement. Making its way across the highway to a canal, it stretched clear across the center line: Snout in the oncoming lane, tail oscillating across my lane. In an instant, I swerved. I missed the gator, but my right front tire hit the concrete abutment of a small bridge over the slough. The car bucked. The steering wheel jerked.

And just like that, I lost control.

EIGHTEEN

THE JEEP'S RIGHT SIDE veered off the road, spitting sand and weeds every which way. I'd taken my foot off the accelerator, but I was fighting forward momentum. Over-correcting could flip me into the canal where the gator now lurked.

Suddenly, I heard a voice, low and calm, in my head: Mama's third husband, who'd taught me to drive. *Take a deep breath. You know what to do.*

Once, when No. 3 was giving me a lesson, an oncoming car strayed into my lane. I went off the road, and he guided me back: *Ease off the gas. No brake. If the drop-off's sharp, turn back sharply. If it's smooth, nice and easy."*

Holding my breath, I executed a turn between sharp and smooth. The Jeep leveled out; tires gripped pavement. Number 3 may have been a bad match for Mama, but he was a good man—and a great driver. I let out my breath, until the Jeep traveled a few more yards.

Bumpedty-bump, bumpedty-bump, bumpedty-bump.

Uh-oh. The right front tire must have blown hitting the concrete curb of the bridge. I punched the button for my emergency flashers and slowed to a stop. Before I got out of the vehicle, I listened for the deep bellow of a big gator. I hoped he'd moved on. A tire iron was no match for a riled-up, nine-foot reptile with seventy-five or eighty sharp teeth.

———

Sweaty, grease-stained, and mosquito bitten, I got back in my Jeep. Still, I was grateful—first, that things hadn't ended worse; and second, that Husband No. 3 also taught me to change a tire.

As soon as I settled into the driver's seat, I noticed my cell phone was lit. Between swearing at the balky lug nuts and swatting at swarms of bugs, I must have missed it ringing. The caller ID said *Maddie*. She'd left a voice mail.

The first thing I heard was a sob, and then a couple of sniffles. "It's me, Mace. I tried you at home, but no answer."

There was a long pause. She took a deep breath. "Kenny never came home from work, and he still hasn't called. He's not answering my text messages, either."

She blew her nose.

"I'm so angry . . . but I'm also wuh-wuh-worried." Breaking on the last word, her voice became a sob.

After a moment, she seemed to collect herself. "I don't mean to pile all this on you. There's no need to come over here. I'm fine. Fine." She repeated herself for emphasis.

"It's such a long way, and it's already so late."

I started my Jeep.

"I'm going to try to get some sleep. Everything will look better in the muh-muh-morning."

That last, choked-out word pierced my heart. I made a U-turn, heading back to Himmarshee and my hurting sister.

NINETEEN

MADDIE'S FRONT WINDOWS WERE dark; the spot where Kenny always parked his truck conspicuously empty. The place looked sad and lonely. Or, maybe I was just projecting my sister's abandonment onto the inanimate house.

When I pulled around to the side of the house, I saw the dim blue glow of a TV coming from Maddie and Kenny's bedroom. So she was still up. I hurried to the front door and retrieved the key from its hiding spot under her pot of dying geraniums.

I called out as soon as I opened the door so as not to startle her… or raise her hopes it was Kenny coming home. No answer came from her room, but I heard the rustle of bed linens being thrown aside. She was up and waiting for me by the time I walked down the hallway.

"I told you not to come. I'm fine."

That was a lie. Maddie's eyes were swollen nearly shut from crying. She wore a ratty bathrobe and just one sock, all stretched out with no elastic at the top. The other was probably lost somewhere in her bed. Used tissues spilled from the pocket of the robe. Beyond her, I saw more tissues all over the bed, a snowdrift of crumpled white.

"I know you're fine. When I got your message, I was in the neighborhood anyway."

She gave me a suspicious look. "You were not."

"Okay, I thought maybe you could use some company."

"Fine. But leave those nasty boots at the front door. You stink like the livestock market after the Tuesday auction."

Maybe her griping about my crap-covered boots was a good sign. When I scuffed back inside in my socks, the TV was playing an ancient rerun of *Matlock*. The sound was off, but Andy Griffith was doing his trademark wily Southerner grin. It made me sad to think Andy was dead and gone.

"Kenny hasn't come home." Maddie looked over her shoulder at the rumpled, empty bed. "He hasn't even called."

I gave her a half-hug. "There, there." As I gave her shoulder an awkward pat, I wished again she'd chosen to tell her secret to Marty instead of me.

As if she could read my mind, Maddie said, "Bet you never thought you'd be comforting me, did you? Haven't I always been the old, happily married lady who has it all together? Haven't you always been the one unlucky in love?"

I didn't think she was looking for an answer. Fact was, she *had* always been happy with Kenny, ever since I could remember. They were junior high school sweethearts. As far as my dismal record in the romance department, everybody was pretty clear on that— thanks to Mama, the Mouth of the South.

"You have to help me find him, Mace. I just want to know what's going on. I have to know before this stupid party on Saturday."

"Have you thought any more about cancelling it? Maybe you should."

She sunk onto the bed, tears in her eyes. "I can't! It's paid for. A hundred people are coming. It's supposed to be Kenny's big night."

She rooted around on the bedspread for a shredded tissue. When she dabbed at her eyes, a snowstorm of white flecks fluttered onto her robe.

"There must be some reason Kenny's cheating. What's wrong with me, Mace? Have I been a bad wife? Am I a bad person?" She blew her nose. "Is it because I've put on a few pounds?"

I gave her shoulders a gentle shake. "Don't even think like that, you hear me? You're a fantastic wife. That mo-ron is lucky to have you." I found a nearly whole tissue and handed it to her. "This is not about you! It's about Kenny, and whatever is going on in his pea-sized male brain."

I figured I should say no more about Kenny. Maddie would never forgive me for trashing him, once they got back together. And they *were* getting back together, I was sure of it. Or, at least, I hoped for it.

Matlock was over. One of the judge shows was starting. Maddie flicked channels on the remote until she landed on a rerun of *Two and a Half Men*. Charlie Sheen's philandering character probably wasn't the best subject for my sister's viewing tonight. I grabbed the changer and found an animal show. Some kind of antelopes raced across an African plain. It'd be only a matter of time before the camera showed the lion chasing after them, death on their trail.

On second thought, maybe a comedy would be a better option.

"Are you hungry?" I asked.

Maddie shook her head.

"All I saw you eat at Mama's was a few bites of that plain chicken breast. Have you had anything else?"

Another head shake, some tissue shredding. "I can't eat."

"Well, I'm hungry. I feel like having some mashed potatoes with butter. You'll have a few bites, okay?"

Maddie shrugged. At least she didn't say no. I headed to the kitchen to prepare our default comfort food.

When I returned, bearing a pot of whipped potatoes and two big spoons, Maddie had washed her face and combed her hair. She'd tossed handfuls of the used tissues into the wastebasket in the corner. Those were encouraging signs, even if what she'd chosen to watch was some woman-done-wrong movie on Lifetime.

I plumped a pillow for my back, and sat beside my sister on the bed. Both of us rested against the headboard. The potato pot created a warm spot between us. When she made no move to dig in, I scooped up a buttered spoonful for her. Just as Maddie had done for me through countless of my nasty or humiliating breakups, I raised the spoon toward her. "Mmm, yummy!"

Obligingly, she opened up and ate.

"Better?" I asked, after she'd savored several more bites.

"A bit." Her smile was wobbly, but at least it was a smile.

"Want to try to get some sleep?"

Maddie glanced out the window to the side yard. No truck.

"I'll stay up and wait," I said. "I'll wake you as soon as he gets home."

I didn't mention that first I planned to have it out with her cheating husband, no doubt calling him a few names the church ladies at Abundant Forgiveness would not forgive.

Despite my best intentions, the Lifetime movie sucked me in. The woman wronged dumped her louse and ended up with a great guy who appreciated her. By the time the credits rolled, and I had the potato pot washed and draining on the sink, Maddie was snoring softly. My own eyelids felt heavy. Maddie's bright red clock—apple-shaped, stamped with the words *World's Greatest Teacher*—read 1:47 a.m.

The house was so quiet, the sound of the refrigerator humming carried from the kitchen into the living room. I sat myself in Kenny's recliner. Would it reek of cheater's musk? All I smelled, though, was Kenny's usual scent: a not-unpleasant mix of engine grease and drugstore aftershave.

The chair was cushiony, and I was exhausted. It seemed like I'd just sat down, but next thing I knew, harsh morning light slanted through the living room blinds.

I'd turned off the alert sound on my sister's phone so as not to wake her overnight. I picked up the phone from the coffee table, and was about to turn it back on, when I saw there was a text message, from Kenny. I hesitated only a moment before I read it.

I did something terrible. I don't think you can forgive me. I'm so sorry.

Outside, his parking spot was still empty.

TWENTY

"ANGEL, DOLL, THIS DRINK is delicious, but could I get just a smidge more vodka?"

Beatrice Graf offered up a pleading tone and what looked like a Bloody Mary to the barmaid at the 19th Hole. I'd just taken my first sip of morning coffee, and the mayor's wife was already pursuing an alcohol buzz.

Without a wasted motion, Angel picked up my money from the bar, spun to retrieve a bottle of premium vodka, topped off the glass of Mrs. Mayor, and replaced the bottle on the shelf. Then, she proceeded to the register to ring up my coffee.

I'd returned to the golf course to take another crack at finding Kenny. I was waiting for an opportune moment to speak with Angel.

She returned with change from my five. "Keep it," I said.

Angel's eyes lit. "Thanks."

"You should at least make it an Irish whiskey." Beatrice chuckled beside me, stirring her drink with its celery stalk. "Who comes to a bar and orders a plain coffee?"

"Somebody who has to be at work in an hour." I wrestled with a couple of sugar packets, managing to get most of the contents spilled into my cup.

Mrs. Mayor fluffed at her poodle perm, then hoisted her Bloody Mary at me for a toast. Her eyebrows had a reddish tint, to match her hair. Her mascara looked like she'd applied it with a paint roller. I clinked her morning cocktail with my mug, and each of us took a swallow of our preferred poisons. Angel performed a quick introduction. I didn't let on we'd met before.

"I'm running a ladies' group meeting for the Newcomer's Club this morning. I always tell the gals to have a little nip. It makes the time go faster. You should try it."

"Think I'll stick to coffee, but thanks."

She saluted us, wobbling a bit as she walked away. I suspected that wasn't the morning's first Bloody Mary. She didn't seem to place me from the dining room the day before, or the library before that. Probably the memory-killing effect of too many drinks.

"Bit early to be hitting the vodka." I nodded toward Beatrice. The purple pom-poms on her golf socks bobbed as she zigzagged across the dining room.

Angel shrugged. "To each his own. I don't judge; I just pour."

"A generous shot, too. Doesn't management get mad if you give people extra booze without getting extra money?"

She looked around the empty bar, then leaned in close. "Can you keep a secret?"

"I'm a vault."

"I only start her out with half a shot. She ALWAYS asked me for more, even when I poured her a double, so now I pour her less to begin with."

"Smart."

"I'm a clever girl." She gave me one of her strangely seductive grins. "So, you're not a golfer, right?"

"Not even on a dare," I said.

"So how come you're back here today?" Wiping down a sprinkle of sugar crystals on the bar, she came close enough to brush my wrist with hers. "Did you miss me?"

I whisked my hands into my lap, folding them there. "I'm still looking for my brother-in-law, Kenny. Thought I might find him here this morning. My sister said he likes to play on Mondays."

"Haven't seen him."

"Will you tell me if you do?"

"I said I would."

"And you keep your word?"

"Always."

She reached out a hand, grazing her fingers across the top of my left breast. I jumped back so fast I nearly fell off the stool.

"Sorry. Didn't mean to scare you." That suggestive smile again. She pointed. "You spilled some sugar all over your shirt there."

I wasn't sure what her game was, but I knew I wasn't playing. I made a show of consulting my watch. "Look at the time."

"Yeah, you better get to work. You do something with animals at the park, right?"

I surely looked stunned, because she said, "You must have mentioned that." She gestured at my shirt again. "Plus, it says 'Himmarshee Nature Park,' right there."

I looked down at the logo. "Oh, right. Thanks for the coffee."

"Thanks for the tip. Hope to see you again, soon."

Angel's gaze now focused on a spot over my shoulder. I turned, to see the mayor coming in the door from the golf course, trailed by a group of four or five younger men. They were loud: laughing, shaking hands, and slapping backs.

"You owe me another game, you son-of-a-bitch." The mayor wagged an index finger in the tallest man's face, but his tone was teasing, not angry. "You stole that one like a whore lifting a drunk's wallet."

An older woman on her way to the ladies' room gave him a disapproving frown. The mayor, bidding the group good-bye, seemed not to notice. His face was red. He mopped his brow with a big white handkerchief. His canary-colored golf shirt showed rings of sweat at the arms and under his saggy pectoral muscles. His jaunty yellow cap was wilted. It was early, but the September sun was already heating up the course.

Angel had filled a glass with iced water, and was moving in the mayor's direction. She nodded toward the door to the outside patio. He opened it, and they both went out.

She gave him the water, which he drained in one long swig. He held the ice-filled glass to each temple, cooling off. Angel waited, arms crossed over her chest. He put the glass on a table and whispered something in her ear. Angel shook her head, lips pressed into a hard line.

She pulled a pack of cigarettes from her apron, took out two. He rushed to light hers first, and then his. As they shared a smoke, he put a hand on her arm. She looked at it like it was a palmetto bug crawling across her skin. He immediately dropped it, and lowered his eyes to the table. Everything about his posture suggested he wanted something from Angel.

Everything about hers said she wasn't giving it.

TWENTY-ONE

THE SOUND OF SUSTAINED applause echoed in the empty dining room of the country club. It seemed to be coming from an open door leading to the room where Beatrice Graf was holding her event.

I'd already paid my tab and finished my coffee. The mayor and Angel were still outside. With no other customers at the bar, there was no telling how long they'd talk. I'd try to catch up to each of them later to see what I could learn about Kenny.

In the meantime, I was curious about all the clapping. I peeked from the dining room into the private room, and saw about twenty-five women inside. Mrs. Mayor was right. Almost every guest had a glass of wine or a cocktail at her plate. I ducked into a dining-room booth with an unobstructed view so I could spy in my preferred manner: Unobserved.

I was surprised to see Prudence Law, wearing a nervous smile and a conservatively cut suit. She walked to the lectern at the front of the room, and waited for the applause to spatter to an end. She stood on tiptoe to reach the microphone.

"Thanks for that nice introduction. I asked Mrs. Graf if I could say a few words to let you know how awfully grateful I am for the gift basket, as well as the kind expressions of sympathy so many of you have sent."

An acknowledging murmur moved around the tables in the room.

"As a librarian, Camilla was terribly keen on book groups. Several of you mentioned that she was helpful with suggestions for reading material. She'd be pleased to know she's remembered in that way."

The mayor's wife stepped to the lectern, claiming three-quarters of Prudence's limelight. "All of us are so sorry for your loss. Your sister was a lovely woman.'

She was singing a different tune today. At Gladys' diner, I'd heard her skewering the murder victim for her sex clothes and sinful ways.

A woman in a mint-green sweater set hesitantly raised her hand at the front table. Prudence and the mayor's wife simultaneously nodded their permission to ask a question. The woman looked momentarily confused as to who was in charge, but she plowed ahead anyway.

"Have the police told you anything about who might have killed Camilla?"

When Beatrice began to speak, the sweater-clad woman raised her hand again, a bit timidly: "I was asking her sister."

Mrs. Mayor aimed a glare at the questioner, but quickly covered it with a fake-looking smile. Prudence edged her aside and reclaimed the lectern. "No, they say they're still investigating. They haven't provided any specific information, beyond the fact she wasn't killed where her body was found. They haven't let me into her home. That leads me to believe they're still looking for evidence there."

The mayor's wife shouldered Prudence out of the spotlight. She spoke directly into the microphone. "I think we have to assume Camilla knew her killer."

Though sidelined, sweet Prudence still managed to put some frost in her voice. "I'm not sure we can 'assume' anything at this point. Why do you say that?"

"Well, surely that clothing was meant for some kind of special occasion. She dressed that way for a reason."

Prudence's eyes were cold enough to make the woman at the front table wrap herself more tightly in that sweater.

"I wasn't aware my sister was required to check with you regarding what she wore in the privacy of her home. I thought you Americans were all for individual freedom."

The look she aimed at the mayor's wife was so scornful, I'm surprised it didn't singe the split ends off her bottle-red hair. But instead of becoming argumentative or blustery, as I expected, Beatrice cast her eyes downward to the floor.

"I'm so sorry," she mumbled, seemingly submissive. "I certainly don't want to offend you, or the memory of your dear sister. Especially not at a time like this."

Prudence sniffed, and smoothed at the sides of her dark jacket. The lapels were trimmed in white piping.

"It's all right," she finally said, sounding like it definitely was not all right. "You can't help being ignorant."

I thought that would get a rise from Mrs. Mayor, but instead she started clapping, and the other women followed her lead. Leaning back toward the microphone, she said. "Thank you so much for coming, Prudence. Anything you need, please call any one of us, right gals?"

Heads nodded and voices murmured in assent. Prudence marched out into the dining room. Her gait was determined; her jaw set. A flush suffused her fair skin. She didn't look grief-stricken. She looked furious.

———

Before I left, I checked in at the pro shop. The young woman behind the counter said she hadn't seen Kenny. I also asked about the club's pro, but Jason wasn't in. Just as well. With no makeup, dirty hair, and red eyes after my nearly sleepless night at Maddie's house, I wasn't exactly looking my best. Not to mention, I still hadn't scraped all the cow crap from my boots.

Not that I felt I had to impress Jason. After all, I had a fiancé.

Now, thanks to all the coffee I'd downed at the bar, I needed to visit the ladies' room before I started the drive to work. While I was there, I figured I'd find that stash of moisturizing lotion and hair supplies again. I could use all the beauty help I could get.

I wended my way from the toilets past the whirlpool tub and back to the changing room. A soft murmur of voices came from a corner, behind a bank of lockers. I paid them no heed. I was on a moisturizing mission, trying to allay the effects of thirty-plus years in the Florida sun with a few free dollops of a silky-smooth cream

I was too cheap to buy for myself. I slathered my bare arms and neck. It smelled clean and spicy, like lemons and rosemary.

I went a little crazy with the pump bottle, and spilled a big glob of moisturizer on the counter. I thought I remembered seeing a stash of towels in a wicker basket behind the lockers. Rounding the corner, I spotted Angel at the far end. I could see she was in deep conversation with someone standing just behind the lockers, out of sight. She held tight to the woman's hand. The look on Angel's face was tender, caring. She didn't appear nearly as hard as she did while working behind the bar.

Uncomfortable that I might be intruding on an intimate moment, I turned to go. From the corner of my eye, I noticed a swath of familiar fabric resting on the bench by Angel's side. I hadn't even reached the door when I remembered where I'd seen it: Navy blue with white piping. It was the jacket to Prudence Law's conservative suit.

TWENTY-TWO

MARTY AND I SAT at our usual lunch table at Gladys' Diner. We were waiting for Mama to quit swanning around the room and come tell us what she planned to order. We would never order the same thing. That would take all of the fun out of stealing from each other's plates.

I crooked a finger to Mama, trying to motion her back to our table. Instead, she moved in on a church lady friend across the room. She stuck a fork in the woman's squash casserole for a generous sample. Chewing, Mama gave me the wait-a-minute finger. With her, that's always more like ten minutes.

"Let's just order," I said. "She's probably going to get the Monday special meat and three."

"Right," Marty said. "Meat loaf, collards, black-eyed peas, and mashed potatoes."

In the distance, Mama's features formed the *mmm-mmm* face. She licked her lips and nodded at her friend. "Make that squash casserole instead of the potatoes," I said.

"But she'll definitely have the butterscotch pie for dessert." Marty tapped on the menu. "So, I'll order the vegetable plate and coconut cake."

"Barbecued pork sandwich and banana pudding for me," I said. "Now, what kind of sides do I want—"

"Oh my!" Marty slapped her hand over her mouth, whispering between the fingers. "Look who just walked in to sit at the counter."

I quit considering the side orders. Prudence Law stood at the front of Gladys', crisp in a light blue blouse with a Peter Pan collar, her navy jacket folded over an arm. I wanted to tell Marty I'd seen her that morning at the golf course, but I didn't want to have to create a lie about why I was there. It felt strange, keeping my baby sister out of the loop.

"We should ask her to sit with us." Marty elbowed me.

"She probably wants to be alone," I said.

"Not at a time like this. She's hurting, and she's so shy. I'm sure she doesn't have a single friend in Himmarshee."

I recalled Prudence looking not at all shy when she coolly put the mayor's wife in her place at the morning meeting. And she seemed to have at least one very special friend in town: Angel Fox.

"C'mon, the woman just lost a sister. Imagine how any of us would feel." Marty looked at me, her blue eyes brimming with compassion.

I nodded okay. Marty stood and waved Prudence over.

———

"I can't stay long." Prudence took a seat. "I've only just put in an order for takeaway."

"You must have a lot to do," Marty said. "Will you let us know if there's any way we can help?"

The resemblance between the two women was amazing. Marty was blonde, and Prudence's hair was dark, but both were petite. Both had enormous blue eyes and a fringe of bangs that gave them a waifish appearance. Their pale complexions were similar, too, as was the pink curve of their rosebud lips. Did men—or maybe women?—want to protect Prudence, like they always did with Marty? It was clear at least one man had felt no protective instinct toward Prudence's murdered twin, Camilla.

"Thank you, Marty. What a kind person you are."

"Everyone says that about Marty." Our cousin Henry had materialized at the table, and was standing next to Prudence with an expectant look. "Are you going to introduce me, cousins?"

I did the honors.

"I'm sorry for your loss," he said, holding on to Prudence's hand. "I hear your sister was a wonderful woman."

"That's a thoughtful thing to say. It appears kindness to strangers runs in your family," she said.

"You must not have met Maddie yet," Henry said.

He found an extra chair for the table, stuck it right beside Prudence. As she scooted a bit to let him in, her jacket fell off the chair back. Henry bent to the floor to retrieve it, dusting off some cornbread crumbs. Shaking it out, he returned it with a flourish. "I believe this belongs to you, pretty lady."

Her cheeks flushed adorably. She fluttered her eyelashes, Mama-style. "So gallant!"

Henry waved a hand. "It's nothing."

"You're right about that," I muttered.

Marty kicked me under the table, but Henry and Prudence ignored me.

"I just love your Southern manners. British men are not nearly so courtly." What sounded like a giggle escaped her lips. My cousin puffed out his chest.

"So, Henry, how are those young'uns of yours?" I asked. "And how 'bout your sweet wife? Is she pregnant again?"

Taking my hint, Henry announced he had to meet some colleagues for lunch. Prudence pushed back her chair to stand. Shooting out of his seat like it gave him a shock, he helped her out of the chair. "Don't let Mace scare you away," he said.

"She hasn't scared me." Prudence put a hand on his sleeve, stroking his arm through the fabric of his button-down shirt. "Don't be daft. I'm making a quick stop in the loo, then I'm on my way out."

As soon as she was out of hearing range, I lit into my cousin. "Slimy much? Are you really flirting with a woman whose sister was just murdered?"

He looked wounded. "I most certainly was not flirting! I was just being a gentleman; 'gallant,' in fact."

"What's even weirder is she was flirting back. Right, Marty?"

"I didn't see it that way," my sister said. "Don't be so critical, Mace. Her sister was just brutally murdered, as I shouldn't have to remind you. She's entitled to act a little strange."

Strange? Oh how I wanted to tell them about Prudence at the golf course.

"I'm right and you're wrong." Henry stuck his tongue out at me. "Just because Maddie's not here doesn't mean you have to stand in for her role as bitchy sister."

He looked around the diner, waggled his fingers at Mama. She was now cadging a spoonful of creamed spinach off someone else's plate.

"Where is Maddie anyway?" Henry asked.

They both cocked their heads at me. Maddie's whereabouts was the last question I wanted to discuss. I shrugged.

"Henry's right, you know." Marty buttered a biscuit. "You're doing a pretty good job of playing Maddie's role. You're acting all judgmental, just like she always does."

Henry rose. "I'm going to find a table for my meeting, before you two start throwing cutlery."

With barely a nod at our departing cousin, Marty continued in the same vein, telling me how she understood people far better than I did; how I should rely on her judgment about Prudence.

"Maybe you should stick with the critters and let me handle the people," she said.

Henry had announced I was acting like Maddie. But listening to Marty harangue me, I realized *both* of us were taking on some of our absent sister's least lovable traits. Maybe Marty suspected something was amiss. Maybe imitating Maddie was a way both of us were dealing with that unvoiced suspicion.

I decided to let my little sister blow off steam. I'd curb my impulse to take offense. As she talked, my gaze wandered around the room. Prudence was at the counter, waiting while Charlene collected her take-out order. Brewing hot tea—an uncommon request in Himmarshee—was taking some time. Prudence seemed to be explaining that hot tea isn't made by microwaving a glass of sweet iced tea.

Charlene rushed past us to a serving station at the rear of the diner, muttering as she went. "I know I've seen a single-size tea bag around here somewhere." She called over her shoulder to Prudence. "Just give me a sec, hon."

A good-looking cowboy waited at the register to pay his bill. He tipped his hat to Prudence, and they struck up a conversation. Before long, the two of them were chatting away like old friends. They gazed into each other's eyes as if they were the only two souls in the place. He said something to make her smile, and she leaned toward him, placing a hand on his broad chest. He put an arm around her. She stepped close. Her tiny but well-developed frame fit neatly against the intimate contours of his body. Surely, they'd just established a record for quick canoodling.

"Look at Prudence now," I hissed, interrupting Marty's rant. "You can't tell me *that's* not flirting."

I was rewarded by seeing Marty's mouth drop open just after she'd finished the phrase "... your very bad judgment, Mace." She looked at Prudence and then back at me, and then back again at Prudence. The cowboy was nuzzling the English woman's pale neck. Prudence giggled.

Finally, Marty said the six words I loved above all others.

"I was wrong. You were right." She nodded. "That is *definitely* flirting."

TWENTY-THREE

"WELL, IF THAT DOESN'T beat all." Mama sopped up the last of the gravy on her plate with a chunk of meat loaf.

As soon as Charlene brought our lunch orders, Mama had come running back to our table at Gladys.' Between bites, Marty and I filled her in on Prudence's encounter with the cowboy at the counter.

Marty wasn't completely ready to pass judgment, though.

"We don't know what's going through her head, y'all. Everybody grieves differently. You've always said that, haven't you, Mama?"

"Grieving and making a spectacle of yourself in public with a cowboy you've never met are two entirely different things, honey. I can't get my head around that gal's behavior."

Mama patted her mouth with a napkin, and then whipped out her Apricot Ice. Using the screen on her smart phone as a makeshift mirror, she delivered a *smack-smack* kiss to her reflection.

"Now." She snapped shut her lipstick. "Enough about Prudence and her impropriety. What do you girls suppose we can do about Maddie?"

Uh-oh. I didn't like where this was heading. What would I say if Mama mentioned she was concerned about my older sister's emotional health? What if she started talking about saving Maddie's marriage? She took a small sip from her water glass; regarded us with a grave expression.

"We simply cannot let her wear that yellow dress."

I shouldn't have worried. Mama would let nothing dissuade her from her mission: Making sure none of her daughters ever embarrassed her with misguided color choices.

"Henry!" Mama called across three tables to where our cousin's lunch meeting was breaking up. "Come and give your Aunt Rosalee some sugar, honey."

Like most everyone else, Henry rushed to do Mama's bidding. No sooner had he kissed her cheek than she whipped out her phone to show him the picture she'd taken of Maddie's dress at Fran's Fancy Frocks and Duds.

"Isn't that just awful?" she asked.

"Looks fine to me. The color's nice and bright, like a flashing yellow traffic light. And I like those little short sleeves. They look like bells."

Mama shook her head, not hearing the answer she wanted from Henry. "That's another thing. Maddie's upper arms will look like hams in those sleeves."

"Why don't you leave her alone, Mama? Maddie already bought the dress." I signaled Charlene for some more coffee. "So what if it's not perfect? Big deal. Let her wear what she wants."

Mama narrowed her eyes at me. Before she could start in on my snippiness or my fashion faux pas, Henry headed her off.

"Are you going to bring a pan of your lemon squares to Kenny's big bash, Aunt Rosalee?"

"Ooooooh, I love those!" Marty said.

"It wouldn't be a party without them." Henry grabbed one of Mama's hands in both of his; smiled into her eyes. "No one can bake like you do."

Smooth, I thought. It was no wonder my charming cousin had a way with a jury, particularly ones with lots of women members.

Mama patted her hair. "Well, of course I will, Henry. I know how you love them."

Talk among the three of them turned to detailed descriptions of their favorite party foods, despite the fact we'd just finished lunch. My appetite was definitely off. I was feeling guilty about what I knew—and they didn't know—about Maddie. I wanted to tell them she was in real trouble, far more trouble than having an ugly party dress. I couldn't violate her confidence, though.

I was deep in thought when a caress of warm breath and a kiss on my cheek brought me back to my surroundings. I smelled faint aftershave, sandalwood and spices. Carlos!

Turning in my seat, I pulled his face to mine for a real greeting. "Am I ever glad to see you!" I planted an unusually public, and long-lasting, smooch on his lips.

Carlos looked surprised, but pleasantly so. He returned my kiss with equal enthusiasm.

"My, my." Marty smiled. "Must be something in the water at Gladys' today."

Henry clapped Carlos on the back. They shook hands.

"Looks like 'on-again' is lasting longer than usual with Mace and her boyfriend," Mama said.

I waved my ring hand in front of her face. "My *fiancé*."

Marty and Henry chuckled. Mama smiled her approval.

"Let's call Reverend Delilah. You two can set the date. It's about time you made an honest woman out of my daughter, Carlos."

"Soon," he said.

"You hear that, honey? He's ready to be caught! All you have to do is toss the net. And make it snappy. You're not getting any younger."

"I'm not a quart of milk with an expiration date, Mama."

"Mace grows more beautiful every day," Carlos said.

Marty coughed. I felt my cheeks flush.

"I am not the one setting up blocked roads, Rosalee. Your daughter doesn't want to be caught, or else she'd slow down and let me catch her."

He was grinning, which made me smile. I thanked my stars Carlos didn't seem to be embarrassed or put off by Mama's constant nagging about our wedding. I was about to invite him to sit down, when the cow bells at the door jangled. I got distracted when I saw who was walking in.

Jason gave a big cheerful wave. In a polo shirt and cap emblazoned with the name of the golf course, he headed straight for our table. Nodding quickly at the others, he zeroed in on me.

"I was passing by and saw your Jeep parked outside." He dropped a casual hand on my shoulder. "I hear you were asking for me at the pro shop this morning."

Charlene picked that moment to come pour my coffee. "Who's the hottie," she whispered, loud enough to be heard in the kitchen over the roar of the dishwasher.

"Jason," he answered, with a flash of white teeth. "I'm the pro at Himmarshee Links. You should come out sometime. I'll help you work on your swing. I keep trying to get Mace to let me finesse hers."

At the next table, a couple of women from the courthouse swooned. Flustered, Charlene knocked over the creamer on our table with her coffeepot. The cream splashed out to where Carlos still stood, landing all over the front of his slacks. He jumped back, and then grabbed a handful of napkins. I wasn't sure whether his frown was due to Jason's shameless flirting, or his fastidiousness about his clothes.

"Sorry," said Charlene, flushed with embarrassment.

"Not to worry," Carlos smiled at the waitress. "I keep a second set of clothes in my locker at work, which is where I need to be right now." He glanced at his watch, gave me a peck on the cheek, and headed out the door.

"Was it something I said?" Jason aimed his tanned dimples at me. "I've got to get back to work, too. I just stopped to ask if I'm going to see you again."

The glances exchanged by my family members caromed around the table like pool balls. I lifted Jason's hand off my shoulder.

Mama frowned. "Since when do you play golf, Mace?"

Marty said, "The last I remember, you were saying you wished you'd left that gator you trapped in the pond at the golf course. You said maybe he'd do us a favor and eat a few newcomers."

"Ouch!" the pro laughed. "I don't think that's what the course's architect had in mind when he designed our water hazards."

"Talk about your penalty stroke," Henry said.

I mumbled something about stopping by the course soon. Jason left shortly after, to sighs from two tables of women.

Once he was out of earshot, Mama got serious. "Why are you going to the golf course?"

I tried to think of a convincing lie. I came up blank.

"None of your business."

Even as the words escaped my mouth, I knew Mama would not rest until she made it her business. I had to discover what Kenny was up to before my family imploded under the weight of what I was hiding

I threw a ten on the table and rushed out the door after Jason.

TWENTY-FOUR

"Wait up!" I yelled from the sidewalk outside Gladys' Diner.

A big ol' boy in bib overalls and a cap touting Nutrena cattle feed turned with a hopeful smile. I shook my head and pointed at the golf pro in the parking lot.

Jason stood beside a red BMW convertible, which is a pretty fancy car for a pro who works at a small golf course built on a former cow pasture in middle Florida.

"Well, well." He leaned against the driver's door, and crossed his arms over his chest. "Looks like you did want to see me again, sooner rather than later."

"Don't flatter yourself," I said. "I needed to ask you some questions, but I didn't want to talk in front of my family." Not to mention my fiancé, I thought.

He glanced at his watch; lit a cigarette. "I've got a few minutes." He exhaled. "Knock yourself out."

I decided to stick to my cover story, about trying to find out who might owe my brother-in-law money. Kenny hadn't been back to the club since we'd spoken earlier, Jason said.

"Did you notice if he seemed particularly close to anyone out there?"

Jason stroked the handsome cleft in his chin; appeared to give my question some thought.

He finally said, "He spends a lot of time at the bar, talking to Angel."

I hoped the surprise didn't show on my face. She had told me she barely knew Kenny. It also seemed she was more into girls than guys. I decided to take the plunge; ask the question right out.

"Isn't Angel gay?" I said.

He took a drag. "That's complicated. I think her sexual leanings depend on what's in it for Angel."

"Do you think there's something in it for her to have some kind of sexual relationship with my brother-in-law?"

"Nah. He's not her type. Not enough money or power. I think it's more a bartender-as-confessor thing for him. Lots of people pour out their problems to bartenders."

An image formed in my mind of Prudence's jacket on the locker room bench; the tender look on the barmaid's face. "Well, who is Angel's type?" I said. "Is she serious about anyone?"

He cocked his head. "Why? Are you interested in girls? Didn't you say you were engaged? I assumed to a guy."

He grabbed my left wrist, holding up my hand to examine my ring. His grip was a little rough.

"That hurts."

He squeezed—hard—before releasing me. "Sorry. I can be a little dominant at times. Guess I don't know my own strength."

I rubbed my wrist; decided to let it pass. In my mind, golf was kind of a girly sport. Maybe he was trying to show what a man he was with a crushing grip. I said, "What about the mayor?"

"And Angel?" he asked.

"Well, I meant the mayor and Kenny, but yeah. What's the deal with Angel and Mr. and Mrs. Mayor? It seems like they walk on eggshells around her."

He laughed. "Probably afraid if they offend her she'll pour a stingy shot." He put thumb to mouth in the sign for drinking. "Both of them like their booze. A lot."

"Kenny, too?"

He crushed his cigarette underfoot, and then glanced at his watch.

"Nah, Kenny seems like he's strictly a beer man. Doesn't over-indulge, like a lot of folks do out there." A strange smiled played across his lips. "Oh, yeah. There are *all* kinds of over-indulgences at Himmarshee Links."

"What's that supposed to mean?"

He put up his hands, signaling he'd say no more. "I really have to get going. Like I told you before, it's complicated."

"You can't say that and just leave me wondering. That's not fair. Is there something shady going on out there? Is my brother-in-law involved?"

That would be all Maddie would need: a husband walking the criminal path.

Jason gazed around the parking lot. The after-lunch crowd was starting to stream out. He lowered his voice. "I don't think so. But you wouldn't believe the stories I could tell about what goes on at the club."

"Like what?"

He hit the key fob to unlock the BMW; eased himself into the front seat.

"I really do have to go. I've got a lesson scheduled. Honest, I'll fill you in on everything, just not right now." He turned on the engine. It purred. "Meet me at the club for a drink."

I narrowed my eyes at him. Was he playing me?

He returned my look with a guileless grin. His cheeks dimpled, and the skin around his eyes crinkled with sincerity. "I swear I'm not coming on to you, Mace. It's just a friendly meeting. Maybe I can give you some information that might help you find out who borrowed Kenny's money."

If I was going to help Maddie, I did need information. It was just a drink. What could it hurt?

TWENTY-FIVE

A LOUD LAUGH ECHOED through the cypress trees, shattering the quiet sanctuary of Himmarshee Park. Startled, a great blue heron took flight from the creek bank near the nature path. Another laugh sounded, even louder than the first. A group of men in business dress rounded a curve in the path near the park office. I was outside the office, in a vending machine alcove, battling a recalcitrant package of Corn Nuts.

The noisy crowd of suits and ties came to a halt on the boardwalk over Himmarshee Creek. The mayor, at the center of the group, nodded toward the water: "You know what they say about waterfront property in Florida, don't you?" His voice boomed, and he slapped one of the suits on the back. "Get it while you can. They're not making any more!"

The man chuckled, a bit too heartily I thought. A second suit, much taller, stepped forward to peer over the railing. He pointed to the dark water below. An expensive-looking gold watch peeked out from the monogrammed cuff at his wrist: "So this stream also fronts the parcel we've been talking about?"

Parcel? What parcel? These guys looked like developers. No telling what kind of proposal they'd cooked up.

I stepped out of the vending area and onto the wooden boardwalk, my indestructible snack bag in hand. My boss's lectures about being more friendly and welcoming to park visitors ran through my mind. Well, here were some park visitors. I injected a smile into my voice.

"Can I help y'all?"

Except for the mayor, the men looked like they'd all selected their outfits from the Timeless Fashions for Business Guys Shoppe: white shirts, dark suits, black dress shoes, red ties—with a couple of striped-blues thrown in to mix things up. It had to be 95 degrees outside. They stood in the full sun, and not a one of them had thought to take off his jacket. It was clear they weren't from around here.

The mayor gave me a campaign-poster smile. I was surprised to see a diamond stud winking from his earlobe. Pretty hip for a guy sporting polyester beltless slacks, white loafers, and a T-shirt that screamed BILL GRAF FOR MAYOR in red block letters.

"I know you, don't I?"

"We've met at the country club." I didn't add that when we met, Mama had informed him she'd voted for his opponent, and then tried to browbeat him and his wife into attending her church. "I think you also play golf with my brother-in-law. Kenny Wilson?"

He pursed his lips like he was thinking. "Nope. The name doesn't ring a bell."

"The staff out there said you two played together. Big guy? Drives a pickup truck with silver mud flaps?"

He grinned. "Oh, yes. The flaps with the naked girl silhouettes. You don't see too many of those at the club."

"Naked girls or mud flaps?" said the tall man with the watch. A couple of the other suits smirked.

"I think I might have played a round or two with your brother-in-law, when one of my threesome didn't show."

The tall suit leered. "Threesome? I've heard you like to play with a foursome."

The mayor ignored the comment. "Your brother-in-law's a lousy golfer, by the way."

I didn't reveal I'd heard the same assessment of the mayor's game.

"Have you seen Kenny lately?"

"Can't say that I have. Look, we're kind of busy here." His tone was impatient. "We're looking for the park supervisor. We need to have a cornfab about business."

Opening the office door, I pointed inside to my boss, Rhonda.

" 'Cornfab' away."

A familiar wave of relief that I wasn't management material washed over me. When the mayor and the four suits had filed into the office, I slipped in behind them and took a seat at my desk. I'd been working on an exhibit about the mating habits of the Sandhill crane. I arranged it so I could disappear behind it.

Rhonda, trapped in a dull phone conversation about budgets and such, quit talking in mid-sentence when she spotted the mayor. "Anyway, those are the salient points about personnel." She quickly wrapped up the call. "I'll have to get back to you. Something's just come up."

As soon as she placed the receiver on its cradle, she unfolded her lithe body from her chair, and stretched her hand out toward Graf. "Mr. Mayor, what a pleasant surprise."

A smile spread across her lovely face. Only I recognized it as one the former fashion model reserved for people she didn't really want to see. It reached her angled cheek bones, but stopped short of warming her hazel-flecked eyes.

A couple of the suits seemed awestruck to find such a beauty wearing park department khakis. The mayor, though, barely gave her a second look. "Where's your boss, doll?"

Her smile was cool. "I am the boss."

Which of Rhonda's characteristics confused him, I wondered: The fact she was black, or that she was a woman?

"So, you're in charge?"

She extended a long graceful finger, tapping the supervisor title on her desk nameplate. "That's what it says."

"Well, screw me like a rabbit, I'm surprised." It didn't seem to register with the mayor he was pissing off a possible ally in whatever plan he was hatching. "We're trying to find out anything we can about the owners of the properties next to the park."

"All you have to do is go to the county courthouse." Rhonda took her seat again, started shuffling papers. "Property ownership is public record."

The mayor glanced furtively around the office. He didn't seem to notice me slumping down behind a stuffed Sandhill crane—a tall, regal bird with a red cap of feathers.

He lowered his voice. "We're more interested in off-the-record kind of information. Are any of the property owners having financial problems? Anyone contemplating divorce? Or, maybe one of the families is struggling with a tragic—and costly—illness?"

I came out from behind my bird.

"In other words," I said, "is there anybody in a bad way so a bunch of developers can take advantage and buy their land cheap?"

"That's rude," one of the suits said.

"What's rude is outsiders coming in here and buying up property to build ugly crap that nobody wants."

Rhonda lifted her palms in the air in the traffic cop position. "That's enough, Mace."

"You know it's true," I said. "Why don't you ask them what they have planned? No doubt it's something that will compromise every living tree and critter, not to mention the water supply, in this end of the county."

"It's a subdivision," the mayor said. "Country Haven. New homes for five-hundred residents. The park will become a very important amenity. Everyone wants a house conjoining a park."

"Adjoining," I said. "But nobody wants to live next to a shoddily built subdivision with cookie-cutter houses and too many cars and people."

The face on one of the suits turned thoughtful. "What's the possibility of getting a zoning change for the park itself?" He looked out the window to acres of pristine woods and water. "That's prime real estate, just going to waste!"

The mayor glared pointedly at him, and then cut his eyes to Rhonda and me as if to make sure we noticed. "We'd never do anything to compromise this beloved park, or Himmarshee's precious eco-system, for that matter. It's what makes this part of Florida very unique."

I bit my tongue so I wouldn't correct him again. Lord knows, Maddie drilled it into my head enough: Unique is unique. Something can't be "very" unique. Even beyond his grammar, though, I wasn't buying his words.

A frown creased the face of one of the suits, the gold watch guy who'd first gazed over the railing at the creek. "I'm still troubled about the image of the community itself. Marketing Country Haven as 'How Things Were Back When' is difficult with headlines screaming about a sexually tinged murder."

The mayor tugged at his collar. Swallowed a couple of times. He looked nervous. Stalling for time, maybe? The suit had a point.

"Mrs. Graf and myself were just discussing this at breakfast."

I could stand the mayor's misspeaks no longer. "That's 'Mrs. Graf and I.'"

He looked confused. "You and her have talked?"

Rhonda caught my eye; shook her head. "Never mind," I said.

"Big city sin can touch even the most innocent of towns. Satan likes nothing more than to wreak havoc where he's not wanted. He loves it when he can get his hooks into the weak and the idle." His voice rose like a hell-fire preacher. "The point is, all this about the murder will be forgotten by the time we break ground."

"It won't be forgotten by the victim's friends and family," Rhonda said.

I nodded in agreement. "I'll bet that's exactly what's troubling everyone who knew that poor girl: How will her brutal murder affect Himmarshee's image?"

At least one of the suits had the good grace to look embarrassed. But the mayor blustered on. "It was a horrible thing, but it's over. Once we get this project off the ground, people are just going to be happy we're bringing jobs and a boom to the tax base."

I think he meant *boon*. I said, "That's assuming you do get it off the ground. Don't underestimate how much people are tired of runaway growth. Maybe they don't want yet another fake community to replace what's real and natural about Florida."

One of the suits smirked. "Natural? Swamps and snakes? Bugs and humidity?" The others laughed.

He was hunting bear without a rifle, attacking my native state. Rhonda caught my eye again, though, and gave me the cease-and-desist glare. She'd heard me rant before about people who can't appreciate Florida's original beauty.

She said, "I think we can all agree we want what's best for Himmarshee, and for justice. That's where Mace comes in. Give her a few days, and she'll be on her way to solving Camilla's murder. She's done it before."

A couple of the suits aimed curious looks at me. I wanted to hide again behind my bird. Sputtering, the mayor waved away Rhonda's comment. "That's preposterous! I'm confident the police have it in hand. They hardly need a redneck Agatha Christie sticking her nose in."

"Mace isn't a redneck," Rhonda said.

"That's all right, boss. If the boot fits…" I lifted my foot, showing off my size-ten clodhopper. Some dried manure flaked off the heel and onto the floor.

"Well, she's not the dumb kind of redneck, anyway," Rhonda said. "She's super-smart, even if she isn't great with people. She keeps her mouth shut and her eyes open. I'll tell you right now, Mace might know who killed Camilla before the police do."

The mayor pulled at his collar again, wiped some sweat from his forehead. He gave me a suspicious look. "Irregardless," he said, as I winced at the extra *ir*, "surely the police don't encourage amateurs to help solve crimes?"

"I don't have a bull in this rodeo, Mr. Mayor. I didn't even know the victim. Besides, the Himmarshee police hardly need my help," I said. "Carlos Martinez is the head of the homicide division, and he's quite capable."

I didn't elaborate that Carlos IS the homicide division.

"He earned his stripes solving murders in Miami," Rhonda added.

"He'll have this one wrapped up in no time," I said.

The suit with the posh gold watch glanced at it. "I hope so. The sooner people forget about this murder, the more houses we can sell."

"I'm sure that will help Camilla's soul rest in peace," I said.

———

It was quitting time. The mayor and his cronies had taken a couple of maps, and left to survey the park's outlying areas. Along with the Corn Nuts and a Coke, one thing sustained me over the afternoon: The image of all those shiny black dress shoes and the mayor's white loafers slogging through dank muck and soggy marshes. I only wished we'd had a drenching rain to make things worse.

In the parking lot, a huge Hummer commanded two spaces. I was sure it was the developers' vehicle—a fitting symbol for an invading army. It sat in the full sun, soaking up heat. I hoped they all burned their legs on the Hummer's black seats when they climbed in.

At the far end of the lot, the driver of a small school bus had wisely parked under the shade canopy of a live oak. She read a paperback in the front seat while a field trip group finished up. The kids were getting close. Childish laughter and piping voices filled the woods.

I heard a car engine start as I was putting some research files about birds in the back of my Jeep. The first children were just beginning to lope into the parking lot from the nature path. They were hot on the trail of a squirrel, which was making for the safety of the oak tree.

"Slow down!" a teacher's voice called out.

A cluster of kids raced after the leaders, trying to close the gap on the squirrel. Only a few children heeded the teacher's command.

The car engine revved. With a squeal of tires, a dark sedan rocketed out of a blind parking space, hidden by the big Hummer. The car's tinted windows were rolled up. I saw the faint outline of a man in a white T-shirt behind the wheel, talking on a cell phone. He wasn't paying attention.

The children skipped excitedly across the lot. The squirrel scampered up the tree. Gaining speed, the car came closer. The kids were directly in its path.

"Watch out!" I shouted.

TWENTY-SIX

THE ATTENTION OF THE first boy in the line of children snapped from the squirrel to the speeding car. His eyes widened in fear. He seemed rooted to the pavement. The car came closer. Inside the parked bus, the driver pounded frantically on the horn: *Beep! Beep! Beeeeep!*

Kids scattered. The teacher screamed. Just in time, the black car swerved.

Safe, but scared, some of the kids began to cry. As the teacher hustled toward them from the woods, she tripped and fell to the parking lot pavement.

When the car zoomed past, it was close enough that I could see through the dark windows. The mayor was behind the wheel. He yakked away on his phone as if nothing had happened. As he sped for the exit, I saw a red-white-and-blue campaign sticker on his bumper: "A Mayor Should Care. Vote Graf."

I ran to help the teacher.

"Are you okay?"

Wincing in pain, she tried to rise to one knee. She sank back to the asphalt. "The students?"

I looked toward the bus. The driver was comforting everybody. Some had already taken their seats inside. "Fine. Probably a little shaken."

"I think I twisted my ankle."

I bent; she looped an arm around my neck. I hoisted her to her feet, steadying her at the waist. "Good thing you're strong," she said. "I'm not exactly a delicate flower."

"Me, neither." I grinned. "Let's get you over to the bus and the kids."

I quickly introduced myself.

"Elaine Naiman," she said. "We'll shake later."

She was pretty, in a studious-looking way: Thick, dark hair cut short; horn-rimmed glasses; a build that was sturdy but not fat. If Mama were here, she'd advise Elaine to grow out that glossy black hair. It was her best feature. And, of course, Mama would try to convince her to put on some Apricot Ice.

"I feel so stupid," she said, as we slowly made our way to the bus. "I shouldn't have brought the kids out here without an aide. But there were only ten signed up for the trip, and they seemed so disappointed when our aide called this morning to say she couldn't make it."

She looked in the direction the car had gone. We could still faintly hear it, battering the boards of the bridge over Himmarshee Creek just before the park's exit to the highway. "It's a weird coincidence," she said. "The aide had to cancel because some idiot on a cell phone ran a stop sign this morning and hit her car."

She shifted her weight, moaned. I paused, to give her a short rest.

"Speaking of idiots," she said, "who was driving the black sedan?"

"You won't believe it," I said. "That was Himmarshee's mayor."

————

I sneezed when I walked through the door to the 19th Hole Lounge. The smell of cologne and spilled wine was so strong, it was like a punch in the nose. Everything in the bar was overdone: the laughs were too loud; the backslaps too hard; the hair and makeup on the women too much. The only thing that wasn't too much was Angel's outfit. That was too little, with a midriff top that barely skimmed the bottom of her breasts.

Men stood two deep at the bar—ordering, of course. But also ogling, perhaps wondering if the next time she reached for a top-shelf bottle, the blouse would ride up and reveal everything she had.

She was trim and taut, with bumps and curves in all the right spots. Even I had to admit, her body was hot. As the comedian Dom Irrera always said, *That don't make me gay, does it?*

I didn't want to spend too much time at a place that clearly wasn't my style. But I did want to talk to Jason. I saw him on a stool at the end of the bar. He sat with his legs spread. The mayor's wife stood between his knees, facing him and swaying slightly. Had she been out here all day, drinking?

I edged closer in the crowded bar so I could see and hear them. A burly guy with his arm around a big-boobed blonde provided the perfect camouflage. I slid onto a seat at a high-top table, hiding myself behind the big guy and busty babe.

"Aw, c'mon," Beatrice said to Jason. "It's just a little Sex on the Beach. I know for a fact you like that."

Jason raised an eyebrow at her.

"Them. I mean I know you like them." She giggled. "Y'know, the *drinks* called Sex on the Beach."

"You're a naughty girl." He shook a finger at her. She bit it, and then sucked, doing an excellent imitation of a banana-eating contest I saw once during Spring Break in Daytona.

Jason grinned, and extracted his finger from her mouth. He moved it south, tracing her bare cleavage. She closed her eyes and shuddered, and then placed her palm on his thigh. With a devilish smile, he lifted it, and moved it several inches closer to his lap. When she tried to kiss him, though, he bobbed his head out of her reach.

I looked around to see if anyone else was catching this action, and nearly fell off my stool when I noticed who was. The mayor sat alone, just a couple of seats away from his wife and the golf pro. He followed every move they made, his eyes glued to the mirror behind the bar. I expected him to jump up and pound Jason to a pulp. That's what would have happened in most every bar I knew. Oddly, the mayor didn't look angry. He looked interested, like a man watching a fascinating documentary. There was some other expression there, too, but I wasn't sure just what. The bar was dark, and the mayor looked away when he caught me staring at him in the mirror.

Suddenly, I realized Jason was standing next to me. While I'd been preoccupied with trying to read the mayor, the pro had broken away from Beatrice.

"So, you came."

"Yep, been here awhile. I didn't want to interrupt you, though. You looked like you were pretty into Mrs. Mayor."

" 'Into' her. Good one." He plucked a peanut from the bowl on my table, popped it into his mouth. "I'm just keeping the members happy. It's part of the job."

"Maybe you should find another job."

"Why?" He sounded genuinely surprised. "I like it here, and I'm not hurting anybody."

I gestured down the bar with my chin. "Except her husband, maybe?"

Jason's gaze followed mine. He didn't seem the least bit taken aback to see the mayor so close by. He smiled slyly. "Don't be too sure of that."

Someone pinched my waist. Hard. A familiar voice rang out in the noisy bar. "Well, well, if it isn't my daughter—my *engaged* daughter—talking to this handsome man. This handsome, *single* man."

I turned to see the Mama Glare aimed full force at Jason.

He dimpled, pouring on the charm. "I was just telling Mace about another gator we've found on the course. Don't worry. I have no designs on her at all. We're just friends. I still can't get over the fact you're her mom, though. You're so beautiful; you seem far too young."

Mama thawed a bit.

"I know your husband, Sal. He brags about you all the time, saying how he can't believe he managed to catch you. I have to say, though, all his bragging hasn't done you justice. Sal's a very lucky man."

Mama smoothed at her hair. Jason had her at "brags about you."

"What are you doing here?" I asked.

"Sal and I have an early dinner engagement. I was on my way to the Ladies when I spotted you." She sniffed. "I smell manure. What's that all over your boots, Mace?'

I grabbed a handful of peanuts, stuffed all of them in my mouth. Mama slid the bowl to the far side of the table, out of my reach.

"Calories, Mace. If you and Carlos ever do get married, you want to make sure we don't have to push you down the aisle in a handcart."

I chewed. Mama shook her head. "Just like a cow and her cud. Where are your manners?" she said. "Now, why did you say you're here?"

"I didn't," I mumbled through a mouthful of peanuts.

"The gator. Mace helped trap our last one." Jason shot me a look. "Remember?"

Was he more clever than I gave him credit for?

"Rosie!" A Bronx bellow vibrated the air. Sal stood in the doorway, beckoning Mama. "Our table's ready, sweetheart. C'mon, I'm hungry!"

Jason waved at Sal. The big man waved back, and yelled across the room. "I'm ordering the steak, Mace—that big T-bone you liked so much."

Now that everyone in the lounge knew Sal's and my meat preferences, Mama took her leave. But not before taking my peanut bowl. "Sal's hungry, honey. And Lord knows you don't need these."

When she was gone, Jason said, "Your mother's a trip."

"Yeah, but no vacation," I said. "So, you told me you'd fill me in on all the secrets of Himmarshee Links. I hope I didn't waste the drive out here."

Jason looked around, leaned in close to whisper. I thought he was going to reveal something scandalous. Instead, I felt his hot tongue in my ear. Before I could smack him, Angel grabbed him from behind by the shoulder. It must have hurt, because Jason jumped off his stool and let loose with a few curse words. He spun around. When he saw who it was, the expression on his face turned in an instant from angry to contrite.

"Manager needs to see you in the office. Right now." Her tone was brusque. "You're probably in trouble. Again."

"Sorry, Angel."

He should have told *me* he was sorry, seeing as I was the one whose ear he tongued. Angel didn't bother to acknowledge his apology. She just glared at him until he scurried away.

She took the spot he left, next to me. "You're back."

"Yep. Jason promised to tell me all the dirty secrets about this place."

She snorted. "And you believed him?"

"Why wouldn't I?"

"He's trying to hit on you. There's nothing to tell."

I looked at her. She looked back, seemingly assessing me the same way I was assessing her. Could I trust her? My concern for Maddie outweighed my suspicions about Angel telling the truth.

"I'm worried about my brother-in-law, Kenny. My sister hasn't seen him in a couple of days. Something's going on. I'm just trying to find out what."

"Why do you assume it's something out here?"

"Because all of this mess with Kenny and Maddie started when he suddenly got interested in golf. It's so out-of-character, I just know there's got to be a tie-in."

We eyed each other. Silence stretched between us.

"I hear you know Kenny better than you let on. He likes to hang out at your bar."

She shrugged. "So do a lot of other guys."

"Can you tell me anything about his friends? What he says? How he acts?" I said. "It'd mean a lot to me."

"I don't know his friends, but I can tell you Kenny's a stand-up guy." Angel spun a cocktail straw like a tiny baton between her index and middle fingers. "He's a good tipper."

Kenny? The same man who used a five-percent-off coupon for a three-dollar peach cobbler at the Pork Pit?

She stopped spinning the straw. "He's not in any trouble, is he?"

I thought about Maddie, and what she might do to her cheating husband once she moved past the betrayal stage into rage. "Yeah, you could say Kenny's in a little trouble."

"Well, whatever it is, it's got nothing to do with the club. This is a family environment."

I looked around. Everyone was drinking heavily. Men flirted with anyone but their wives. A clutch of well-preserved women in their fifties surrounded Jason, who'd returned to the bar. One tweaked his nipple through his golf shirt; the rest giggled and urged her on like hormone-addled teenagers.

"Yeah, you're right, Angel. This place is so wholesome I'm surprised you don't have a spot in the bar just for Bible study."

I slid off the stool, gathered my purse, and headed for home. I'd need a hot shower to wash away the nasty images from the 19th Hole.

TWENTY-SEVEN

"Ice cream man's here!"

Sal bulled his way through the kitchen door at Mama's house, carrying two sacks filled with quart containers. Himmarshee had a brand new ice cream parlor. After I showered and ate a quick dinner at home, we'd all met up at Mama's for a late evening sampling of their wares. No one had to twist our arms to help support local business, not when the business featured frozen flavors like Rodeo Red Velvet and Cracker Trail Coffee.

So far as I knew, the parlor had no plans to play off the local Speckled Perch Festival by naming an ice cream Fried-Perch Peach.

I fetched bowls from the cabinets; Marty got the spoons. Mama put out a couple of plates so the scoopers wouldn't drip all over the table. Sal provided commentary as he lined up the ice cream:

"Here's Kissimmee Kandy Kane. This one's Chief Wild Cat Chocolate. Here's Brahman Butterscotch, Growling Gator Tracks, and vanilla."

"Vanilla?" Mama said. "Couldn't they come up with something more exciting?"

"The girl in the shop told me vanilla is vanilla. No one felt inspired."

"Well, Maddie and I both love vanilla. They could have tried a little harder, don't you think, honey?"

Mama looked across the table at Maddie. She didn't seem to realize Mama was waiting for her to chime in on the virtues of vanilla. Maddie stared off into space, tracing her finger around the rim of her empty bowl.

"What say you, Maddie?" Sal said. "Can you think of a cute name?"

"Just a spoonful or two, please. I'm not that hungry."

Maddie uninterested in wordplay *and* not hungry? Silent shrugs were exchanged.

Once all our bowls were filled, I asked Sal, "How was dinner at the golf course?"

"Delicious! That place might be a little strange, but there's nothing off about their food."

Maddie suddenly went as still as a rabbit when a hawk flies over.

"Strange how?" Marty asked. "*Mmm-mmm*, that chocolate flavor is good."

"Well, you can start with all the women with their big bazooms," Mama jumped in before Sal could answer. "That can't be natural, can it? Fifty-year-olds showing off their boobies like strippers. It's not right."

"Add to that those hideous outfits the men wear to go golfing." I slid a spoonful of Cracker Trail Coffee into my mouth. Heaven.

"Hey, we never complain when you ladies want to mix it up with the jazzy colors and patterns," Sal said. "Golf gives men an excuse to strut our stuff, fashion-wise."

"That's not the only strutting the men are doing out there," Mama tsked.

Maddie was so immobile, I wasn't sure she was breathing.

"What do you mean?" Marty asked.

Mama leveled a stern look at Sal. "Do you want to tell them, or should I?"

He grabbed for the carton of Brahman Butterscotch. With a pleading look, he held it out to Mama.

"I got this just for you, Rosie. I know how you love your butterscotch."

She turned, showing him the back of her head. Mama refusing butterscotch? Would the world soon stop spinning?

"Why don't you girls ask my husband about men strutting?"

"Which husband?" Marty said.

"I think she means her current one," I offered.

Marty and I raised our eyebrows at Sal. Maddie regarded him seriously.

He waved a hand. "Your mother thinks I have a thing for the barmaid. It's ridiculous."

Mama huffed. "Not so ridiculous when I had to wipe the drool off your chin after you got an eyeful of that mini-midriff she was wearing. Not that you were the only one staring."

"Everybody knows I only have eyes for you, Rosie."

"That's true, Mama. It's common knowledge," Marty said.

Mama snorted. "I know one thing. That gal's no natural blonde. Not with that olive skin and those dark eyebrows."

"Not a natural blonde, huh?" I rolled my eyes at Mama, the original peroxide-bottle belle. "The horror."

Teensy chose that moment to jump into Mama's lap. Like furry sprinkles, a dusting of white dog hair settled on the ice-cream scoopers. "Gross!" I took them to the sink and rinsed them in super hot water.

"Do you mind, Mama?" Marty plucked the little dog off his owner's lap and deposited him back on the floor. "I prefer my ice cream unadorned with shedding Teensy."

"Don't pay any attention to them, darlin'," Mama cooed to the dog. "You'll never forget you're mama's baby. You'll never forget what good care Mama takes of you, will you? Not like some ungrateful daughters I could mention."

Maddie finally moved, pushing her chair back. She'd tried just a few bites of ice cream.

"Didn't you like it, Maddie?" Sal peered into her bowl. "There's no dog hair in there."

"I need to make a phone call." She took her cell into the living room.

I tried to steer the conversation back to the golf course again. I wanted to know what Sal thought was strange, because I certainly thought something was. "Sal, about what you said—"

Mama shushed me. Putting her finger to her lips, she crept to the kitchen doorway to eavesdrop on Maddie. Marty followed. I began again. "The golf course, Sal—"

This time Marty put a finger to her lips; shook her head at me. Mama whispered: "I'm worried about your sister, Mace. Something's wrong, and I aim to find out what!"

From the other room, I could hear the faint electronic beeps of Maddie hitting the keypad on her phone. There was a pause. Then she spoke, her voice shaking with anger and frustration.

"Not voice mail again! Where are you? This is ridiculous. We need to talk. You owe me that, at least. I'm leaving another message: 'Call. Me. Back.' "

The next thing we heard was the door close on the hallway bathroom. The pipes in the old house were noisy. Water running to the sink's faucets sounded through the wall.

In a hushed voice, Mama asked, "What do you suppose that was all about?"

She and Marty cocked their heads at me. I shrugged.

"She doesn't sound happy," Sal said.

"No kidding," Marty said. "She's not eating, either. Maybe she's dieting to get into her yellow party dress. Maddie's always in a bad mood when she diets."

"I wish she'd rethink that dress," Mama said. "Very few people can wear bright yellow. I'm lucky I'm one of them."

From Maddie's misery to Mama's lovely skin tone, another record set.

"What do you suppose Kenny will wear?" Marty asked.

"Something new, I bet. Have you noticed he's lost weight?" Mama said. "He looks great."

Sal scooped seconds of the Kissimmee Kandy Kane ice cream into his bowl; considered for a moment, and then plopped in another mound of chocolate, too. "Must be all the exercise he's getting, playing golf," he said. "Kenny's making all sorts of new friends at the club."

From my angle, I could see Maddie, listening just outside the kitchen door. Her face was damp and her eyes were swollen. I didn't let on she was there.

"He'd better not be getting too friendly with that barmaid," Mama said. "Maddie will tee up for a hole-in-one right off his forehead."

"That's a ridiculous idea, Mama," Marty said. "Maddie's not insanely jealous, like you. Besides, she has nothing to worry about with Kenny. He's the most loyal husband on earth."

A stifled sob came from the hallway. Maddie rushed from the house, slamming the front door behind her. Teensy scampered to the window in the living room to watch her go. Within moments, a car engine started. Tires squealed. The dog's fevered barking outlasted the sound of Maddie fleeing.

TWENTY-EIGHT

"I DON'T WANT TO make the call, Mace. You do it."

Maddie held a cocktail napkin with a phone number scribbled on it in lipstick. She'd found it deep in the pocket of a pair of Kenny's slacks. Hand shaking, she shoved the napkin at me. I didn't want to make the call either. But this was my sister. I took the number.

I hadn't waited around at Mama's to hear any more of Teensy's yapping—not to mention any further dissection of Maddie's strange behavior. I made a quick excuse about having to be up early, and was out the door right behind her. I tailed her to her house.

Now, the two of us were in her living room. The telephone beckoned on a table between us. The room was so quiet, I could hear the motor whirring on the decorative fountain in Maddie's front yard.

I punched in the phone number. It rang and rang, maybe a dozen times, before someone finally answered. The clink of glasses and laughter echoed in my ear.

"19th Hole Lounge; Angel speaking."

I pressed down the button on the phone to disconnect.

"Who was it?" Maddie asked.

"Nobody," I lied. "They never picked up."

"No answering machine? No voice mail?"

I shrugged. "Maybe they can't afford it."

I folded the napkin and slipped it deep into my pocket. I wasn't going to make it easy for Maddie to call again. I wasn't sure how the golf course's bar—and its gorgeous barmaid—played into Kenny's unfaithfulness. But I'd rather find out first than let Maddie assume the worst and act rashly. Angel didn't seem like a good person to cross without having all the facts in hand.

Later, when Maddie's mind was less burdened, she might think about hitting redial on her home phone. For now, the number was hidden in my pocket. I tried to distract her. "Why don't you try Kenny again?"

"I've dialed that number so many times the cramps in my fingers have cramps," Maddie said. "I have the feeling he's hiding out at his hunting camp. Would you go look for him? I'm so angry, I honestly don't trust what I might do if I find him."

I knew Maddie was right about that. The mood she was in, she might just shoot him and mount his head like a hunting trophy on the wall. "Absolutely, I'll go. If I find him, I'll fetch him home again." I didn't say I'd probably knock some sense into the cheating bastard first.

"You can find it, right?"

"Yep, I was just out there last winter when y'all had that big pig roast. It's almost to the Okeechobee County line, not too far from the dump."

Maddie nodded. "I owe you one." Her voice was so soft I had to lean in to hear her.

She looked miserable. It seemed every ounce of the self-confidence she'd always possessed had been sucked out. Putting my arm around her, I pulled her close. I wanted to protect her.

"You'd do the same for me, sister. You don't owe me a thing."

I smoothed at Maddie's fiery red hair, and brushed my lips against her cheek. It tasted salty from the tears she'd shed.

———

My Jeep bounced over the rutted entrance to Kenny's camp, more a claustrophobic pathway than a road. Live oaks raised gnarled limbs overhead, creating a dark tunnel. I remembered how sweet bay and wax myrtle crowded in from both sides. The cramped lane gave me the sense I was sliding blindfolded into a long, narrow chute.

I tried to keep my eyes out for potholes, while my mind focused on what I'd find when the Jeep came out the other side. Even in the dark, I could see the white blossoms on a wild sour orange. The tree's branches scratched at the Jeep, rubbing paint off my already-battered ride.

Finally, I broke free of the woodsy tunnel and entered a small clearing. My high-beam headlights played over what would be the camp's front yard, if Kenny had ever bothered to plant grass. No lights shone in the windows of the ramshackle camp house—a scrap-wood building with a broad screened porch and patched tin roof. Kenny's truck was nowhere in sight. Weeds were flattened and small shrubs crushed in the area he and his hunting buddies normally used for parking. No one was parked there tonight.

The Jeep rolled over what looked like a huge anthill. I pulled to a stop about twenty-five feet from the front porch door. Grabbing a flashlight from the glove box, I got out and made my way to the structure.

I knew the camp was larger—and nicer—inside than it seemed from the yard. Kenny had put in electricity and indoor plumbing, which was a plus when it came to convincing Maddie or Mama to ever visit. Marty and I definitely got all our family's nature-girl genes. Aiming the flashlight at the top of the door jamb, I ran my finger along the wood. There was the key, just where Kenny always hid it. Once inside the door, I flipped on the lights.

The first thing that struck me was the smell of cigarette smoke. Aside from Sal's occasional cigars, no one in our family smoked. Kenny didn't either, as far as I knew. Judging by the pungency, the smoke was fairly recent.

Only after the cigarette odor registered did I notice another, fainter smell. It was lemony, like perfume or cologne. I'd smelled it somewhere before. When I sat down on the couch, the sweet scent was stronger. It seemed to rise up from the cushions. I definitely preferred it to the smoke stink, or the stale beer I could smell in a bottle on an end table next to the couch.

The bottle was about two-thirds full. Cigarette ashes littered the top, and someone had dropped their butts into the remaining beer. Lovely. The ashtray on the coffee table also overflowed, and lots of those discards were stained with lipstick. I poked through the ashtray with a pencil, and found at least three different shades on various cigarettes.

It looked like more than hunting was happening at Kenny's camp. Fearing what I'd find, I made my way to the bedroom.

The bed was rumpled, a jumble of black satin sheets and tossed pillows. No way were those linens Maddie's. My prudish, fiscally conservative sister would be more likely to sleep on a bed of nails than on slinky, pricey, black satin.

Thong panties, bright red with lacy insets, draped a lampshade. Again, not Maddie's. On the nightstand sat two empty cans of diet Mountain Dew, Kenny's favorite. Next to those were three packages of condoms in camouflage colors. An unopened bottle of Dom Perignon rested on the bed.

I may be more Budweiser than fine champagne, but even I knew that was some pretty pricey hooch. Another two bottles, empty, were up-ended in silver ice buckets half-filled with water. The water was still cool to the touch, but all the ice had melted. I counted five champagne flutes. Three were on top of a bureau. The other two were on the floor by the head of the bed, one on each side. I checked them for lipstick stains. All but one had the telltale marks.

I fetched the ashtray from the living room to see if the shades matched. At least one did—the lipstick on several of the cigarette butts matched one of the champagne glasses.

I stood there, trying to make sense of what I was seeing. No matter how I figured, it didn't look good for Kenny. Several women had been here—or maybe just one woman with an unusually diverse lipstick palette. There was drinking—which Maddie didn't approve of. There was the appearance of sex. And there were those camouflage condoms. Those had Kenny and hunting camp written all over them.

I hadn't found him, but I'd certainly found something. What in the world was I going to tell my sister?

I was about to leave when I remembered the napkin with the phone number I'd shoved into my pocket. I pulled it out and held it next to the champagne flute that matched one of the cigarettes. The rosy red phone number to the 19th Hole Lounge was written in exactly the same shade of lipstick.

———

Outside on the front porch, I let my eyes adjust again to the dark. Beneath a waxing moon, there was light enough to see the sabal fronds beginning to shudder in a gusty wind. The temperature had dropped. A storm brewed. Silvery clouds swollen with rain scudded across a black sky.

A limpkin screamed from a nearby creek, raising the hairs at the back of my neck. No matter how many times I heard the wailing cry of the bird, it always gave me a start. Not for nothing did early Florida settlers call the limpkin the Crazy Widow.

Rustling sounds came from all around the dark landscape. It might have been the wind; or maybe wild hogs. Between the mournful bird and the imminent storm, I was feeling uneasy. Soon, the weather wouldn't be fit for man or beast—or woman, either. I had planned to look around for signs of Kenny. He might have parked the truck somewhere else on the property. But the thought of tramping through the dark woods in a pounding rain didn't hold much appeal.

Truth be told, I wasn't sure what I'd do with Kenny once I found him. Where would I start in trying to unravel the story of that scene inside the camp-house? I needed to think about the best way to extract the truth from him. I decided to head for home, a good night's sleep, and a chance of staying ahead of the storm.

The breeze picked up. Leaves skittered over the tops of my boots. The wind changed direction. I smelled rain coming, and something else: the acrid odor of cigarette smoke.

I was not alone in the woods.

TWENTY-NINE

I hurried to my Jeep, stumbling a bit over the rough ground. The wind gusted harder. Still, I could smell the cigarette. It was probably just a hunter, settling in for a smoke before the rain began. But something about this whole episode at the camp hadn't set right with me. I didn't intend to stick around to find out exactly who was puffing away on Kenny's isolated property in this lonely stretch of the county.

Grabbing the handle, I flung open the driver's side door. My fingers scrabbled nervously at the waistband of my jeans, where I'd tucked my keys. They slipped from my hand, jangling to the floor. I bent to find them, just barely catching a reflection moving across the passenger side window. In the same second, my brain recognized it as an aiming dot, and I heard the loud crack of a rifle. I ducked my head as a tree limb shattered to my left. Leaves and chunks of bark rained onto the hood of my Jeep.

Hand shaking, I retrieved the keys and jammed them into the ignition. The engine clicked, but didn't kick over. I cursed my reluctance to spend money on a new battery. Still slumped low in the seat, I turned the key again. The Jeep started. The relief that flooded through me was short-lived.

Another rifle shot split the air. A new branch burst, this time to my right. Chips of wood dinged off the fenders. A scatter of leaves clung to the windshield. Still ducking, I hit the gas. The tires spun in the sandy soil, and finally grabbed. Backing over the ant hill, I swept the steering wheel in a wide circle. Straightening the Jeep, I thrust it into drive. Peering up and over the dashboard, I spotted the rifle's aiming dot dancing above the tree branches.

A third shot sounded just as I made it to the pot-holed driveway. Whoever was shooting had aimed very high. No storm of foliage followed the last shot.

Still, I hunched low in the seat, taking no chances. Toward the end of the tree tunnel, open space appeared ahead. The paved road was within sight. I hung a wide right off Kenny's property, jouncing over the shoulder onto the pavement. Just as I made it, the first fat drops of rain slapped against the Jeep's roof.

My eyes searched the rear-view mirror, but I saw only darkness behind me. What in the hell had happened? It was either a hunter with appalling aim, or a marksman aiming to intimidate. I swallowed; took a deep breath. My mouth was desert-dry. The thumping of my heart echoed in my ears. My hands were so tight on the steering wheel my knuckles ached.

I was beyond intimidated. I'd been terrified. Now I was ticked-off.

———

My mood hadn't improved much by the next morning. Mama was pouting. I would not concede a point. It wasn't pretty.

"Well, I don't understand why it's such a big deal, Mace. It's just a tiny bit out of your way, and it sure means a lot to me. Any other daughter would be happy to give her poor mama a ride to work."

"You happen to have two other daughters. Why didn't you call them?"

Mama stuck out her lower lip. She punched the scanner button on the radio to find a Christian music station.

"Hey, I was listening to that!" I punched it back to country.

"You are sure in some kind of snit, girl. Who licked the red off of your candy?"

I didn't want to tell her my foul temper might be a result of being shot at—or at least *thinking* I was being shot at. I couldn't be absolutely certain about last night. Was it the most inept hunter in the county? Maybe someone held a weird grudge against trees. Whatever, it felt an awful lot like the series of shots was some kind of message meant for me.

If Mama knew what I'd found at Kenny's camp, let alone that I was alone out there on the wrong end of some moron's target practice, she'd throw a fit. My stomach churned when I considered how easily those shots could have ripped into me instead of the trees. I shook off the thought, and returned to picking at Mama.

"I'm just saying that old convertible of yours is in the shop so much maybe you should get rid of it. You should have dumped it after you found the body in the trunk." I glanced over, my face deadly serious. "Maybe it's cursed!"

Mama snorted. "You know I don't believe in that supernatural mumbo jumbo. It's against the Bible."

"So what is it, if not a curse, that you've stumbled upon dead body after dead body ever since?"

Silently, Mama took out her lipstick. She turned my rear view in her direction. Surely the base was stripped by now. She Iced, then smacked her lips a couple of times.

"I've just been at the wrong place at the wrong time, honey. Several times." She kissed a tissue to blot off the excess. "Besides, it's not like I've found all the bodies stashed in the back of my convertible."

We were both quiet for a moment. I thought about the dead girl in the dump. Mama must have, too, because she asked, "Has Carlos found out any more about Camilla?"

"Nothing he's said to me. You know how he is when he's working a case."

I eased to a stop on Main Street, at one of Himmarshee's two traffic lights. She tilted the rear-view mirror back toward me. It showed me a narrow slice of the left rear window and the top of the driver's side seat belt. Sighing, I realigned it. As the light turned green, I eased into the intersection with U.S. Highway 441.

"By the way, I did try Maddie and Marty before I called you for a ride to Hair Today Dyed Tomorrow," Mama said.

"So I wasn't your first choice? Imagine that."

"Marty had a doctor's appointment bright and early. Maddie never picked up. That girl is avoiding me for some reason. I don't understand it."

"Maybe she's sick of hearing about how you hate that yellow dress."

Mama cut her eyes at me.

"What's the problem with Marty?" I changed the subject. "She's not sick, is she?"

Mama waved a hand. "She and Sam are ready to have kids. Marty wants to have the doctor check her over, make sure she's in good health."

I nearly swerved off the highway. "Kids?! What? How come nobody told me? This is big news."

Mama looked smug. "You don't know everything, Ms. Smarty Pants. Of course, Marty would turn to her mama to have a talk about children. It's not like you're the most maternal woman on the planet."

I was still shaking my head about my little sister when Mama hit me with something else to ponder.

"She'll do fine. It's not Marty I'm concerned about, honey."

I motioned a 4 X 4 hauling a stock trailer to pull out from the feed store parking lot. Tipping his cowboy hat, the driver slowly turned in front of me. My raised eyebrows signaled to Mama to continue.

"It's Maddie." Mama's forehead wrinkled with worry.

I knew I had to tread carefully. I didn't let my face reveal a thing. "How so?"

"For starters, she's lost weight."

"Isn't that all you ever nagged her to do? Now she has, and it's a problem?"

Mama folded her arms over her chest. "Something is not right. I know my girls. I just hope whatever's wrong won't ruin Kenny's birthday. Maddie has worked so hard to plan that celebration for him."

A speeding driver in a red luxury SUV zoomed past us with inches to spare. He veered so close to a sod truck in the oncoming lane I could see the truck driver's eyes widen. His lips formed the F-word. The SUV cut back into my lane. He darted into the car length I'd left between my Jeep and the stock trailer so as not to tailgate and spook the cattle.

Mama stuck her head out the window and screamed, "Watch your manners, buster!"

"Newcomer asshole," I muttered.

"Language, Mace."

Mama was momentarily distracted from the Maddie issue by the prospect of the wild driver in the SUV killing someone, like us. I didn't mention that a ruined party barely registered on Maddie's problem-o-meter right now.

In the distance, the salon's sign beckoned. A huge pair of mechanical purple scissors snipped at the air. The SUV pulled out to pass again, terrifying a white-haired couple in a Buick, and earning a one-fingered salute from the cattle-hauling cowboy.

I prayed we'd make it without the SUV causing a crash. If we did, it'd be the first time I was ever relieved to pull in under those scissors to park at Hair Today Dyed Tomorrow.

THIRTY

"Oh my goodness! My hair looks a fright."

Mama caught a glimpse of herself in the mirrored walls of Betty Taylor's shop. I trailed her into the salon, toting her box filled with aromatherapy candles and Color Me Gorgeous pamphlets.

"Windswept hair is the price you pay for sticking your head out the window to scream at rude drivers, Mama."

D'Vora glanced at us. Then she ducked her head and hurried into the stock closet. I was beginning to take her avoidance personally.

"What's up with her?" I asked Betty, as I put down Mama's supplies.

She shrugged. As she stood back to examine the haircut on the woman in her chair, I realized it was the dark-haired teacher from the scary incident with the kids at Himmarshee Park.

"Elaine, right? How's the ankle?" I asked her.

A smile slowly replaced her look of confusion. "Oh, hi! I didn't recognize you since I'm not hanging on to your neck and limping." Lifting her leg under the purple drape, she showed off her taped ankle. "Not bad. Still swollen. I won't be running around after the kids for a while."

The bells at the front door jangled. An older woman entered. Another customer waited to pay at the cash register .

"D'Vora, get out here! I'm busier than a short-tailed cow in fly season." When Betty yelled, the young stylist came running.

Nodding a quick hello at Mama and me, D'Vora rang up the departing customer, and then settled the new one in a chair at the shampoo sink. I took a seat. Since I had to work over the weekend, I had the day off from the park. There was no better place in town than Hair Today to catch up on gossip, both useful and not.

I introduced Elaine to Mama. Exactly as I predicted, she offered the teacher some advice: "Honey, your hair is so pretty. You ought to let it grow out."

"Welcome to my world, Elaine. My mother's not one to hold back on helpful beauty tips. Helpful tips of any sort, actually."

The teacher's dark eyes sparkled. She seemed more amused than offended. "I'll give it some thought, Rosalee."

I filled everyone in on how the mayor had nearly run down Elaine's school class.

"I've done some checking up on that man. People say he bought the election. I didn't like him before. Everything I've heard since makes me like him even less," Elaine said.

"Join the club," I said. "He's bringing in some developers to build a big subdivision right next to Himmarshee Park; maybe even pave over the park itself."

"Our nature park?" Betty turned Elaine's head back to the mirror. "Can he do that?"

"This is Florida," I said. "Anything's for sale if the price is right. I made an appointment for this afternoon to talk to him about it. Mama's coming along for moral support. Right, Mama?"

She fluffed her hair. "It's more like I'm coming along to charm the mayor. We all know which of us loses her temper and who smoothes things over."

"I can certainly understand losing your temper about the prospect of ruining that lovely park." Elaine said. "When my family visited from Canada, that's the first place I took them."

"See if you can find out anything from the mayor about that poor girl's murder," Betty said. "The sooner we know what happened, the safer I'll feel."

I noticed D'Vora hadn't chimed in on the conversation. Not on the prospect of development, our sleazy mayor, or the murder. She didn't even ask where Canada was. She concentrated on her shampoo job like she was curing cancer.

"Seriously, Betty… what's wrong with D'Vora?" I whispered.

"Man trouble, I'll bet." Betty whispered back. "That man of hers fell out of the loser tree and hit every branch coming down."

More loudly, she called out, "D'Vora, you're so quiet you're scaring the customers. Is that no-account Darryl up to no good again?"

D'Vora shook her head, kept right on scrubbing at the customer's hair. Scabs were probably forming on the poor woman's scalp by now.

Under her breath, Betty caught us up: "She tells me that moron bought brand new custom wheels for his truck, even though they can barely cover the rent. I guess that's better, though, than him being out there spending money on other women."

"Oh, I've been there," Mama said. "My girls have been a lot luckier picking out men than I was. Well, it took Mace a while, but she's got a keeper now."

Betty sighed. "That Carlos is sure gorgeous! Such thick, dark hair. And skin that looks like buttered rum. You're a lucky girl, Mace."

"They all three are," Mama said. "Marty and Maddie got a couple of princes, too."

A troubled look flitted across D'Vora's face. She finally joined in, abruptly changing the subject to the charms of the golf pro. "I saw him at Gladys,' speaking of men. He's one tasty-looking hunk."

"I don't get the attraction of golf," Elaine said. "Hitting a little ball all day? Bor-Ing!"

"Golf may be God's dullest gift to the world of sports, but D'Vora's right about the pro," I told her. "This guy will make you want to find the sweet spot."

Mama slapped my hand.

"Ouch! I meant on a golf club, Mama. That's where you're supposed to hit the ball."

She narrowed her eyes at me. "That boy's forbidden fruit, Mace. You're almost a married woman. You're spoken for."

"'Spoken for?' What am I, a heifer at the Himmarshee Livestock Auction?"

Elaine smiled.

"You know what I mean," Mama said. "Once you're engaged, you cannot waltz around flirting with anything in pants."

"Since when have I done that?"

Betty butted in, nipping our squabble in the bud. "Speaking of flirting, I saw Sal's man-crazy cousin C'ndee at the Booze 'n'

Breeze drive-thru. She told me about some of that I-talian food she's serving for Kenny's party. I can't pronounce it, but it sure sounded good. Who's that Jersey sparkplug seeing these days?"

Mama slapped her forehead. "I can't believe I forgot to tell y'all. Guess who's been beating his head against the wall, trying to get C'ndee to go out with him."

A salon full of women raised their eyebrows at Mama. Even D'Vora stopped her torture by towel. She cocked her head, waiting. Mama hadn't shared any C'ndee gossip in awhile, so this news was bound to be fresh.

"Who?" D'Vora asked.

"Guess."

Not this routine again.

"The music director at Abundant Forgiveness," Betty said.

"Nope."

"The cook at the Pork Pit," said D'Vora.

"Guess again."

"Juan, from Juan's Auto Repair and Taco Body Shop," offered Elaine.

Mama shook her head.

"Oh, for God's sake, Mama. We don't have all day. Who?"

"The honorable Big Bill Graf. Our new mayor."

Mama looked satisfied when the woman at the shampoo sink gasped. She peeked out from under D'Vora's towel. "But he's married! Didn't he run on a family values platform?"

Betty waved off the question with her purple comb. "He sure wouldn't be the first hypocrite to hold office."

Mama lowered her voice. "Now, I'm the very last one to countenance cheating, but have you met Mrs. Mayor? That woman always

189

looks like she's been sipping vinegar. What a sourpuss! Maybe the mayor wanted somebody cheerful and lively for a change."

"C'ndee is lively all right," I said.

"She has some real fun events planned for Kenny's birthday party," Betty said. "Maddie and Kenny must be looking so forward to it. What a celebration they're going to have."

D'Vora dropped a big bottle of shampoo. When all of us looked her way, she tossed the towel on a chair and pointed her chin at the customer, "She's ready for you, Betty."

She hurried toward the door, averting her eyes from Mama and me. "Sorry, I've got to run an errand real quick."

She left the shampoo bottle where it fell. The bells jangled as the door swung shut.

"Weird," Elaine said.

Mama and Betty exchanged knowing smiles. "Want to bet the errand has something to do with her checking up on her man?" Mama said.

"Nothing like hearing someone else's husband is cheating to make you suspect your own," Betty added.

I didn't think it was Darryl troubling D'Vora. Why was she avoiding Mama and me? Did she know something about Kenny and Maddie she didn't want to talk about?

I followed her out the front door to find out.

THIRTY-ONE

D'VORA SAT ACROSS THE street, on a bench under a magnolia tree in the courthouse square. She faced the building, where a handful of clerks and legal workers were arriving to start their day. I watched her for a while. She was fidgeting with the hem of her purple smock and chewing at her thumb like it was a Tootsie Roll.

I crossed the street and sidled up behind her. "Hey," I said, and she nearly jumped off the bench.

"You scared me!"

"Sorry, I didn't mean to." I pointed at the space next to her. "Mind if I sit for a bit?"

She shrugged, and I was afraid she was going to bite clear through her thumbnail.

As I took a seat, D'Vora's gaze lit everywhere but on me. "Listen..." I began.

She quickly called out to a couple of youngish women who looked like they could have graduated with her from Himmarshee High: "Hey, y'all. Already hot as hell's hinges, isn't it?"

"Hot enough the trees are bribing the dogs," one answered, as they entered the courthouse.

I tried again. "I feel like you've been avoiding me. There's something I want to talk…"

D'Vora glommed on to another acquaintance, who was wearing a form-fitting dress in royal blue. "Hey, Amber," she shouted. "You're sure looking good. That's definitely your color."

Amber beamed. "I'm coming in next week for blonde highlights. I didn't lose all this weight to go through life with mousy brown hair."

"Give me a call, anytime. Better yet, let me give you a card." D'Vora rocketed off the bench, but Amber motioned her to sit down.

"I know Hair Today's number by heart." She looked at her watch. "Gotta run! I'm just about late."

The stylist sat again, reluctantly it seemed. Her eyes darted here and there, but Himmarshee's miniature morning rush hour appeared to have ended.

"Why do you keep running away from me?" I asked her.

"I'm not." Now, she was worrying both thumb and index finger between her teeth.

"D'Vora, if you know something you think I should know, you need to tell me. I've always been straight up with you, haven't I?"

She nodded, twisting her hand at her mouth to gnaw on yet another fingernail.

"Are you afraid you'll get in trouble?"

She shook her head. She looked like she was about to cry.

"Are you afraid of getting someone else in trouble?"

She nodded. Sure enough, a tear rolled down her cheek.

I put a hand on her knee. "Honey, it's probably not as bad as you think. You'll feel better once you get it off your chest. I can share some of the burden of knowing with you."

I saw her wavering. "D'Vora, you need to do the right thing."

That sealed it. She started blubbering, trying to get the words out: "Iiiii… ttttt… it's…" She pulled a tissue from her pocket and blew her nose. Slipped it back into her smock.

"It's what?"

"Not what. Who. It's Kenny."

The thumb flew back to her mouth. She was biting so hard, I could hear her teeth nicking the nail. I gently took her hand, holding it still in mine.

"What about him?"

"He's cheating on Maddie."

I sighed with relief. Not that the news wasn't bad. But I'd already dealt with the anger and disappointment of finding out about my brother-in-law's philandering.

"I saw him out at the lake at sunset, in his truck. I knew it was his because it had that bumper sticker on the back, *Proud Graduate of Bubba University*." She pulled a folded slip of paper from her smock, and placed it on my lap. "I also took down his license tag number, just so no one would think I was imagining things."

I put the paper in my pocket. "We know about it, D'Vora."

Shock played across her pretty face. "You do? Maddie, too?"

"Unfortunately, yes. Even the best marriages get into trouble. I just hope Maddie and Kenny can get past this."

I stared off into the distance, wondering whether that would even be possible.

D'Vora took out her tissue and blew her nose again. As she composed herself, my gaze settled on the moss hanging like gray lace from the oak trees. I thought of the old Southern folktale that told of its origins. Supposedly, a Spanish woman was captured by Indians. They cut her long hair and tossed it high into the trees. In no time at all, the black hair turned gray. It spread from tree to tree, and that was the beginning of Spanish moss.

I was imagining the fear that dark-haired woman must have felt, when I realized D'Vora had stopped sniffling. She was speaking again.

"…and that's why I've been wracking my brain, wondering if I should tell them."

"Tell who, D'Vora?"

"The police, of course."

A shiver ran up my spine. Suddenly, my attention was riveted.

"Why would you tell the police Kenny's cheating? If they got called out every time a man in Himmarshee cheated, that'd keep them pretty busy, wouldn't it?"

I searched D'Vora's face. Her eyes were on the pavement. Her voice came out hushed.

"It's not so much *that* he was cheating. It's *who* he was cheating with."

The shiver in my spine turned into a fusillade of pinpricks.

D'Vora continued, the words flowing now like water. "I saw him, Mace. I saw Kenny parked in a public place, doing things with that librarian. With Camilla."

A sob worked its way up from deep in her chest. "It was the night before you and your mama found the poor thing murdered, lying dead in piles of garbage out at the dump."

THIRTY-TWO

BOOKSHELVES LINED THE WALLS of the living room at Camilla Law's small, but tastefully furnished, home. A framed quotation by Jorge Luis Borges held a place of honor over a fireplace. In black letters bordered with gold, the words were illuminated by two small spotlights mounted in the ceiling:

I have always imagined that Paradise will be a kind of library.

I said a silent prayer that after what Camilla suffered, she had found just that paradise.

The police finished searching for evidence at her house. Camilla's sister had been permitted to move in from the hotel. She planned to remain in Himmarshee to follow the details of the murder investigation. She also had to handle all the arrangements that follow any sort of death. Planning a funeral. Sorting out finances. Deciding what to do with the possessions left behind by a loved one.

I didn't envy Prudence those tasks, even as she mourned her sister. I didn't want to bring on added pain, but given the information I finally dragged from D'Vora, I had to find out more about

Camilla. If I also happened to discover something about Camilla's mysterious twin, that would be all the better.

I'd taken a seat on a sofa in the living room. A shrill whistle sounded from the kitchen. Prudence poked out her head. "I'm sorry there's nothing to eat. I had to throw out some spoiled food. Will you have a cup of tea with me?"

I thought about the kinds of questions I wanted to ask about her dead sister. It was almost lunch time. I weighed my need for fortification against her judging me to be a pre-noon lush.

"Have you got anything stronger than tea?"

I saw the tiniest frown of disapproval before she banished it. "I'll take a look. I never touch alcohol myself, but Camilla may have kept something in the house."

I recalled Prudence polishing off those brimming glasses at Mama's house. Maybe the English didn't consider sweet pink wine to be "alcohol."

She opened a closet door in a small hallway. She felt around on the top shelf, and then held up a dusty bottle of bourbon. "Will this do?"

I gestured with thumb and forefinger to indicate a small amount. "Just a swallow or two. I'm driving."

She put the bourbon on the coffee table in front of me, and then went to retrieve her tea. She returned, carrying a small tray. On it was a delicate porcelain tea cup, a miniature pitcher of water, an empty juice glass, and a second glass filled with ice. The glassware looked like expensive crystal.

"I wasn't sure how you'd drink it." Her smile was apologetic as she eased into a chair facing the sofa.

"Undiluted," I said, tipping the bourbon into the empty glass. I knocked back a generous swallow. It burned my throat. She sipped daintily. Light glowed through the rose-covered teacup, so fine it was nearly translucent.

"Thank you for coming by," she said. "Your family has been very kind."

"It seems like other people have, too. You and the bartender at the golf course looked pretty close. Was she comforting you"

The tea cup paused at her mouth. She looked at me over the rim, waited a beat. "Yes, exactly that. She apparently cared a great deal about Camilla." She sipped. "Her name is Angela, I believe."

"And then there was that cowboy at Gladys' diner. It looked like he was also being ... kind."

The room was silent. We stared at each other. Prudence finally sighed. "Your family was spot-on when they described you as an amateur detective. You don't miss much, do you?"

I shrugged.

"Yes, well, one must take comfort where one can. If that happens to be with a bit of harmless flirting with a handsome American cowboy..." She raised her palms as if to surrender.

Knowing I was about to besmirch the reputation of her dead sister, I cut her some slack. Then I steeled myself with another hit of booze.

"I'm really uncomfortable asking you this," I began.

She cocked her head at me.

"It's about Camilla," I said.

Her blue eyes clouded with suffering. I felt like I was crushing the life out of a baby bird.

"Would your sister have messed around with a married man?"

Prudence carefully placed her cup on the saucer. "I think I told you Camilla and I had become estranged."

I nodded.

"Frankly, I didn't know what she was up to in the last couple of years. She had certain … 'tastes.' We didn't speak much about her love life, because she knew I didn't approve." She dabbed at a drop of tea on the tray. "I wouldn't rule out adultery, or much of anything else, for that matter."

"So you don't know who she was seeing before she was killed?"

Prudence shook her head. "The police had the same question. Why do you ask?"

I didn't know how much to tell her. I didn't want to give anything away about Kenny. I didn't want to believe Maddie's husband was involved in Camilla's murder. But I knew he'd be a suspect if what D'Vora told me was accurate.

I'd begged the young stylist not to say anything to anyone else until I had the chance to talk to Kenny. Carlos would be angry, but I couldn't think about that. I was more concerned with protecting my sister and her family than I was with my fiancé's murder inquiry.

I shrugged. "I guess I just can't break the habit of sticking my nose into investigations. The more that's known about your sister's comings and goings, the more likely the police can find links to her killer. Jealousy, love, lust … those are strong emotions. Strong emotions can become motives for murder."

She narrowed her eyes. "Don't you think that's dangerous, poking into the investigation? Suppose you ask the wrong question of the wrong person? You could be hurt."

"Nobody's managed to murder me yet."

Prudence recoiled as if I'd hit her. I felt like slapping my own face.

"I'm so sorry. That was a stupid, insensitive thing to say."

She gave a small nod, silently letting me off the hook. The room was so quiet, I could hear her breathing. When she finally lifted the teacup again, it clattered against the saucer.

"This has all been so hard for me." Unshed tears thickened her voice.

I fished in my jeans for a package of tissues. I offered her one, but she waved it away.

"I'm fine. Really."

Eyes welling, lower lip trembling, she didn't look fine.

"It's just so bloody awful to think that in some way, my sister might have brought this killing on herself."

She rose from her chair and walked to a bookcase. From the bottom shelf, she extracted a photo album, bound in rich leather. She sat beside me, placing the book across our knees, and opened it to the first page. "This was us in grade school. We were inseparable."

Two dark-haired girls in matching outfits sat astride a pony.

"Which one are you?"

"I'm behind Camilla. She was *always* the leader." Prudence traced her sister's hair in the photo, a wistful look on her face.

She turned a few more pages. "Here's another." The sisters were teenagers, crammed into a photo-booth with two boys. Eyes closed, one of the girls was entwined in a make-out session. I pointed: "Camilla?"

Prudence laughed. "How'd you guess? It was a double-date. We were each supposed to kiss our lad as the camera snapped. I lost my nerve."

On the opposite page, the girls were older. In a grassy field, they posed holding over and under shotguns. "I didn't think the English believed in firearms," I said.

"We're not the wimps you Yanks imagine us to be." She smiled. "Our dad was quite active in the British Association for Shooting and Conservation. Of course, Camilla always won our competitions."

She paged through several photos, and then stopped. Flanked by a well-dressed man and woman, the twins leaned against a Mercedes. One of the sisters scowled at the camera, arms folded. "Camilla was cross with our parents. They'd punished her for sneaking out at night."

She closed the album. "That's the last picture of the four of us. Our mum and dad were killed within the month in a crash on the M1 motorway."

My heart went out to her; first her parents, now her sister. "I'm sorry," I said, knowing the words were inadequate.

She returned the album to its shelf. Her fingers lingered on the spine, but when she turned, her eyes were clear. Her shoulders were squared. "Yes, well. One must carry on."

So that was the stiff upper lip the English had made famous.

"I do wish we'd remained close." Prudence's gaze traveled around the house, lighting on a sickly looking plant in the corner; the walls of books; the framed quotation. "She never even invited me to visit. This is the first time I've seen her home."

She picked up a cushion in a vivid silk print, and cradled it to her chest. "It's a shame we wasted so much time."

I thought of how close I was to my sisters. I thought about Maddie, and how I'd do just about anything to see her happy again. How hard it must be for a grieving sister to "carry on."

The bourbon sat uneasily in my nearly empty stomach. I needed food to soak up the alcohol. "I've imposed on you long enough." I hauled myself off the couch. "You want to grab lunch somewhere?"

She shook her head. "I'm waiting for a call from Camilla's bank." She indicated an array of folders on the dining room table. "I'm trying to make sense of her assets. She always was the one with a head for figures."

A thought surfaced: As Camilla's closest relation, Prudence would likely inherit this home with all its expensive furnishings. I remembered the diamond bracelet we'd seen on Camilla's wrist. How much money was in the bank, I wondered?

Even with the bourbon under my belt, I couldn't bring myself to ask Prudence that question when her sister's body was barely cold. Instead, I said I had to get going.

"Can I offer you some other beverage before you leave?"

"I wouldn't turn down a Coca-Cola to go. It'll give me a jolt just as the bourbon is trying to make me sleepy." I leaned against the kitchen entryway while she rummaged in the fridge.

"That's another thing I never developed a taste for," Prudence said. "Frightfully sweet."

"You would have learned to love it if you were born in the South," I said. "Down here, babies are weaned on Coke."

"Success!" She pulled out one of the classic contour bottles, and then reached around to the wall side of the fridge, where a bottle opener was affixed by a magnet.

Prying off the cap, she handed me the cold bottle. "Your Coke, madam."

I thanked her and made my exit, drinking as I went.

Out front in my Jeep, I drained the last syrupy swig. Glancing toward the window of the house, I caught Prudence watching me. Before she stepped out of sight, I saw she'd traded her teacup for a long-stemmed wine glass. She seemed to be acquiring quite a taste for the alcohol she said she never touched.

THIRTY-THREE

Mama and I sat on a leather loveseat at City Hall, waiting to see Big Bill Graf. The phone rang on the desk of his fifty-something receptionist, a holdover from the previous mayor. Turning in her swivel chair, she angled her body away from us and answered the call.

"Bill Graf's office," she said in a practiced purr. "A Mayor Should Care."

"He should, but he doesn't—at least not about scaring kids or ruining the environment," I whispered to Mama.

"You'll catch more flies with honey than with vinegar, Mace. Be nice!" She leaned close to hiss in my ear, and then pinched my side before she sat back.

"Ouch!" I wheezed from the pain.

The receptionist scribbled a message on a phone pad. She hung up and swung back to give us the evil eye. "Do I have to separate you two? You sound like hissing cockroaches."

"Is the mayor going to be much longer? We had an appointment for one o'clock. It's already twenty after."

Mama feinted with her left, and then came in with her right for another pinch, but I'd slid to the far corner of the mini-couch to escape her attack. "What I meant to say is I know the mayor's busy with important city doings. I just wondered if we should reschedule."

Mama nodded approval at my smiling suck-up.

Just then, the door to the mayor's office opened. He ushered out a young woman with long blonde curls and five-inch heels. Her dress clung to the curve of her butt and bustline like dark pink plastic wrap. He made a show of giving her a business-like handshake as he bid her goodbye.

"Thanks for coming in, Bambi." His fingers caressed the small of her back as he propelled her toward the door. "We'll let you know about the administrative assistant job. We're still interviewing."

"Bambi?" I mouthed to Mama.

"Assistant?" She mouthed back.

"Maybe an assistant stripper," I whispered.

The receptionist hid a grin behind her hand. "Miss Mace Bauer and Mrs. Sal Provenza to see you, Mayor Graf." She began tidying papers on her desk.

The mayor turned to us, arms outstretched, grin in place. I really hoped he didn't intend to dispense a hug. Mama rose and grabbed both his hands for a friendly shake. I hung back until I was certain he wasn't going to end-run in for an embrace.

Claiming it was "such a treat" to see us again, he gestured us into his office. The walls looked like a taxidermy exhibit. Hunting trophies included a huge buck, with antlers as wide as the window; a wild boar with lethal-looking tusks; and a couple of leaping largemouth bass. An upright grizzly dominated a corner of the room, mouth open in a soundless roar.

Mama stood on tiptoes, peering up at the bear.

"Does your husband hunt, Mrs. Provenza?"

"Only for take-out pizza and ice cream, Mr. Mayor. And please, call me Rosalee."

I had nothing against hunting. My personal preference, though, was to see animals alive and out in nature, where God put them. Before the mayor could meander down hunter's memory lane, relating how he bagged each stuffed critter, I got to the point of our visit.

"You might remember I saw you and your developer pals the other day, hatching plans to ruin Himmarshee Park. I've been upset ever since."

The paper-shuffling in the outer office went silent.

"What Mace means is she wants to find out how all of us can work together to bring progress to the county while still preserving its natural beauty." Mama fluttered her eyelashes.

He cocked his head at her. "Speaking of beauty, has anyone ever told you how gorgeous you are?"

I muttered, "Only a million times."

Ignoring me, Mama rewarded the mayor with a dazzling smile and a double lash flutter.

"I'm told you were in that movie they filmed here," he said. "I hear you were luminous. A real star."

"Make that a shooting star," I said. "The part was so brief, Mama will be there and gone before you even notice she's on the screen."

"Well," the mayor said, "you know what they say in Hollywood: There are no small parts—"

"—only small actors!" Mama finished the line. "That's just what I always told Mace!"

The two of them chuckled together like lifelong pals. Mama was such a pushover for flattery. She was about two compliments away from being ready to drive the bulldozer to develop the park.

"When does the movie come out?" he asked.

"They ran into a little trouble while they were filming. It pushed back the release date," Mama said.

The mayor's fake smile turned into a sad frown. "Yes, I heard about the 'trouble.' A murder on the movie set won't make it easy to woo Hollywood back. We'll have to offer tax cuts and other incentives."

Not to mention a no-murder guarantee. Was everything about business with this guy?

"Getting back to the park," I said, "I hope we see some public discussion before any deals are made. People here don't take kindly to outsiders pushing through proposals without giving the natives a say."

"I'm not an outsider." Graf puffed his chest at me. "I'm the mayor. I was elected fair and square."

"Of course you were." Mama was employing her most placating tone. "I think Mace just meant you're not from around here."

"It's true my wife and I are newcomers. But I love this part of Florida just like I was born here. I only want what's best for Himmarshee."

Sure you do, I thought. "A friend of mine writes for the 'Himmarshee Times.' The paper may be small, but they're mighty when it comes to watching out for the community. I'm warning you, if there's even a whiff of the misuse of public land, the paper will raise a ruckus."

"Is that a threat?"

Just as Mama laid a hand on the mayor's arm, ready to smooth things over, his wife bustled in through the outer office. The receptionist followed right on her heels. "I'm sorry, Mr. Mayor. I tried to tell Mrs. Graf you were in a meeting."

"Threat? What's this about a threat?" Beatrice narrowed her eyes at Mama's hand on the mayor's arm.

Wisely, Mama slid it out of sight, into the jacket pocket of her lime-sherbet pantsuit.

"You misunderstood, darling," the mayor said to his wife. "We were just talking about the threat of hurricanes this summer. We're not out of the woods yet, are we, ladies?"

"Let's just hope there are some woods *left* in Himmarshee," I said darkly.

"I'm not a fan of the woods; too many bugs and poisonous plants." Beatrice shuddered. "Give me a nice, manicured golf course any day."

Still standing behind Beatrice, the receptionist caught my glance and rolled her eyes.

As if she sensed the mimed criticism, the mayor's wife turned. "Run get us two coffees, would you? Cream and two sugars. Hurry. Quick now, like a bunny."

A hint of resentment played on the receptionist's face before she pasted on a professional smile. The mayor said, "Thank you, Ellen. Would you mind sending in Diamond? I believe she's in her office."

To me, he said, "Diamond will take down your information. We'll let you know if the proposal for the development near the park comes up for public review. I'm all about conducting business in the open, in accordance with Florida's Sunshine Law."

I'll bet you are, I thought.

Mama said, " 'Diamond.' That's an awful pretty name."

"More awful than pretty, I'd say." Beatrice took a seat on the mayor's desk, assessing Mama and me with a superior look. She crossed one leathery, tanned leg over the other. I was mesmerized by the sight of the salmon-hued pom-pom on her golf sock shaking as she jiggled her foot.

"Do you enjoy golf?" Mama tried making conversation.

"What's it to you?" Beatrice countered, plucking an imaginary piece of lint from the hem of her salmon golf "skort."

She seemed to sway a bit on her desktop perch. I wondered if she'd been drinking.

The mayor leaped in to the silence. "We both love golf," he said. "It's a wonderful game. I believe your son-in-law has taken it up, Rosalee."

To his wife, he said, "You know Kenny Wilson, dear."

Her face brightened. "Oh, I love Kenny. He showed me a wonderful place to shoot skeet. Not too far from here, either."

Skeet? Kenny? As far as I knew, Kenny's only knowledge of the shooting sports was plinking beer can targets. What else didn't we know about Maddie's cheating husband?

Just then, Diamond sashayed in. Seemingly a dark-haired replica of the blonde Bambi, she had the same long curls, same curve-hugging clothes, same spike heels. Maybe they'd worked side-by-side poles at the same stripper bar.

Before the mayor could say a word, Beatrice shoved a legal pad and pen at Diamond. "The mayor needs you to get the particulars of how to reach…" she looked at me, snapping her fingers impatiently.

"Mace Bauer," I said. "We've met before. Twice."

She waved her hand, as if she couldn't be bothered remembering the little people. "Give your name and other information to Diamond."

She aimed a scornful glare at the younger woman. "You can handle that, can't you, Miss Sparkling Diamond?"

Eyes on the rug, Diamond nodded.

With an oily smile, the mayor put one hand at Mama's back, the other on mine, herding us through the reception area. "I hate to rush you, but my wife and I need to discuss some family business."

"Family business!" Beatrice Graf snorted. "That's a good one."

His cheeks reddened, his lips compressed to a thin line. But he didn't stand up to Beatrice. She leaned in, so close I noted booze on her breath, along with a familiar lemony smell. Now I remembered the scent. I'd smelled it at the golf course locker room, and at Kenny's cabin, too.

"Toodle-loo, ladies." She shoved Mama into me, pushed us both into the hall, and then slammed the office door behind us.

We caught the receptionist returning, carrying two cups of coffee. I wondered if she spit in the one for Mrs. Mayor. I jerked my head toward the closed door. "She's a piece of work, isn't she?"

"You have no idea," the receptionist said. "Did she brag about her kills?"

I raised my eyebrows at her.

"Mayor Graf lets visitors assume he's the Great White Hunter, but his wife is responsible for animal death row in there." She lowered her voice to a whisper. "Some days I picture her head up there on the wall."

The outer door opened. Diamond stepped into the hall—pad in hand, blank look in place. Sighing, the receptionist went back inside.

"*Mace*," Diamond said, painstakingly putting pen to yellow pad. "Now, do I spell that with a big letter *M*?"

THIRTY-FOUR

CARLOS SPOONED UP SOME *picadillo* from a pan on the stove for me to taste. Flecked with olives, chopped green pepper, and raisins, the ground beef dish was a favorite Cuban recipe.

"How is it?"

"Mmmmmm ... perfect," I said, licking the spoon.

"Does it need anything?"

"Just a plate, so I can start eating it."

"Rice?"

"That will take too long."

Carlos and I had met at his place near downtown for a late lunch. Just in time, too, because I was starving. The Coke and a package of peanut butter and cheese crackers I'd had between my visit with Prudence and the appointment at the mayor's office was hardly enough to hold me. When he'd called to invite me over for some home-cooking, Cuban-style, I dumped Mama back at Hair Today, and jumped at the opportunity.

I tried not to think about the fact I was withholding important information from the caring man who was about to satiate my growling stomach.

"Okay, no rice. But a piece of Cuban bread, at least?" He peeled the white paper from a loaf of the crusty bread, and quickly sliced it into rounds.

Before he could get the bread off the cutting board and into a basket, I grabbed a slice, slathered it with butter, and popped the whole thing in my mouth.

"Nice manners. I'm going to tell your mother."

"Amfythimg butf thatf!" I said, my mouth busy with the bread.

He gave me one of his sexy smiles, and bent down to brush his lips against my forehead. "This kiss to be continued, when you aren't chewing a mouthful of food. I have to pick my moments with you."

Once we started eating, conversation was kept to a minimum:

"Would you like some *mojo*?" he asked.

I shook my head. "Doesn't need any sauce. It's great just like it is."

"Were you planning to share the bread?"

I offered him the basket, he took a piece.

I pointed at about a half-cup of *picadillo* left in the pan. "Okay if I finish it off?"

He nodded.

Finally, I quit eating, and collapsed back against the chair. Carlos grinned at me.

"I don't know where you put it." He dabbed at my chin with a napkin. "I do see one little piece of an olive that got away, right there."

I ran a hand over my face, checking for any more errant morsels.

"Man, that was good." I gave a satisfied sigh. "You're going to make some lucky girl a very fine husband one day."

He lifted my hand to his mouth and kissed my palm. "That's just what I intend to do. Soon, I hope."

Our eyes locked. His were like deep, dark pools drawing me in. I basked in this molten warmth that washed over me. It was a feeling of contentment; of safety; of love.

"Yes, soon," I said. "But first..." I threaded my fingers through the hair at the back of his head, pulling his face close to mine. "How about us enjoying some dessert?"

He kissed me, nipping gently at my lower lip. "I couldn't eat another bite of food," he said.

"Who's talking about food?" I asked.

———

Later, as we showered together, I rubbed Carlos's back. "How's that?"

"Little higher, to the right."

With the hot spray of water and a soapy washcloth, I worked the familiar spot at the base of his neck. All the stress of his job often parked itself right there.

"Ahhhh," he said. "*Gracias, niña.*"

Hearing him thank me stirred my guilty feelings again. I was so tempted to say something about Kenny, but I didn't. First, I had to find out more about the relationship between my brother-in-law and the dead librarian. D'Vora was pretty specific about Kenny's truck, but she could have been wrong about seeing them together. Even if she wasn't, there could be a reasonable explanation.

Couldn't there?

I had to talk to someone who could help me sort out what I knew. But who?

"…about the case."

"Sorry, what?" I said. "I zoned out there for a minute."

"I said I appreciate the fact you haven't grilled me about the case."

"Camilla," I murmured.

"Yes, the murder of Camilla Law."

"Well, it's really none of my business."

"Since when has that ever stopped you?"

I didn't want to tell him my real reason for not trying to pick his brain. I was afraid if I did, he'd work his detective magic and end up discovering my secrets instead. I needed to create a distraction before I spilled everything I knew. I spotted a bottle on the window ledge in the shower.

"Shampoo?"

"That depends," he said. "Do I have to tip the shampoo girl?"

"I'm sure we can think of an appropriate reward."

The smolder in his smile told me he'd already conjured up a fitting idea. I put away the bottle as he wrapped his strong arms around me. I was willing and eager to collect my pre-shampoo tip.

THIRTY-FIVE

Henry closed the door between his office and the reception area. He opened it again a moment later, and stuck his head out to speak to Amy, the college student who helped him run his legal practice. "No phone calls, okay? My cousin and I need some uninterrupted time."

I'd settled on Henry as the most likely person to help me sort out what I'd come to think of as The Kenny Crisis. He knew the law, and he wouldn't reveal anything that would harm Maddie. It wasn't simply a question of attorney-client—or attorney-cousin—privilege. He truly cared about my sister, despite the fact that he poked fun at her like a kid with a stick every chance he got.

"You said on the phone Kenny and Maddie are in trouble. Please don't tell me somebody's sick." He touched a golden gavel on his desk, like a talisman.

"Kenny's running around. He's cheating on Maddie."

Henry stared at me, and then gave his head a forceful shake. "I don't believe it."

I outlined the evidence. As I spoke, Henry's face betrayed his emotions: Sorrow when I told him how devastated Maddie had been when she found out. Anger when I said Kenny had left their home, simply disappeared. Finally, shock when I revealed his apparent involvement with Camilla, and how Kenny may have been among the last people to see her alive.

I'd rarely known Henry to be speechless. But there he sat, uttering nary a word. Eventually he closed his eyes, as if to clear away images of Kenny's actions. He rubbed his hands over his face. "Well, this is one heck of a shit-storm, Mace."

"Tell me something I don't know. What are we going to do about it?"

Henry's face turned thoughtful. He lifted the gavel from his desk, and pounded it into the center of his palm: *Smack. Smack. Smack.*

Before he could injure himself, I asked if he had any water. "I had *picadillo* for lunch," I said. "Good, but the olives were salty."

He took a water pitcher from a small table beside his desk, turned two glasses right side up, and poured one for each of us. I wondered if he'd reach into his bottom drawer for a shot of something stronger, but he didn't. Just as well. Clear minds would help us decide our next step.

"There's something else, Henry."

His grip on the glass tightened. "It gets worse?"

I nodded. "It's Carlos. I haven't told him what I found out about Kenny and Camilla, even though it's relevant to his murder investigation."

"Great. One cousin's husband might be a murderer, the other cousin could be brought up on obstructing justice charges." He put down his glass and started massaging his face again.

"Can he arrest me?"

Henry peeked at me through his fingers. "Realistically? Probably not. Technically, yes. We all remember how Carlos once tossed your mama in the slammer without a second thought."

He dropped his hands from his eyes, took another minute to think about it. "He's going to raise holy hell and prop it up on a block when he finds out you've withheld information."

"Yeah, that's what I'm afraid of." I looked out the window; wondered what Carlos was doing at this moment. Maybe he was fondly remembering his loving interlude with his lying fiancée.

"I don't want to hinder his investigation," I continued, "but I do want to protect Maddie. If all Kenny's guilty of is cheating, maybe they can save their marriage. That becomes a lot less likely once her husband's name has been dragged through the mud as a murder suspect."

He pointed at me with the golden gavel. "If Carlos asks you a specific question about Kenny, and you lie or mislead him, you're on shaky ground, legally."

"I'm going to be on shaky ground emotionally if I don't tell him what I know. We're engaged, Henry. It's a trust issue."

We both sipped at our water. A soft knock sounded at the door. Amy looked in. Conservatively dressed and serious seeming in dark-framed glasses, she was the antithesis of the "administrative assistants" at the mayor's office.

"Sorry to interrupt, but it's after five o'clock," she said. "I just wondered if you need me for anything before I go."

Henry thanked her, told her he'd see her in the morning. I heard the outer door close, the lock slip into place.

"There's only one thing I can do, Henry. I have to find Kenny and prove he had nothing to do with Camilla's death."

"And how are you going to do that?"

Thinking about that question, I gazed around the room. A blue blazer hung on the back of an office chair. Law volumes crowded the bookcases. My eyes lingered on an antique radio displayed on a shelf.

Suddenly, I knew what to do. "I have an idea how we can flush Kenny out from whatever rock he's been hiding under."

Henry cocked his head at me.

"You and the morning show DJ from the country music station are good buddies, right?"

He nodded.

"You think he'd do us a favor?"

THIRTY-SIX

HENRY EASED HIS LAWYER Lexus into a spot in the empty lot at Kenny's insurance office.

He'd phoned his radio friend, to set my plan in motion. Then we'd left Henry's place, intent on doing what we could to find Kenny in the remaining hours of daylight.

The one-man insurance shop was closed, the door locked up tight. I looked in through the streaky windows. A small pile of unopened letters had collected on the floor inside, by the mail slot. The only thing in the trash basket by Kenny's desk was an empty can of diet Mountain Dew, crushed.

"Maddie and I have tried calling him here," I told Henry. "It rings, but the voice mail is full."

Henry put his face against the window. "Looks like he hasn't picked up his regular mail for a few days, either."

I brushed a dirt smudge from the tip of my cousin's nose. Kenny's office is right on Main Street. The big stock trailers and sod trucks rumble by and stir up road dust. A fine gray powder coats all the store fronts.

I wrote a message with my finger across the dusty door: *Call me, ASAP. Mace*

———

Henry worked the happy hour crowd at the 19th Hole like a politician at a pancake breakfast. With his gift of gab and easy charm, he moved a lot more easily than I did between the old and new factions of our hometown. We hadn't found Kenny, but it wasn't for want of my cousin trying.

Henry had slapped backs, bought drinks, and told jokes in pursuit of information. So far, the most valuable tidbit we'd uncovered was that Kenny had trouble with his bunker play and needed to work on his short game, whatever that meant. Fortunately, Henry spoke golf, so I could ask him later to translate. According to reports from the other golfers, Kenny had played a few rounds with the mayor, and he liked to talk to Angel at the bar, both things I already knew.

My ears perked up when a big-bellied retiree in plaid pants mentioned Jason.

"Sure," Plaid Pants told Henry. "I know Kenny. He handles my storm insurance. Boy, hurricane coverage costs an arm and a leg in Florida. It's more than quadruple the price of a homeowner's policy back home. In Ohio…."

"About Kenny?" I interrupted.

"Right, the pro's been spending a lot of time with him, working on his putt. It's all in the grip."

Plaid Pants got off his barstool and demonstrated, holding an imaginary putter.

"You're talking about Jason, right?" I asked.

"Sure, he's the only pro here. It can't be cheap, as many lessons as Kenny's had."

Funny, Jason hadn't mentioned he'd given Kenny lessons. I leaned over to whisper in Henry's ear. "We need to talk to the pro."

We found him closing up the pro shop, alone thankfully. I asked Jason why he hadn't told me he tutored Kenny. "Somebody said he'd probably paid a lot for all the lessons you gave him."

He shrugged. "Not everything is about money, Mace."

"It is when you have a daughter at an expensive college, like Kenny does, and your wife has no idea you're throwing away tons of green learning to nudge a ball into a little cup."

"Maybe I didn't charge him."

Henry and I exchanged skeptical looks.

"At least not in cash," Jason clarified.

Henry put a hand on Jason's shoulder. I could tell he was squeezing, because the younger man's teeth were gritted. "Look here," he used his most intimidating courtroom voice, "maybe you should just tell us the nature of your relationship with Kenny."

Ohmigod, I thought to myself. What if Jason revealed he and Kenny were gay lovers? That'd end Maddie's marriage for sure.

"Kenny has this hunting cabin, way out in the middle of nowhere," Jason said. "It comes in handy for certain…activities…our club members are interested in pursuing."

"Activities?" Henry asked.

Having seen Kenny's hunting camp, I had a pretty good idea what that meant, but I wanted to hear how the pro would describe it.

Jason glanced at his watch. "It's past my quitting time, and I need to close the shop. A man can get awful thirsty when people are asking him to reveal secrets."

Henry took the hint. "Drinks in the bar, on me."

We waited as Jason locked up the cash register, shut off the lights, and grabbed the keys to that fancy BMW off a peg on the wall. Henry tried again as we walked across the parking lot to the bar. "Could you elaborate on the kind of 'activities' you were referring to?"

Jason coughed a few times, pointed to his throat. "I can barely speak, I'm so parched."

A few moments later, we'd slid into a booth in a quiet corner of the 19th Hole. Revelers stood two and three deep at the bar for happy hour. Angel was a blur of motion, mixing drinks. A server helping out from the dining room took care of our orders.

After our drinks arrived, Jason took a few swallows of his Long Island Iced Tea. Henry then slid the drink to the side of the table. "Less parched now, I presume?"

"Whatever, dude."

"Why don't you tell us what kind of activities the members enjoy?" I said.

"Fine. A lot of people here like to swing," Jason said.

"I think Mace meant activities aside from golf," Henry said.

"I'm not talking about golf swings."

I saw comprehension dawn in my cousin's eyes. "Sexual swinging?" he asked.

"Bingo," Jason said.

Henry shifted into courtroom mode. "Who's been a party to this activity?"

Jason's forehead wrinkled. He looked at me to translate. "Is he asking about parties? Because we have lots of swingers' parties."

"He means who all's involved in the sex."

A sly smile spread across the pro's face. "Well, you'd be, if Angel had her way." He explained to Henry: "Our barmaid thinks Mace is hot."

I felt my face flush. "I'm straight."

"That's all right, so is Angel, for the most part. But she knows a few swingers who would think the two of you together are just their type." He leaned across the table to caress my arm.

"Mace is engaged," Henry said.

"I sure am."

"Well, you're not married yet." Jason winked at me.

I tried to ignore the fact my arm tingled a bit where he'd stroked it. What was wrong with me? How could I even think about some sleazy country-club Romeo when I had a good man who wanted to marry me? Maybe Maddie's current crisis combined with Mama's checkered history really had spoiled me for true love.

I glanced at Jason. He gave me a ravenous look. Suddenly, I thought of a Florida panther zeroing in on a fawn. I dropped my arm into my lap, safely out of caressing distance.

"Let's get back to this swingers' club," Henry said.

"Is Kenny involved?" I asked.

The pro shrugged. "He's not a charter member. He may have fooled around a little. Hard not to when everything's going on right there in the house at his hunting camp."

"Well," Henry prodded, "who *is* a charter member?"

The pro looked over each shoulder, perhaps gauging if anyone was eavesdropping. He nodded toward the bar, where Angel was pouring shots from a vodka bottle into a long line of mixers.

"You already told us about Angel," I said.

"I'm not talking about Angel." He pointed to the end of the bar nearest us. Beatrice Graf sat alone, golf skort hiked up nearly to the Promised Land. She stared into her who-knows-how-many umpteenth Bloody Mary of the day.

She must have sensed us looking at her. She turned, and spotted Henry. Drunkenly, she picked up the celery stalk from her drink, holding it in both hands. Lasciviously, she ran her tongue up it and down it, and around and around it. When she finished her show, she crooked a finger at my cousin and waggled her tongue wickedly.

"Oh, my Lord," Henry breathed. "She's old enough to be my mother."

"A senior citizen swinger? No way," I said.

"Oh, yeah," Jason said. "Mrs. Graf swings like a front porch glider, and so does his honor, the mayor."

THIRTY-SEVEN

I ELBOWED HENRY, DRAWING his attention away from Beatrice Graf and her sexually explicit celery stalk. "Speak of the devil."

I pointed with my beer bottle to the foyer of the dining room. Big Bill had just entered, and was busy glad-handing his constituents.

"At least *he* looks sober." Henry tossed some money on the table to cover our tab. "Meet me over there when you finish your drink, Mace. Given the choice, I'd rather talk to His Honor than to the drunken wife. She might construe it as my being interested in buttering her muffin."

On his way to the dining room, Henry attempted to give Beatrice a wide berth. But the bar was crowded, leaving little room to navigate. She beckoned him to come closer, waving her celery at him and performing a hoochie-coochie hip rotation. Henry was doing his best to ignore her.

"Looks like you've lost your Sugar Mama," I said to Jason. "She seems quite taken with my cousin."

"No worries. There's plenty more where Bea came from." Jason's narrowed eyes and angry frown belied his words. He watched Beatrice with what looked like jealousy.

"You care about her!"

"Please. We have a business arrangement. I don't want it compromised."

Realization dawned. "So that's how you afford the BMW?"

He shrugged.

"Women pay for your, uh … affections. How can you do that?"

Another shrug. "It's a living. It beats the hell out of baling tobacco or picking up garbage, which are only two of the crappy jobs I've had."

He drained his drink, ice clinking against the glass. "Speaking of which, I've got another hot date waiting. I better scoot."

I put out a hand to stop him as he got up. "Does your 'date' involve Kenny's hunting camp? I'm still trying to find him, you know."

"You've only told me a million times. And I've told you I haven't seen the man. As much as I'd love to see *you* at the camp, wearing only a coat of flavored body oil, there's nothing going on there tonight." He grabbed my hand. "I'll be sure to let you know the next time we're having a get-together, though. I can guarantee you'll be very popular. You may even earn a few bucks, if you're willing to … experiment."

His finger circled suggestively in the center of my palm. I yanked my hand away. This time, my skin crawled where Jason had touched it. The leer on his handsome face disgusted me. Who were these people? And how had they infiltrated Himmarshee?

As soon as he left, I went to join Henry. In the few moments it took me to cross the bar and dining room, I watched the mayor's expression change from jovial to wary. Henry had backed him into a corner by the restrooms. Judging from His Honor's body language, he wasn't thrilled with the cross-examination.

As I sidled up beside them, Henry gestured. "I know you've met my cousin, Mace."

Smiling tightly, the mayor gave a curt nod.

"I was just asking Mayor Graf what he knows about activities of a sexual nature at Kenny Wilson's camp."

The mayor's beefy face was more scarlet than usual. He'd puffed up his broad chest, until it was almost as big as his substantial belly. He stood about six-foot-two, and was looming now over Henry. Physically imposing, he probably was unaccustomed to seeing a man who was at least five inches shorter get up in his face. But, like a small dog who fancies itself a Great Dane, my cousin had never been one to back down—not in the courtroom; not in life.

"Mayor Graf?" Henry prodded. "Have you attended any of the swingers' parties at the camp?"

Graf crossed his arms over his chest. "I have no idea what you're talking about, Counselor. And I resent you inferring that I would."

"Implying," Henry corrected.

The mayor said, "I ran for office on a family values platform."

I laughed out loud. "And we all know there's *never* been a family values politician caught with his pants down."

The mayor glared first at me and then at Henry, regarding us like we were two rats using his dinner plate as a toilet. He stepped so close, the toe of one shoe touched mine; the other shoe touched Henry's. I smelled lemons. Maybe the men's locker room at the club provided the same fancy lotion as the women's did. When Big Bill spoke, the chill in his voice dropped the temperature in the cramped foyer.

"You two redneck hicks do not know who you're dealing with. Cross me, and I swear you will regret it."

"Is that a threat?" Henry asked. "Did you hear that, Mace? Did it give you a reasonable fear of bodily harm? If it did, that's what we redneck hicks and the Florida Criminal Statutes like to call 'assault.'"

Henry's questions hung in the hallway. The door to the ladies' room swung open, and the mayor's expression changed in an instant. From raging bull to avuncular boss.

"Diamond, dear, I thought you may have gotten lost. We need to grab a quick bite to eat so we're not late for the city council meeting."

I nodded at the young woman I'd met earlier in his office. With spiky heels and a sparkly halter top, she was dressed for a disco instead of some dull government meeting. The mayor introduced her to Henry as his aide.

My cousin, with his typical appreciation for the feminine form, got all googly-eyed over the bra-less cleavage her halter exposed.

"Pleased to make your acquaintance," she said.

I pinched Henry's arm. "Me, too," he answered lamely.

The mayor shifted into his friendly politician persona again. He slapped Henry on the back. "Sorry we're going to have to cut our conversation short, Counselor." His smile was wide, his sincerity false. "I'd be glad to explore this topic some more, in private."

He hustled Diamond to the dining room, and slipped a ten-dollar bill into the hand of the woman at the hostess stand. She whisked the two of them toward a staff entrance. I wondered whether that was because they were in a rush, or so they could avoid traipsing past the mayor's wife at the bar.

Henry was still staring after the departing Diamond and her various jiggling parts. Her skirt was so tight, her rear end looked like two baby possums tussling in a potato sack.

"Jesus, Henry! Pick your eyeballs off the carpet, why don't you? You're a married man."

He tore his gaze away, just as the staff door closed on Diamond's 24-carat butt.

"Answer me something. If Miss Diamond Doll came on to you like the mayor's wife did, would you take her up on it? Would you cheat on your wife?"

I waited a beat, then asked the question I really wanted to know: "Are you and all other men just like Kenny?"

Shock registered on his face. He put his hand over his heart. "Please tell me you don't really think that, Mace. I love my wife. And I've never once strayed, not in twelve years. A married man can flirt. He can look. But he can never touch. That's where Kenny went wrong."

His eyes searched mine. I had the feeling he was trying to see into my soul.

"I would never, never cheat on my wife."

That was just what I thought he'd say. I would have expected Kenny to say the same thing, before. Look what happened with him.

"Never say never, Henry."

THIRTY-EIGHT

MAMA'S DOOR WAS LOCKED. I knocked, cueing a cacophony of barking from inside.

Henry plugged his ears with his fingers, grimacing like he was standing next to a tree-cutter with a chainsaw. "My Lord, how is it Sal hasn't permanently silenced that awful creature by now?"

"Believe it or not, he loves Teensy as much as Mama does. While he's stretched out in his TV chair, watching sports, Sal lets the dog sleep on his stomach. He hand-feeds him cheese curls out of the same snack. One curl for Sal; one for Teensy."

Henry mimed a gagging motion.

"Tell me about it,' I said. "I love dogs, but that doesn't mean I want to eat after one."

We heard the approach of heavy footsteps on the other side of the door. Gently toeing Teensy aside, Sal cracked it open an inch and peeked out. "Mace?"

"Who else?" I asked. "Mama called me and insisted I come over."

I'd had a strange phone conversation with her as Henry and I headed home from the golf course. She called in a huff, raging and raving, saying she'd never forgive me.

"You'd better ggmph over here and mfmph slllph."

"What?" I'd shouted into the phone. "I can't understand you."

"Explain..." Mama yelled, before the phone cut off.

The reception was bad in that slice of the county, and Mama ranted disjointedly. I couldn't tell what the hell she was talking about. Of course, that wasn't unusual.

I'd convinced Henry to make an emergency detour to her house to figure things out in person.

"Your mother's furious at you, Mace." It became "mudder" in Sal's Bronx accent.

"Yeah, that's about all I managed to understand. Henry's out here with me, Sal. Are you going to open the door and let us come in off the stoop, or should we just wait until the mosquitoes suck out every drop of our blood?"

As if for punctuation, Henry slapped a hungry specimen on his neck. I flicked two at once off my wrist.

The door opened. Sal was dressed for bed, wearing a pair of men's pajamas that would give any normal person nightmares. Black, they featured bright red cartoon characters. Boy devils with tails and pitchforks chased after girl devils. The girls, complete with horns and the subtle bud of breasts, jumped over flames of orange and yellow.

Sal padded in his red leather slippers from the living room into the kitchen, where he'd been feeding Teensy. We followed him.

"Where'd you buy the pajamas, Sal? Hell-Mart?" Henry asked.

231

I giggled, but Sal didn't crack a smile. He spooned food from an open can into Teensy's bowl, set it on the floor, and then leaned against the kitchen counter. "She's really upset, Mace. She won't tell me what's wrong. She's in the bedroom, with the lights out and a cold compress on her head."

I looked at the Elvis Presley clock over the sink. Above the King's swiveling hips, the time read 8:05 p.m. That was early for bed, even by Himmarshee standards. Chances were Mama was not asleep.

"You want to come with me to talk to her, Sal?"

The big man backed up as if I was asking him to bungee jump off a cliff, minus the bungee cord. I opened the door of the refrigerator, took out two beers, and poured a hefty glass of sweet pink wine for Mama. I handed Henry one of the beers. "You may need this, cousin. You're coming in with me. No way I'm facing her alone."

I pushed Henry to the bedroom door ahead of me. He was always her favorite among all the cousins. I figured whatever bee was in her bonnet about whatever I'd done, she wouldn't make a scene in front of Henry—or, at least not as big of a scene.

I rapped gently on the half-closed door with the top of my beer bottle. "You awake?"

I heard a dramatic sigh from inside. "Yes." Her voice quavered.

"I've got Henry with me. Are you decent?"

"Of course." Another sigh. "Hey, Henry."

"Hey, Aunt Rosalee," he said from the hallway.

"Well, don't just stand out there like a couple of ninnies," she said. "Come on in and turn on the lights."

As we did, Mama tossed the washcloth from her forehead onto the floor. She plumped three pillows behind her and sat up against a peach-colored headboard.

"Pink wine?" I held out the glass to her.

"Henry, please tell my daughter I'm far too upset to drink more than a couple of sips."

"Mace, your mama says—"

"—I heard her, Henry." I handed her the glass.

"Tell my daughter thank-you."

"She said—"

"—Yeah, I got it."

Henry and I perched about midway down the king-size bed; me on Mama's left; Henry on her right. She gave Henry a sad look. I got a furious frown.

"I'm madder at you than a wasp with a ruined nest, Mace. I'd have never believed you'd keep information like this from me. Maddie's in pain, and I'm sitting on my hands. I could have helped before it got this far."

I was quiet. I learned long ago the best offense against Mama is silence. She can't stand the sound of it. As I knew she would, she jumped in to fill it with words.

"I got this text tonight." She handed me her cell phone.

I've had enough. Don't bother coming home. I want a divorce.

The words hit like a punch to my solar plexus.

"At first I thought it was somebody poking fun at my matrimonial record. Then I saw it was Maddie who'd sent the text, and Maddie never pokes fun. Of course I called her right back to find out what that meant."

"What'd she say?" Henry asked.

"That she hit my number by mistake; Kenny's right next to me in her phone directory. I wasn't supposed to receive the message. Like I didn't know that." Mama took the phone from me; stared at the text again. "She said it wasn't any of my business what the text meant."

Mama raised her face to mine. Tears pooled in her eyes. "How can it not be a mother's business when her daughter wants a divorce?"

"Mama, I…"

She cut me off. "Maddie was crying, but she hung up on me when I tried to ask her what was wrong. I called right back, and she hung up again. The next time I called she said she simply couldn't talk about it. Maddie said, 'Mace knows the whole story. Ask her.'"

Mama's phone timed out, and the screen went dark. She placed it upside down on the bed and then covered it with a pillow, as if by hiding it, she could erase that text from existence.

"So, I'm asking my middle daughter why my first-born never saw fit to mention to me that her marriage of twenty-some years was crumbling."

Mama's voice sounded more sad than angry. A look passed between Henry and me.

"So, Henry knows about this, too?" Her voice rose. "I'm the only one in the dark?" Now, anger was back in the lead over sadness.

Henry took her hand. "Mace only brought me in because there may be criminal issues involved."

"Criminal?" Mama wailed. "Is Maddie going to jail?"

"Nobody's going to jail, Aunt Rosalee." Henry aimed for a soothing tone. "At least not right away."

Her eyes widened. "Maddie would look a fright in those awful orange jumpsuits they make you wear in jail."

And so we had another record shattered: From fury to anguish to fashion in less than five minutes.

Teensy gave a sharp yip in the living room. A car door slammed. A crescendo of barking began.

"That'll be Marty," Mama said. "I called her, too. She couldn't believe Maddie would choose to tell you about this instead of her."

"Believe me, I've asked myself that same question."

I headed to the front door to corral Teensy. I'd reveal to Mama and Marty that Kenny was cheating. I'd tell them everything, except who his secret lover had been.

THIRTY-NINE

First thing Wednesday morning, I turned on the radio in my bedroom to the country music station. I listened to five commercials, the latest Jason Aldean song, and some back-and-forth between Henry's disc jockey friend and a clueless caller. The guy thought he'd dialed his girlfriend's number when a deep-voiced man answered the phone.

"Uh, I was calling for Donna Jean. Did I dial the … wrong number?" the caller's voice was hesitant.

"Donna Jean's in the kitchen, making me breakfast. Who the heck is this?" the DJ demanded.

When he finally let the poor guy off the hook, the announcer did the bit I'd been waiting for: "We've got a terrific prize for some lucky driver today. Two tickets to the big monster truck show later this month. I'm going to read off some numbers, and if your license tag is a match, you're the winner. Got a pencil? Here we go…"

Then he read off the tag number D'Vora handed me when she revealed she'd seen Kenny parked at the lake.

The station, ranked No. 1 in most of the counties ringing Lake Okeechobee, ran frequent giveaways and contests. If Kenny was in range, he was listening. He wouldn't be able to resist the monster truck jamboree, especially for free. Henry had asked the DJ to help us razz a relative. Since the man spent most of his mornings pulling pranks, he was happy to do it. He agreed to repeat the pitch five times throughout the morning.

"You'll have to pick up your tickets in your vehicle so we can make sure the tag matches," the announcer continued. "Stop by the station between noon and one o'clock, and we'll hand 'em over. You'll be sittin' pretty, watching Maximum Destruction crush everything in sight…"

———

"Duck!" I said to Henry, as I slid down in the front passenger seat of his wife's minivan.

Talking on his cell phone, he wasn't paying attention. "Sorry, hang on," he said into the phone. "What are you doing?" He stared at me, as I'd folded myself nearly in two to get under the dashboard.

"Get down, I said!"

"Yoo-hoo, Henry!" The horn on Mama's convertible tooted. "It's Aunt Rosalee."

My cousin ended his phone conversation, too late. Our cover was blown. "Way to go, Henry."

It was 11:50 am. We were staked out in the parking lot of the radio station. I heard the familiar rumble of Mama's vintage car as she pulled up beside us. If Kenny saw that distinctive turquoise cruise liner, he'd never drive into the lot. That's why we were in the white minivan. It wasn't as recognizable as any of the cars we usually drove.

I hopped out of the van.

"Where'd you come from, Mace?"

I opened the driver's door of her car, and talked fast. "Scoot over. We have to hurry. It has to do with Kenny. I'll explain while I drive."

I gave her a little push, and to my surprise she moved. With the minutes ticking away until Kenny might show, I didn't have time to argue with Mama, or devise an elaborate subterfuge to get rid of her. She'd never leave simply because I said so. I had no choice but to include her in the plan.

"Henry and I set up a fake radio contest to lure Kenny to the station. We're waiting for him right now so we can finally confront him about what's been going on."

Gunning Mama's car, I crossed the street and drove around to the rear of a convenience store across from the radio station. A cluster of dumpsters would provide a serviceable hiding spot.

"We don't want him to spot us, so we're going to have to hurry back and get in Henry's van. How'd you come to see us, by the way?"

"I was driving past. I just picked up my car from Juan's Auto Repair and Taco Shop."

I eased her big blue boat in between the dumpsters and turned off the key. *Cla-clunk, cla-clunk, cla-clunk.*

"Engine's still knocking," I said as I opened the door.

"That's not the only thing that'll be knocking once I see my cheating son-in-law."

Setting her mouth in a grim line, Mama gathered up her pineapple-sherbet purse and marched back to the parking lot of the radio station.

———

Henry watched the street entrance from the driver's seat. Mama was in the passenger seat. I was stretched out in the back, waiting for the word that one of them had sighted Kenny's big truck. Mama swiveled in her seat toward me.

"Is there any chance we can patch things up between them by Saturday?" Mama said. "I'd hate to see all those party plans Maddie's been working on just go down the drain."

Henry caught my eye in the rear-view mirror. I hadn't told Mama or Marty that Kenny had been cheating with the murdered Camilla, or the implications of his involvement. Not even Maddie knew that yet.

"Saturday doesn't seem likely," Henry said, with lawyerly understatement.

"How long do you think it was going on?"

"We're not sure, Mama. He'd lost weight, bought those spiffy clothes, and took up golf. All that made Maddie suspicious. The more she investigated, the guiltier he looked."

Mama's eyes took on a faraway glaze. "With Husband No. 2, it was cologne. That man would usually go around smelling like the bottom of a dirty laundry basket. I always knew he'd started running around on me again when he started pouring on the Eau D'Cheater."

I remembered. When No. 2 got ready to go out at night, there'd be cigarette ashes in their bathroom sink and wet towels all over the floor. The moist air would smell like clouds at the men's fragrance counter of a department store at Christmas.

"Heads up," Henry said. "Here comes his truck."

Our plan was to let Kenny park, and make it halfway to the door of the station before we intercepted him. Mama hefted her purse into her lap. Having her along actually improved our odds. If Kenny gave us any trouble, she'd swing that big satchel right for his crotch. I knew she wouldn't hesitate. I'd seen her go for the groin before—once at a would-be assailant wielding a shotgun, and several times after she'd gotten fed up with Husband No. 2.

I didn't expect Kenny to put up a fight. But I felt along the side of the back seat for the tire iron I'd stashed, just in case.

He eased his truck into a spot at the far end of the lot, where he could have vacant spaces on either side. Kenny was a fanatic about his paint job, and careful to avoid dings and scratches. This worked in our favor. If we had to get rough with him, it was better not to have to do it right in sight of the station's front door.

"What in the hell?" Henry muttered.

"Would you look at that!" Mama said.

"Let me see." I popped up my head between the two of them to get a better view out the front windshield. Kenny sported fake facial hair, dark sunglasses, and a black cowboy hat with a costume fringe of brown hair. He looked like Hank Williams Jr. after a very bad night.

"Let's go get him," I said.

Henry and Mama hurtled out the front of the car. I lost some time, looking for the safety button to slide open the minivan's automatic door. I caught up with them midway across the lot.

"Stop right where you are, Kenny." Mama's voice was as cold as the beer fridge at the Booze 'n' Breeze. "You've got some explaining to do."

I thought he might run. Instead, he turned slowly. He looked at Henry, whose big fists were clenched at his side. Henry may have added a bit of fat over the years, but he still had a lot of the muscle and speed of the high school wrestler he'd once been. Kenny's gaze moved to his mother-in-law—purse at the ready, eyes singeing him with the "Mama Glare." Finally, he focused on me, tire iron tucked alongside my thigh.

"Are y'all going to kill me?" he asked.

"I ought to," Henry answered.

I raised the iron, touched it lightly to Kenny's zipper. "I can think of a better fate for a cheating husband."

Mama put her hand over mine, lowering my makeshift weapon. "There's no need for violence, Mace. Kenny knows he's done Maddie wrong."

She turned to him, eyes searching his face. "Surely there's an explanation for all this? You don't just throw away more than twenty years of marriage."

He hung his head. The ridiculous shag-cut wig formed a curtain over his face.

Henry was blunt. "Are you involved with the swingers' club at the golf course? Is that what all of this is about?"

"How's a club to practice your golf swing related to anything, Henry?" Exasperation edged Mama's words. "Let's stay on the topic."

Kenny's face was as scarlet as the feathers on a redbird's cap. "I… I mean … I …"

"My goodness, Kenny, spit it out. There's no shame in having a bad swing. Lord knows Sal goes to the driving range to practice his all the time. He told me the swing is one of the most important elements in golf."

My cousin and I exchanged a look. "Are you going to tell Mama it's a different kind of swinging, or should we?" I asked Kenny.

Silently, he shook his head.

Henry and I took turns revealing to her what we'd discovered: About the sexual swingers' club; how the mayor and his wife were members; that Jason, the pro, and Angel, the barmaid, were also involved.

Mama's face had paled. The heavy purse hung forgotten from one limp arm.

"The reason Henry asked if Kenny was involved is that they meet out at his camp near the county line," I told her.

Throughout, Kenny's eyes had remained fixed on the parking lot pavement. At the mention of his camp, he raised his head. "I didn't invite them, and I didn't want them there. But once I got involved with ..." his voice tapered off.

"I know who you were cheating with," I said.

His head shot up. He slid off the sunglasses to look at me.

"D'Vora saw you with her in your truck out at the lake."

Mama, startled from her trance, asked, "Who's 'her'?"

"Camilla."

I heard her gasp when I said that name.

Kenny nodded. "She was at the center of the whole swingers' group, but I didn't know that. Once I started ... seeing ... Camilla, Jason threatened me. One day, when I took him and the mayor's wife out to the shooting range, he cornered me and said he'd tell Maddie about Camilla if I didn't let them use the camp for parties."

"Did you?" Henry asked.

Kenny's voice was barely a whisper. "Yes. Camilla kept pushing me to party with them, but I wouldn't do that. I only told them how to get to the camp and where I hid the key."

Henry lifted one eyebrow, the same one he used in the courtroom when he wanted the jury to believe a witness on the stand was lying.

Kenny raised his right hand. "I'm telling you the God's honest truth."

"I don't think God had much to do with this," Mama said.

"I felt awful," he continued. "All I could think was how hurt Maddie would be."

He sneaked a glance at Mama. Arms folded tight across her chest, she simply shook her head. He sniffed, knuckled at an eye.

"Unfortunately, you'll have the chance to find out just how much you hurt her," I said.

"I know y'all won't believe this, but I was only with Camilla … in that way … the one time. She started flirting around with me at the golf course. A few times, she sat down while I was having lunch or dinner. She complimented me. She tried to kiss me. It made me feel like I was young again. Sexy."

Kenny took a deep breath. His voice shook when he continued. "We hadn't had sex until that night at the lake."

"Whose idea was that?" Henry asked.

"I swear it wasn't mine. Camilla asked me to drive her to Lake Okeechobee to see the sunset. She just about jumped me when we got there, doing things I'd never dreamed a woman would do." His face reddened. "I couldn't resist."

"Was she wearing that outfit we found her in at the dump?" I asked.

I saw a gleam of comprehension in Mama's eyes. She butted in. "When exactly was this you were with Camilla at the lake?"

He'd clamped his lips shut again; his eyes cast down.

The gleam became a flash. "Oh my Lord Jesus! You're not just a cheater, you're a murderer, too." Mama clutched her throat. Her face had turned grayish-yellow. "I'm going to be sick."

And she was, all over Kenny's shoes.

FORTY

MAMA DABBED HER LIPS with a pineapple sherbet-colored hankie. She must have eaten a big breakfast, because the delicate handkerchief wasn't up to the task. I handed her a super-sized bandana from my back pocket.

I figured the vomit all over Kenny's shoes was his punishment for cheating. My cousin, though, took pity on him. He ran to his wife's minivan to get Kenny some wet wipes. It was either sympathy, or Henry had a lower tolerance for nasty smells than I did.

"How could you think I'd murder that girl, Rosalee?" Kenny scrubbed at one shoe, his voice tight with hurt. "As long as you've known me?"

Mama turned her back on him.

Henry said, "We all thought we knew you, Kenny. If I've learned one thing from all these years practicing law, it's that any man—or woman—has the capacity to surprise those who know and love them."

Kenny scrubbed even harder, shredding the paper wipe against his shoe.

"Camilla was alive when I dropped her off at her house; and she wasn't wearing any kind of black leather getup, either."

Brakes hissed in the road. A horn blared on a tractor trailer hauling sugar cane. I waited until the big truck rumbled past, narrowly missing an oblivious tourist in a rental car.

"What about the text you sent to Maddie?" I quoted it word-for-word, since it was seared into my heart the moment I'd read it: "*I did something terrible. I don't think you can forgive me. I'm so sorry.*"

Kenny's mouth dropped open. The paper wipe went still against his shoe. "That was private, Mace!"

"Yeah, well, sorry if I offended your 'privacy' by trying to help my sister patch together her shattered life."

"That message had nothing to do with anything except the fact guilt was eating me up because I'd cheated. I betrayed my wife, the only woman I ever loved. *That's* what I was saying I was sorry for!"

Mama turned, cocking her head at Kenny. Her expression told me she was judging his story.

He looked at each of us in turn. It seemed he was trying to gauge whether we believed him. I wasn't sure if I did or not. He'd shaken my faith. Not just in him, either. In all men. The fact I couldn't tell if my brother-in-law was lying troubled me more than I wanted to let on to Mama or Henry.

Finally, Mama spoke up. "I'm angry at you, son. What you did to Maddie makes you low enough to walk under a trundle bed wearing a ten-gallon hat. But I don't believe you killed anybody, either."

I heard a whoosh of air escape, as if Kenny had been holding his breath. He moved toward Mama with his arms outstretched for a hug.

"Not so fast." She took a step back. "I want to know how you're going to fix this. How much trouble is he in, Henry?"

My cousin stroked his chin, thinking. "He'd be in a lot less trouble if there was somebody else who saw Camilla after he did. What time did you drop her back home after you left the lake, Kenny?"

"Right before eight o'clock. I wanted to get back to the motel in time to watch that reality show I like about the bounty hunters."

"How appropriate," Henry said. "Let's hope you don't end up starring in a real-life episode."

I was surprised to hear Kenny had anted up the cash to get a room. It did explain, though, why I couldn't find him. Given his reluctance to open his wallet, I hadn't even thought to look for him at the handful of accommodations in the area.

"Where've you been staying?" I asked.

He pressed his lips together; put his sunglasses back on.

"Mace asked you a question," Mama said.

He turned his face my way. The sun glinted off the dark lenses of his glasses. "How do I know you're not going to send Carlos after me?"

"Believe me, if this whole mess didn't involve Maddie, you'd already be sitting, dripping sweat, in his suspect's chair." I ran my fingers through my hair; encountered snarls. "Before it becomes common knowledge, I'm going to tell my sister what's been going on. I owe her that. In the meantime, you ought to talk to Henry about the best way to frame all this when you do sit down to talk to Carlos."

Henry gave a curt nod. "Good advice." He dropped a hand on Kenny's shoulder; not too lightly, either. "Why don't you ride back to my office with me?"

"What about my tickets to the monster truck show? They said on the radio I'm a contest winner."

Henry rolled his eyes. "You're a winner all right."

"It was a ruse," Mama said. "There are no tickets."

I sent up a silent thank-you to the Lord for seeing that their daughter, Pam, inherited her brains from Maddie instead of from Kenny.

Kenny trudged along beside Henry toward the minivan. They were almost there when I called out to stop them. "Kenny, what's the name of the place you're staying?"

"The NoTell Motel."

———

My supervisor at Himmarshee Park was an understanding woman, but even she had her limits.

"Get your ass into work, girl. Your lunch hour has come and gone. I've taken a half-dozen phone messages, and now there's a teacher waiting to see you in the breezeway." Even through the cell phone's crappy speaker, I could hear the testiness in Rhonda's voice.

"I'm just pulling in now, boss. I'll be there in two shakes of a lamb's tail." My Jeep bounced over the slatted wooden bridge at the park's entrance. "I got caught up in some family trouble."

"Humph! Your family is nothing but trouble," she said.

I parked under the meager shade of a slash pine. The asphalt lot baked under a mid-afternoon sun. Sprinting through the woods, it took me just a few moments to arrive at the breezeway outside the park's office. Elaine Naiman sat on a cypress log bench, whistling off-key.

"Sorry I kept you waiting." I was a bit out of breath.

"No problem." She gave me a friendly grin. "I was just enjoying sitting under the trees, listening to the birds singing."

"Yeah, I heard you accompanying them just now."

"Hope it didn't hurt your ears. I love all kinds of music, including birdsongs. But I'm actually tone deaf. No telling how I sounded."

I flashed a thumbs up, withholding my opinion she'd never get a job as a professional whistler.

"I got your supervisor's permission to steal you for a few minutes."

I raised an eyebrow. "I'm on Rhonda's bad side today. Did she say you could keep me for good?"

Elaine smiled. "Not exactly. She said we should make it snappy so you could get some work done. For a change."

"Sounds like Rhonda."

"I'll get to the point: I've found out some things about our mayor. If you're going to fight him on that development he's pushing, you might be able to use the information as ammunition against him."

She seemed so eager. I didn't want to tell her I already had one pretty big battle on my hands. Proving Kenny was innocent of murder had to take precedence over saving Florida from another development scheme. The sad thing was, even if we stopped this one, another ill-conceived project would pop right up to take its place. Out-of-control developers were the state's version of Whac-A-Mole.

Elaine pulled a notebook from her purse and shuffled through the pages. "First, the honorable Bill Graf is into some pretty weird things."

"So I've heard. You mean sex, right?"

Her head jerked up from the notebook. Surprise showed on her face. "Yes, and it's creepy! One of my fellow teachers has a niece, just out of high school. She interviewed for a filing job in the city manager's office. The mayor followed her out to the parking lot at City Hall, and then asked if she'd consider 'hooking up' with him and his wife. It was pretty clear he didn't mean for a nice family dinner."

"What a sleaze ball.'"

"Clearly." She touched the tip of her pencil to her tongue, then made a check mark in her notes.

The door to the park's office opened. Rhonda stuck out her head. "You two found each other?"

I nodded. "I'll be in soon, and then I'm yours for the rest of the day. I'll even spread that pile of mulch on the nature path."

A city crew had dumped it, smack dab at the beginning of the path. Rhonda had been calling ever since to try to get somebody to come back to even it out. Hey, if a little manual labor would get me back on her friendly side, I was not above lifting a shovel. She shook her finger at me and closed the door.

Elaine consulted her notes again. "Next, he was connected to a business up north that got into trouble for trying to bribe some local government officials."

That I had *not* heard. It looked like the Himmarshee paper fell down on reporting the stories it ran about the candidates in our recent elections. I wasn't surprised. Newspapers nationwide were struggling to survive. The local paper was so short-staffed and strapped for the advertising that paid its bills I was amazed it still managed to publish anything at all.

"Was that case common knowledge?" I asked.

Elaine lowered her eyes, suddenly modest. "No, it was a little bitty town in Rhode Island, and the charges were pretty small potatoes. But I'm a good researcher. It's a passion of mine, along with supporting the hapless St. Louis Rams."

She paged through the notes. "The company belonged to his wife's family, so the mayor's name wasn't directly involved. No charges were filed against him, though his wife worked there when the trouble arose. Now, I can't say whether our mayor managed to cover his tracks, or he really didn't have anything to do with their business. I intend to keep looking into it, though."

"Why are you so interested in all of this?"

She looked out across the breezeway, her gaze lingering on Himmarshee Creek and then the cool greenness of the woods beyond. "You know, I love it here. I didn't like the mayor, even before he showed such disregard for the kids' safety in the parking lot. I liked him even less when I found out he had plans to bring in a lot of big development to ruin this place."

She turned to me, her eyes meeting mine. "Maybe someone else would be a better mayor for Himmarshee."

I waited for her to go on. A cardinal chirped from an oak branch, filling the silence.

"You?" I finally asked. *I* sure as hell wasn't mayoral material.

She chewed her lip. "Is that crazy?"

I shook my head. "I've heard nuttier ideas. You're smart. You show great attention to detail. You love the community, and you love kids. The town could do a lot worse."

She grinned. "Mayors here serve a two-year term. I've got time to decide."

"And gather more dirt on His Honor in the meantime." I stuck out my hand. "You've already got my vote."

We shook, and said our good-byes.

"I better get to work before Rhonda explodes." As I walked toward the office, I started making a list in my head:

Return phone calls. Spread mulch. Feed animals. Decide how to tell Maddie her husband had shagged a murder victim ...

The sound of Elaine calling me from the breezeway stopped me at the door. "Sorry," I said, "what'd you say?"

"I forgot to mention Mrs. Graf's family's business. It was trash hauling."

My hand was on the knob when Rhonda yanked open the door. The scowl on her face told me she was not happy.

FORTY-ONE

I HELD BACK MY sister's hair as she retched over the toilet in the bathroom Kenny had remodeled for her thirty-fifth birthday. I remembered how excited she'd been: They'd splurged on beautiful, custom glass tiles, forming a cobalt-blue border around the shower. The tiles were still in fine condition.

I couldn't say the same for Maddie.

She coughed, and blew her nose. Shaking, she sat back on her heels. Her breath came out as a shudder.

"You done?"

She nodded. "I'm sorry, Mace." The words were muffled by a washcloth pressed over her nose and mouth.

"Don't worry about it." I tucked a loose tendril of hair behind her ear. "I love you. What's a little barf between sisters?"

She shifted the cloth, revealing a weak smile.

I didn't mention it wasn't the first time today I'd watched one of my relatives upchuck. I hoped Kenny's behavior hadn't triggered an epidemic of family vomiting.

Earlier, at work, I'd finished my chores. I groveled until I patched things up with my boss. When not chasing down murderers or dealing with family drama, I was a reliable employee. Rhonda was a forgiving sort, usually willing to meet me more than halfway.

I left the park and headed for Maddie's house, dreading the conversation I knew we needed to have. I brewed chamomile tea and sat her at the kitchen table, where I broke the news that her husband was in fact a cheating bastard. It seemed she was taking it pretty well. Then I got to the part about the swingers' club, and how Kenny may have been the last person to see Camilla Law before she was murdered. Maddie clapped a hand over her mouth and galloped for the bathroom.

She threw up two full cups of chamomile tea, turning the water in the toilet bowl bright yellow. I flushed.

"Did you eat anything today, sister?"

She shook her head, putting two fingers over her lips to cover a burp.

"You have to eat, Maddie."

Even as I said the words, I thought how weird they sounded. Maddie never needed encouragement to eat. Usually, we encouraged her to stop. She collected herself, and began getting up from the bathroom floor. I helped her to sit on the bathtub edge. Then I gathered the balled-up, soggy tissues from the countertop, and tossed them in the wastebasket. One hit the rim, bouncing onto the floor behind the toilet. I got on my knees to pick it up. The angle brought my face right over the top of the wastebasket.

I spotted a white plastic test stick at the bottom, peeking out from a rolled up wad of toilet tissue. There was a miniature display window near the tip of the stick. A plus sign, for positive, beamed in bright blue.

The water ran in the sink. My sister brushed her teeth. My mind raced.

"Is there something you want to tell me, Maddie?"

———

We were in Maddie's kitchen again. She had a glass of room-temperature ginger ale in front of her. Outside the window, night had fallen. Maddie was so still, I could hear the bubbles fizzing in the carbonated drink.

"How far along are you?"

She rested a hand lightly on her stomach. "It can't be too far. My periods had gotten kind of irregular over the last couple of years, but I remember having one when Pam was home from college."

"So that was mid-summer, and this is September. About two months, then?"

She shrugged; sipped the ginger ale.

"What are you going to do?"

Her eyes cut me like laser beams. She slammed down the glass, sloshing soda all over the table. "I'm going to have it, of course."

"You do have choices, Maddie. A baby may not be the best thing for you right now with…"

My words trailed off when I saw her reaction. Her face darkened. Her hands flew to her stomach, as if she were shielding the embryo inside. I left the rest of that sentence unspoken: … *with a cheating husband who could be facing murder charges.*

Even if Kenny was innocent—and I wasn't 100 percent sure he was—he might have to go to court to prove it. It wouldn't be cheap, and it wouldn't be easy. You could say the same about Maddie, giving birth at her age with one problem-plagued pregnancy behind her.

"I'm having this baby, whatever else happens. After all the trouble I had bringing Pam into the world, I wasn't supposed to be able to get pregnant again. God must have a reason for sending this child my way now."

I was less devout than my sister was. I didn't give voice to the question looping through my brain: What if the Big Guy upstairs had made a mistake?

She drank some more soda, and then squared her shoulders. Her voice came out sounding strong, much more like normal Maddie. "I'll tell you one thing. This kid will never see the sad-sack version of me you've had to witness lately."

She stood and leaned toward me across the table. In her eyes, I saw a spark of the old Maddie igniting. "I'm going to do something I should have done as soon as I discovered Kenny was running around on me."

She stalked into the laundry room, returning with two empty clothes baskets. I followed her down the hallway to hers and Kenny's bedroom. She threw the baskets on the bed and started tossing in his clothes. I saw the sleeve of that fancy shirt, tangled up with several pairs of vibrantly colored men's briefs. If the phone number in Kenny's pants pocket hadn't been enough to make Maddie suspicious, those sexy "man-ties," or men's panties, should have nailed it.

When the baskets brimmed, she nodded to me. "Grab one, would you?"

I did, and trailed after her through the house to the back door. She flicked on an outdoor flood light, turned the knob with one hand, and kicked the door open. Outside, she entered the utility shed where they stored garden supplies, tools, and a grill. She tossed a can of lighter fluid in her basket, and then scrabbled on a high shelf until she found a long box of matches. She was just about to walk out when she spotted a half-empty golf bag with some spare clubs inside.

"Can you get that golf thingy?" she asked.

Shifting the basket to one hip, I hefted the golf bag over my shoulder.

Maddie marched to the fire pit in the yard. How many back-yard barbecues had I attended here, with Kenny as the attentive host?

You like your burger medium-rare, right Mace? Let me get you another beer.

Maddie turned her basket upside down, kicking everything into the hole but matches and lighter fluid. Little puffs of old ash rose around the mound of clothes.

She looked at me, waiting. I stood, considering the wisdom of what we were about to do. I remembered a similar scene in Mama's backyard, after she finally got fed up with Husband No. 2. It was childish and immature and a waste of the good money spent on the lout's clothes.

But I recalled the satisfied smile that spread across Mama's face as flames consumed the possessions of her unfaithful husband. It was the first time in months Mama had seemed like herself.

I chucked the contents of my basket onto the pile. Then I threw in the golf bag, too. As the bag slid sideways, a Florida Gators cover bobbed atop one of the golf club heads. The plush, toothy University of Florida mascot seemed to be grinning.

"Light that sucker up!" I said.

Maddie doused the pile with lighter fluid. *Scraaaatchh* went the match. *Whuuuuff* went the clothes. Once the flames really got going, I stole a glance at my sister's face. No smile in the golden glow; but her jaw was set with renewed strength.

———

Damn! I was halfway down the steps on Maddie's porch when I realized I'd forgotten to tell her that Mama and Marty wanted to help. My inclination was to bring them in. If Kenny hadn't killed Camilla, we needed to find out who had. To clear Kenny, I could use their assistance. Well, Marty's anyway. Mama's help was often more curse than blessing.

I turned back to the front door. Maddie had removed the spare key from the flowerpot once the whole mess with Kenny intensified. My hand was almost on the doorbell when I noticed something strange hanging in the place of the door wreath. I distinctly remembered the wreath being there when I arrived. As I'd waited for her to let me in, I'd straightened a silk sunflower and brushed some dust from a clump of fake berries.

Now, the point of a silver knife pinned a note to the door. From the knife dangled a black leather collar, complete with a leash. It resembled the collar that encircled Camilla's neck when Mama and I found her body at the dump. My breath quickened. Instinctively, I looked over my shoulder, scanning the dark hedges and the street beyond. All was silent. On the wooden porch, no planks creaked. No breath sounded, aside from my own.

I squinted to read the scrawled message under the knife:

Kenny's a murderer. He must pay for his crime. Try to get him off, and someone in this family dies.

FORTY-TWO

My first thought was of Maddie: *She could not see this.*

Was she in danger? I wanted to hide the threat and the sex gear, as if by doing that I could protect my sister from heartache or harm. I snatched the knife, along with the collar and leash, from the door. The note I slid into my pocket.

The fact I was tampering with evidence might have given me pause, if not for what happened next. A car door slammed, as loud as a shot in the quiet night. An engine gunned. Tires screeched. A vehicle roared past—no headlights, careering wildly from side to side on the narrow street. It was large, dark, and there was a Graf for Mayor bumper sticker on the back.

All the windows were dark in the homes of Maddie's neighbors, early-to-bed retirees with notoriously cautious driving habits. One of them might be a Graf supporter, but I'd never heard squealing tires on her street before. Was the speeding car linked to the note and kinky accessories? I raced to my Jeep, determined to find out.

Swerving into the road, I gave chase to the fleeing car. The headlamps were now lit; twin taillights glowed red in the distance. The driver blew through the stop sign at the end of Maddie's street, and turned in a wide arc onto the highway leading away from town. I paused at the sign, and then jammed my foot on the gas to follow. My Jeep shimmied trying to match the other driver's speed. The big car had a head start and greater horsepower. I was losing him.

I urged my old Jeep onward, but as the miles passed, the taillights ahead grew smaller and smaller. When they were barely pinpricks, I knew I'd never catch him. Pounding my steering wheel in frustration, I eased off the gas. No sense in blowing a valve or some other crucial engine part on a lonely road in the middle of nowhere. I pulled my purse onto the seat, and started feeling around inside for my cell phone. I wasn't sure what was going on. I didn't know how Kenny was involved. But I intended to call Maddie to tell her not to open her door to anyone—including her husband.

Picking through the purse, I felt the sharp point of a metal spike on the collar. I pulled it out, hearing the *clink-clink-clink* of the chain attached. I was fuzzy on the details of how and why people got a sexual kick out of being leashed and dragged around like a dog. In my experience with dogs, even they don't seem to enjoy it that much.

If the spiky collar was sharp, it would be nothing compared to the knife I'd also dropped in my purse. I wanted to find my phone, but I didn't want to sever a thumb. With a hand on the wheel, I dumped the purse's contents on the passenger seat. The phone slid under the seat.

Slowing, I ducked down and felt around under there. I encountered an empty cup that once held sweet tea from the drive-thru;

and something soft I hoped was a dirty sock. With the phone finally in my grasp, I straightened up again. Bright lights shone in my rear-view mirror.

"Where'd you come from?" I muttered into the night.

I moved to the right, so he could pass me. He sped up, staying glued to my bumper. When I pressed the on button on my phone, the screen lit. I quickly glanced at it. No bars. Not good.

Behind me, the driver revved his engine. Lights flashed, blindingly bright. We were alone. This stretch of highway, leading north through ranches and citrus groves, was deserted. I felt for the tire iron normally stashed under my seat. Almost at the same moment, I remembered leaving it in Henry's minivan that morning, after we confronted Kenny.

The headlight glare compromised my ability to see who was behind me. But my ears were perfect, and I knew the sound of gunfire when I heard it. A shot pinged off my right bumper. Another pop, and the mirror on the driver's side shattered. *Shit*. That was close.

I hunkered down as much as I could and started watching the dark shapes of trees and brush along the shoulder of the road. Somewhere along this desolate stretch was an abandoned cow pen. Rarely used and almost overgrown, the dirt-road cutoff to the pen was hard to see. I prayed I hadn't passed it.

With the black night all around me and the high beams behind me, I couldn't be sure what type of vehicle was chasing me. My four-wheel-drive Jeep, though, could handle rough terrain. And there it was, just ahead: A bullet-riddled sign from a long-gone ranch, a forgotten cattle brand in barely legible red. On splintered legs, only a few feet off the ground, the wooden sign served as target practice for local yahoos.

I spun to the right, plunging off the road and through thigh-high brush. I cut my lights. The Jeep went airborne over a small rise I remembered, and then clattered over the rusty grate of a weed-choked cattle guard.

On the other side, I took my foot off the gas and jounced for a hundred yards or so over a rutted dirt road. I rolled to a stop and cut the motor. At first, all I could hear was my own ragged breathing. Then, I heard the sound of an engine slowing. I heard tires on pavement, then on the rocks and grass of the road's shoulder. Was the car stopping? No, now the tires rang over pavement again. The driver had U-turned. Gaining speed on the highway, he was headed back in my direction.

I re-started the Jeep. The rutted drive intersected a sandy cattle trail. I made a hard left, gunning it through the dirt. The Jeep fishtailed a bit, before the tires gripped ground. Behind me, I saw a crazy dance of headlights over pasture. My pursuer had found the cut-off, and was bouncing up and down over the rutted drive. I kept going, all my attention focused on getting away. The note on Maddie's door had threatened death for someone in my family. I was afraid to think about how all this might end.

An engine whined behind me. I looked in the rear view mirror. The reflected glow from his headlights was dimmer now, and no longer bouncing. I kept driving. The other engine screamed; tires spun. I guessed he'd gotten stuck in the sandy trail. Slowing, I kept my eyes fastened on the rear-view. Even if his tires were snared, he might still come after me on foot.

I watched—boot on the gas, hands on the wheel, eyes on the mirror. I saw nothing ... until I felt the jolt of my Jeep ramming head-on into the galvanized steel of a pasture gate.

FORTY-THREE

In the morning, I couldn't tell if the aches in my body were from the Jeep vs. gate collision, or from passing an almost sleepless night on the splintery floor of an abandoned storage shed.

I rolled my shoulders. My spine cracked. My left elbow and knee pulsated with pain. I must have smacked them on the steering wheel when I slammed into the padlocked gate. Or, maybe they got bruised when I clambered over it, slipped on the top bar, and tumbled to the ground. It was funny how something that seemed so loose and sandy when you drove over it felt like concrete when you fell on it.

After the wreck, I hightailed it through the woods on foot until I found the old shed. I had no idea if I was being followed. But I figured the safest option was to seek a hiding place and wait it out. I'd kept a vigilant watch, clutching a rusty wrench I found in the corner of the shed. But I must have dozed off for an hour or two sometime before dawn.

Now, I peered outside through a grimy, cracked window. Light was just beginning to edge the sky. Shadows and shapes around the shed were turning into familiar objects: A fence post, encircled with a rusty snarl of barbed wire. An ancient stock tank, upside down and peppered with the bullet holes of target shooters. Mist rose from a cow pond in the distance. I was lucky I hadn't run my Jeep into *that* instead of the gate.

Limping, I made my way back to the scene of the crash. The Jeep listed to the left: Both tires on that side were flat. My satchel of a purse and most of its contents were still on the passenger-side floor, where they'd fallen when I struck the gate. I'd been in a rush, and hadn't wanted the encumbrance of a big purse bouncing against my side as I tried to run. Groping in the dark, I'd located wallet, keys, and phone. Those, I stuck into various pockets. Everything else I left where it fell.

The black leather collar and leash were gone. So was the knife. It probably came in handy for the pursuer to slash my tires.

I climbed onto the gate again, more carefully this time. More painfully, too. I balanced gingerly at the top, a foot on either side of the highest slat. I aimed my cell phone until one bar appeared. First, I called my lawyer cousin and told him to hustle up Kenny for a trip to the police station. Then, I hit the speed dial for Carlos.

———

I swatted with one hand at mosquitoes, and flagged down my fiancé with the other. Driving one of the police department's marked SUVs, Carlos pulled onto the dirt-and-weed-choked shoulder of the highway. I sneezed as a dusty cloud engulfed me. He leaned across the console and opened the passenger door, but didn't apologize for the dust storm kicked up by the SUV. His grim expression and that familiar vein throbbing at his temple almost made me turn around and run.

"Tow truck's on the way." He spit out the words, looking like each one cost him dearly.

"I'm sorry…"

He thrust out his wrist, giving me the silent signal for "talk to the hand."

"But…"

"Don't even start. There is no possible excuse. You could have been killed."

I stared at my fingers, folded across my knees. He was right, of course. And if he was this mad at me now, how would he feel when I revealed what I knew about Kenny and Camilla?

"So, this person who was chasing you—"

"—People," I said. "I left Maddie's house chasing one car. Then another car came out of nowhere and started chasing me. I'm certain the two were linked."

"That remains to be seen. But you're positive someone was shooting from the vehicle behind you?"

"Yes." I pointed to the brush-heavy cutoff. "My Jeep's through there. You can see for yourself."

"I intend to."

He eased the car over the cattle grate, and we bounced for a while without speaking. "Good thing you brought an SUV," I ventured.

He gave me a curt nod, vein still throbbing.

Pointing out the windshield, I indicated where the cattle trail intersected the pot-holed drive. "That's where I think he got stuck. I could hear the tires spinning in the sand."

The car, of course, was gone now. The driver likely had help getting unstuck.

I continued giving Carlos directions. He rolled to a stop, and parked a short distance from my Jeep. The gate was dented and bowed out, caught in my front bumper. If I'd have been going much faster, I might have driven right through it. We got out of the SUV, and I stood by while Carlos sprayed himself with insect repellent.

"Mind if I use that?"

He tossed me the bug spray. "It's a free country." The can landed in the dirt.

He pulled on a pair of gloves and went to examine the Jeep. We both were being careful to try to preserve any evidence that might prove useful. Shoeprints or fingerprints. Discarded trash or cigarette butts. Hair or a shred of fabric. He crouched to take a closer look at the tires.

"Looks like he used a knife," he said.

Now seemed as good—or bad—a time as any to confess. "I might know something about that."

Carlos barely uttered a word as I told him about the swingers' club at the golf course and the collar and knife I'd found on Maddie's door.

"You took it?"

I nodded.

"I wish you hadn't done that."

"Me, too."

"That's evidence, now gone. What possessed you?"

"I didn't want Maddie to see it."

He raised his eyes, consulted the clouds. I had the feeling he was counting to five. "I know Maddie is a bit prudish, but she's a grown woman. She's probably heard about such things before," he finally said.

He still didn't hold the piece he needed to have the puzzle make sense. Reluctantly, I pulled the note from my pants pocket. "This is what I found with the knife and the rest stuck to Maddie's door. I'm sorry; my fingerprints are on it."

"Of course they are."

He read it silently, his eyes widening. Then, he read it aloud, articulating every word:

"'Kenny's a murderer. He must pay for his crime. Try to get him off, and someone in this family dies.'"

I waited for him to say something. He just kept staring at the note.

"Remember when I told you Kenny was cheating on Maddie? The person he was cheating with was Camilla."

The pulsing vein looked ready to burst right through Carlos's skin.

———

The ride back to town felt like it unfolded in slow motion. Carlos was so angry, I could almost feel heat radiating off his body. I tried to explain. He stared out the windshield at the road—jaw clenched, knuckles white on the steering wheel. Finally, he turned to give me a glare—quick, but singeing.

"You deliberately withheld information."

"Only until I could tell Maddie. I didn't want her to find out about Kenny by reading in the *Himmarshee Times* you'd arrested her husband on suspicion of murder."

A beat-up car in front of us traveled at twenty-five miles an hour under the speed limit. Carlos pulled past as the driver nervously regarded the marked SUV in his rear-view mirror.

"The issue here is trust." He glanced at me. "I have to be able to trust you. Right now, I don't. You lied to me. You compromised my investigation. You compromised my *job*."

"I didn't lie. I just didn't tell you everything. Besides, why is all this on me?" I asked. "Maybe if I felt I could trust *you*, I would have told you about Kenny. I didn't want to test you though; make you decide between my family and a convenient suspect."

His grip tightened on the wheel.

"We all know how well that turned out in the past," I added.

"*Coño*, Mace!" He spit out the Cuban cuss word. "Are we never going to forget that incident with your mother?"

"You mean the incident when you moved up from Miami, thought you knew everything, and tossed Mama in jail?"

"When *I* thought *I* knew everything? Isn't that the frying pan calling the pot black?"

Now probably wasn't the time to comment on his grasp of popular sayings. "I don't think I know everything," I muttered.

"No, you don't think you do. You're positive you do. And that's what keeps getting us in trouble. Well, this is my job. My life. And you keep sticking your nose into it, thinking you know best."

"It's my life, too, Carlos. This is my family."

He put a hand to his forehead; squeezed that spot above the bridge of his nose where his headaches began. "Do you hear us?

Each of us says 'my.' My life. My job. My family. Are we ever going to say 'our'? Will two people who feel so separate ever be able to build a life together?"

His voice was quiet. He didn't sound angry; just resigned. I thought about his question. I didn't know how to answer it. Instead, I turned my head to look out the window. When we passed the livestock auction on the outskirts of town, I finally spoke.

"Could you drop me at Mama's?"

"Whatever you say."

With my hands on my lap, I wiggled the engagement ring off my finger. When he pulled up at Mama's curb, I opened the door and got out. "The answer to your question is no." I stood on the street, leaning into the car.

Confusion settled on his face. I held out my hand, palm open. The ring winked in the morning light.

"No, we cannot build a life together." I pushed the ring toward him. "We do seem too separate."

He stared at the ring, making no move to take it from my hand. "Close the door, Mace. Your family's waiting. I have to get to work."

Yanking his cell phone from his pocket, he sped away without a backward glance. I watched him go. In my sweating palm, I clutched our engagement ring. Was the promise it symbolized now broken?

FORTY-FOUR

"WAS THAT YOUR HANDSOME fiancé I just saw, peeling out of here like Dale Earnhardt at Daytona, God rest his soul?" Mama stepped off her front stoop and peered down the street. "How'd you make him mad this time, Mace?"

If only she knew. "I didn't do anything."

She tilted my chin so she could look in my eyes. "You're not a good liar."

I leaned against the wall to kick off my work boots at her front door. Last time I visited, I tracked a smear of possum poop across her peach-colored carpet. I thought she was going to ban me for life from Pizza Night.

Mama rubbed at a dab of dirt on the door jamb where I'd propped my hand. I pretended I didn't see her rolling her eyes.

"Who's here?" I asked.

"Me, Sal, Marty, and Teensy, of course." She smiled down at the dog, prancing around her ankles. He gave a little yip.

"So," she said, "is the engagement off?"

I'm sure my face registered my surprise. How did she read minds like that?

Mama pointed at my left hand. The ring finger was bare. I patted the pocket of my jeans; felt the prongs on the diamond through the denim fabric.

"I took it off to spread some mulch at the park," I said.

"Sure you did."

Marty poked her head out the front door. "Did you tell Mace about Kenny?"

Mama aimed a pointed look at my ring-less finger. "Don't think you've heard the last from me. We'll get to Carlos and you later."

If there still *was* a Carlos and me later.

Marty smoothed my hair; lifted out a twig. "You look like you slept in the woods, Mace."

Since that wasn't unusual, neither of them questioned my lack of response.

"About Kenny, he's staying with Henry," Marty said. "After last night's Wednesday services, they spent hours with Reverend Delilah in the chapel at Abundant Forgiveness."

Mama wet her finger with spit, and swiped at what I assumed was a streak of dirt on my face. "Because of Delilah's history, she has special expertise with cheating husbands," she added.

"What time were they at the chapel?" Images tumbled through my mind: A shots-fired car chase; me galloping through the woods, trying to escape an unknown pursuer; my long night on a hard floor at the abandoned ranch.

Marty cocked her head at Mama in a question. Mama took over the narration: "It was late, Henry said. After you and I left the radio station yesterday, Henry and Kenny spent the rest of the day at Henry's law office. They were planning strategy."

Marty added, "Henry had him spend the night, keeping an eye on him. He says our brother-in-law may be guilty of being stupid, but he's not guilty of murder."

I let out a breath I hadn't even known I was holding. If Henry never let Maddie's husband out of his sight, Kenny could not have been the person shooting at me. Now, I just had to find out who was.

"According to Henry, all Kenny cares about is getting his wife back," Mama said. "He says he's never seen a man so full of remorse."

Marty toed Teensy out of the doorway. She led the way inside and across Mama's new plastic carpet runner to the kitchen. It appeared to be completely poop-resistant. I tried not to wince as I sat down. Once we were settled, Sal carried three oversized mugs to the table.

"Coffee's just brewed," he said. "I figured you girls could use some coffee if we're going to decide how to keep Kenny out of jail."

We began to discuss strategy: Marty would discover as much as she could about Camilla from the library and Camilla's sister, Prudence. Mama would sift through the useful—and useless—gossip at Hair Today Dyed Tomorrow. Sal would grill some of his cronies at the golf course. I planned to discover who wanted to scare me off the search for the real killer.

The phone on the wall rang. Teensy started yapping. I swiveled to answer the call, and spilled my coffee when I hit my sore knee on the table. Mama jumped up to sop at the caffeinated puddle now dripping onto Marty's lap.

"It's Henry," I said, as Sal tried in vain to shush Teensy.

"What the hell's going on over there, Mace?" Henry raised his voice to be heard.

"The usual," I answered.

Mama tried to grab the phone from my hand. "What's Henry saying?"

"I'd tell you if I wasn't having so much trouble hearing him between you yammering and your ridiculous dog yelping."

Sal scooped Teensy off the floor, covering the dog's ears with his bear-sized hands. "Don't listen to Mace. She's just a big meanie. Daddy's widdle boy is not ridiculous, is he?"

Forget the dog's ears. Mine were hurting from Sal's baby talk.

"Sorry. What, Henry?" I said into the phone.

"I talked to your fiancé. He wants Kenny to come in for questioning."

I thought of Maddie. My stomach clenched. "What'd you say to him?"

"Say to whom?" Marty asked. "Say what to whom?"

"I said Kenny certainly would come in. He has nothing to hide. I told Carlos I'd be present as counsel, of course."

"Tell us what's going on, Mace," Sal demanded.

I put the mouthpiece aside and told them. "Carlos wants to question Kenny."

Marty gasped. Mama nodded. "Been there, done that," she said.

I stepped into the hall, cupped my hand over the phone, and whispered my latest news: The threatening note and my highway adventure.

"I can't hear a word Mace is saying," Mama griped.

"She'll tell us when she gets off," Sal tried to appease her.

"Mace always did try to keep secrets," Marty said.

On the phone, Henry said: "Someone's trying to frame Kenny."

"Then why are they chasing me?" I asked.

"Who's chasing you?" Mama had stepped into the hall, and was lurking beside me. I plugged my ear with a finger so I could hear Henry's answer.

"They don't want you looking into this murder," he said. "Like it or not, cousin, you've got a reputation. Kenny's a convenient suspect. Camilla's real killer doesn't want you or anyone else unraveling this particular whodunit."

Marty sidled up, tapping on my shoulder. "Ask him what time Kenny's supposed to be at the police department."

I started to repeat the question. "I heard her," Henry said. "Carlos wants to see him today at six o'clock, sharp."

"I hope he's not using the rest of the day to get an arrest warrant," I said.

"Arrested? Did Henry say Kenny's going to be arrested?" Sal shouted from the kitchen.

Mama wailed. The dog howled. Marty went pale and chewed at her lip.

"I better go," I finally said to Henry. "This is exactly how rumors get started."

FORTY-FIVE

A SKINNY BLONDE WITH bad teeth sucked on a cigarette in front of the police department. Her protest sign, message side out, was propped against a scrub pine: *No Mercy for Murderers!!*

I didn't recognize her. But there were plenty of people in the crowd I did recognize. I'd made plans to meet up at the station after work with Mama, Marty, and Sal. We wanted to be there to show our support for Kenny when Henry escorted him in to answer Carlos's questions. From the looks of the crowd, it seemed Kenny would need it.

I spotted D'Vora. When I waved, she ducked her head and got busy fiddling with the clasp of her purse. I crossed over and tapped her on the shoulder. "What are you doing here?"

"I dunno."

"Well, you must have come for some reason."

She raised her head. "I heard the cops were going to arrest Kenny for killing Camilla."

"That is not true, D'Vora! Carlos only wants to ask him some questions. He may have critical information, since he was among the last people to see her before she was murdered."

She fooled with the clasp. *Snap. Unsnap.*

"But then you knew that, right?" I asked.

Snap. Unsnap. Snap. Unsnap. Snap.

I persisted. "How'd you find out Kenny was coming in?"

"I stopped at Gladys' today for a take-out coffee. Charlene told me while I was standing at the counter, putting sugar in my cup. Her nephew's girlfriend's mama works as a police dispatcher. She said Kenny was probably guilty."

D'Vora went back to playing with her purse, while I unraveled the genesis of a ruined reputation. The mother told her daughter, who told her boyfriend, who told his Aunt Charlene, the waitress at Gladys.' She told D'Vora, and who knows how many other customers. D'Vora buzzed back to Hair Today Dyed Tomorrow, town beehive for gossip. With its usual efficiency, the Himmarshee Hotline went on to convict Kenny hours before he even showed up at the police station.

It didn't matter that he was appearing voluntarily. It didn't matter that he hadn't been charged. The killing of Camilla Law had shaken the community. The community wanted justice—preferably instant justice.

I scanned the crowd of looky-loos, perhaps a few dozen people. I was surprised there weren't more.

A TV news crew from Orlando had made the trip, drawn south by the scent of sex and violence wrapped up in one scantily clad murder victim. A couple of teenaged girls with blown-out hair and freshly glossed lips waved at the camera. The reporter was interviewing Junior Odom, a hulking man-child in bib overalls and a bare chest. Junior normally spent his days sitting on an overturned milk crate behind the supermarket, playing with a ball of string. Everyone knew he wasn't right in the head. Why did TV people always gravitate to the one person who was sure to make the town look bad?

I asked D'Vora the question right out: "Do you think Kenny did it?"

Snap. Unsnap. Snap. Unsnap. Snap ...

"Look at me!" I grabbed her hand. "Do you think he murdered that woman?"

She pulled away, rubbed at her thumb. "I know what I saw with my own two eyes: The two of them bumpin' boots in Kenny's truck. And I know about men." Her tone was defiant. "Maybe they were having sex, and things got out of hand. Maybe somebody threatened to tell Maddie, and Kenny got scared. How much do we really know about him anyway?"

I stared at her, incredulous. "He's lived here his whole life, D'Vora. I bet he sold insurance policies to your parents and *their* parents."

She crossed her arms over her chest. "He wasn't born here."

"You're right. He moved here in the third grade, from one county over."

I could see she'd made up her mind. That worried me. If D'Vora, with her ties to Mama and the rest of my family, was ready to see Kenny fry for murder, then public opinion was definitely building against him.

"Just keep an open mind, that's all I'm asking. There are things going on in this town that you would not believe. Shady things.

Suspect people. Kenny got himself caught up in some dangerous games; but I am certain someone else killed Camilla."

She raised a skeptical brow. "You're certain?"

Until that moment, I hadn't said it out loud. But yes, I *was* certain. I'd seen Kenny cradle his newborn daughter, tears of joy in his eyes. I'd watched him care for Maddie through miscarriages; through a cancer scare; through the years of them growing older and comfortable—maybe complacent? Always, I'd seen nothing from him but love for his family and kindness toward others. He may have set out to have a middle-aged fling. Many men do. But murder? No way.

I nodded. "I'm certain."

She shrugged. "Well, I guess we'll see if your detective beau agrees with you."

On that troubling thought, I went off to find Marty, Mama, and Sal. After my morning phone call with Henry, I'd provided all of them a condensed version of last night's events. I'd told them about the note and sex collar, the shooting, and my collision with the gate. All I left out was my blowup with Carlos. I couldn't even begin to explain that.

The three of them had commandeered a picnic table in the shade, where some of the police department's civilian staff liked to eat lunch. I hoped someone discovered something that would link anyone else but Kenny to Camilla's murder. I joined them, planting my flag on our pro-Kenny island amid an ocean of anti-Kenny forces.

At the TV crew's urging, Junior displayed his sign, complete with misspellings, for the camera: *A Eye for A Eye. Venjance for Camela.*

"I'm amazed he got the word 'eye' right," Sal said.

Mama tsked. "It's a good thing Maddie's not here to see all this." She pointed with her chin to the glamour-girl teens. "Those two are locals. You know they must have had Maddie for their principal in middle school."

"Maybe that's why they're standing with the anti-Kenny people." I winced as Marty pinched my arm.

"I simply cannot believe D'Vora. That traitor!" Mama harrumphed. "Look at her over there, gossiping with the stringy-haired blonde with the sign."

Heads together, the two women whispered. Whatever D'Vora revealed made the blonde rear back. Her penciled-on eyebrows arched up like arrows.

"The mood out here is pretty ugly," Marty said. "Whatever happened to the concept of 'innocent until proven guilty'?"

"Speaking of," I said, "did y'all find out anything useful today? Anything that will help prove somebody else is guilty?"

Mama spoke first. "Those sex swingers are trying to get some new members. Some gal I know from bingo came to the salon today. Told us we should start offering Brazilian waxes to take care of…" Mama cupped her hand to her mouth; lowered her voice to a whisper "… hair down there."

When Marty looked at her blankly, Mama made a ripping motion over her groin. "Apparently, being bald downstairs makes things sexier when they have an orgy."

"Rosie!" said Sal, shocked.

"I'm just telling you what she said. Anyway, she's trying to recruit some new members. She invited me to come sometime."

Sal choked, barely able to get the words out. "Absolutely not!"

Mama narrowed her eyes at him. "I don't need you to tell me no, Sally. I'm a Bible-believing, church-going woman. I don't even have to ask myself What Would Jesus Do? I can pretty much guarantee you He would not sign up for a swingers' party."

"I've got some information, too, though mine isn't Triple X-rated like Rosie's." Sal aimed a pointed look at her.

She smoothed at her hair. "Not Triple-X, Sally. One X, at the most."

When had Mama become such an expert on the relative shadings of X-ratings?

"Whaddever. I think it's relevant. We all know something has been going on out at that golf course. Kenny's been involved. Camilla was, too." Sal pulled a cigar from his pocket. "Angel and I had an interesting conversation about the club pro today."

"Angel?" Mama's mouth was tight with disapproval. "Talk about X-rated."

Sal, wisely, ignored her. "She said not to buy Jason's dumb, good-guy act. He knows a lot more than he pretends to. He pulls a lot of strings out there, Angel said, in cahoots with the mayor's wife."

"Humph! I'm not sure I trust that barmaid. She's definitely no angel." Mama folded her arms over her chest. "By the way, I hope you're not intending to light that stink-bomb cigar out here. It's sure to give Marty a migraine."

"I'm fine, Mama. Really." Marty offered Sal an apologetic smile.

He gave the cigar a last, loving stroke before he slid it back into his shirt pocket. "Angel is just a hardworking gal, trying to make an honest living."

I wasn't sure about Sal's assessment of Angel's upstanding character. But I could see a storm brewing on Mama's face. I wasn't about to let us get sidetracked by one of her jealous snits. I changed the subject.

"Marty, what'd you find out at the library?"

"Something interesting: Prudence is applying for Camilla's old job."

"And the body's not even cold? That's kind of weird," I said.

"I thought she'd be going back to Atlanta," Sal said.

Marty shrugged. "Apparently not. Prudence told my boss it made her feel close to her sister to stay in her house, right here in Himmarshee."

Mama tapped her cheek, thinking. "Hmmm. Now what do y'all make of that?"

All of us were quiet, perhaps considering the question. Something about Prudence and her sister's house tugged at my brain. She'd confessed she and Camilla were estranged. I reran the mental filmstrip of the barbecue dinner at Mama's, and the look that flickered so briefly over Prudence's face. I suspected the rift went deeper than she admitted. She wouldn't be the only person in the world to wait until a relative is dead to wish she'd reached out to reconcile in life.

As I glanced around the crowded parking lot, my attention was diverted by the arrival of Elaine Naiman. I was shocked to see her limping through the ranks of the Kenny-haters. When she waved and smiled at me, I realized she was coming over to join our small group instead. Sal got up to give her his seat.

"How's the ankle?"

"Better, thanks." She eased herself onto the bench; wiggled her foot slowly. "It's not as swollen, but it's still a bit sore."

She peeked over both shoulders and hushed her voice, like a spy trading secrets. "I've got some news."

Four expectant faces gazed at her. She gave me a quizzical look.

"They're family," I answered the question she hadn't voiced. "They know everything I know. We've all been trying to find information that will make anyone but Kenny look guilty."

"Well, I'm not sure this will help, but guess what I found out about our friend, the mayor."

"What?" Sal, Marty, and I asked at once.

Mama put a pout in her voice. "She said 'guess.'"

I felt my eyes roll. "It's not a game, Mama. It's a figure of speech. Go on, Elaine."

"He's into rough sex; and I know where he indulges his fantasies."

FORTY-SIX

THE INSISTENT BLARE OF a car horn made me jump. The protestors in front of the police department stirred. Henry piloted his Lexus through the jostling throng. In the passenger seat, a white-faced Kenny stared straight ahead.

A whisper grew into a wave of sound.

"That's him!" someone cried.

"It's Kenny Wilson, the murderer!" said another.

Mama climbed on top of the picnic table. "Y'all should be ashamed of yourselves!" She was using her Sunday school teacher's voice, and it carried across the crowd. "A lot of you have known Kenny all your lives. He is *not* the killer. He might have information the police need to find out who is. That's the only reason he's here."

Some members of the crowd looked embarrassed, eyes on the ground. Others, more bold, shouted Mama down: "Justice for Camilla!" one yelled.

Another voice rang: "No mercy for murderers!"

The hissing began as Kenny opened the car door. The volume grew, until the whole parking lot sounded like a writhing mass of snakes. Junior stepped forward, shaking his sign in Kenny's face. Henry batted it away. My brother-in-law stuck his hands deep in his pockets, hunching his shoulders as if he wanted to disappear. The skanky blonde leaned in and spat. A glob of mucous coursed down Kenny's cheek. He tilted his head, trying to wipe it off with one raised shoulder.

"Killer!" The blonde's veins popped on her scrawny neck; her voice throbbed with hatred.

The TV camera caught everything.

I was just glad Maddie wasn't there. Her husband was a pitiful sight, the very picture of shame and humiliation. Was it seeing friends and neighbors taunt and belittle him? Or, God forbid, was it guilt over what he had in fact done?

Henry and Kenny had almost made it to the entrance when the front doors swung open. Carlos stepped out. The reporter surged forward, the cameraman right behind her.

"Is Kenny Wilson a suspect in the murder?" She thrust her microphone toward Carlos, who batted it away.

"No comment."

The reporter aimed the mic again, poking it at Carlos's chin. "Are you arresting him?"

Carlos answered the question with a nonverbal glare. He took Kenny by the elbow, pushing back the reporter and the rest of the crowd with his other hand. Our eyes met. Carlos's were unreadable—as cold and dark as a cavern deep beneath the surface of a freshwater spring. My eyes, I'm sure, were sparking fury. Would it have killed Carlos to allow Kenny to walk under his own power through those police department doors?

I knew exactly what footage would lead the evening newscast: My sister's husband, being escorted through a jeering crowd by a grim-faced homicide detective. His defense attorney was plastered to his side—just like every other guilty S.O.B. hauled in to perform a perp walk for TV.

When the doors closed behind the three men, I glanced at Sal. He shook his head. "That don't look good for Kenny."

"No kidding," I said. "And I'm fixin' to do something about that."

———

Marty and I stood outside the NoTell Motel, following up on the tip from Elaine Naiman. Someone in her book club reported a mayor sighting, along with a rumor about sexual bondage, at the sleazy hotel. My sister and I decided to see if we could confirm that.

The sun was dropping in the sky. The motel's neon sign buzzed and popped, lighting up for the evening. Or, at least some of it was. With its burned-out letters, the sign read *NoT M el*. Only a few vehicles besides Marty's were parked in the lot. Beaten and battered, they all had a lot of miles on them—not unlike the beds at the NoTell.

A cluster of aluminum lawn chairs sat empty on the pool deck, their plastic webbing frayed and gaping. Cracks and weeds cut trails across the dirty gray of the deck. A couple of feet of rainwater had collected at the bottom of the unused pool—green, scummy, and harboring who knows what kind of nasty creatures. Not unlike the motel itself.

Marty slapped at a mosquito on her neck. "Lovely place."

"I don't think anyone comes here for the amenities." A roach scurried onto the deck from a wadded fast-food bag. I squashed it under my boot. "You ready?"

"As I'll ever be. Hey, Mace, when we talk to the hotel clerk, could I be 'bad cop' for a change?"

My sweet sister putting the screws to someone to extract info? "Sure," I said. "Knock yourself out."

The front door stuck when we tried to enter the lobby. Heavy rains and humidity had swollen the old wood. I gave it a kick. It inched open, making a horror-film creak. Small and dim, the lobby looked like it was lit with a single twenty-watt bulb. It stank of stale cigarettes and fried food.

An immensely fat man sat behind the counter, watching a game show on TV. He slurped from a sixty-four-ounce convenience store soda in a superhero cup. It looked like a small keg in his hand, which was boyish and surprisingly delicate. His stained T-shirt, ripped at the neck, failed to cover the bottom third of his substantial gut.

The TV switched to a commercial, and he looked up at us. "Well, two beautiful ladies. Don't see that too much here. Y'all can get a room for an hour; or pay the half-day rate and have yourselves a nice, long session of fun."

I realized he thought we were a couple. Marty must have caught on at the same moment, because her face turned as red as a cherry tomato. So much for her playing the tough one.

"We don't need a room," I said. "We're just looking for a friend of ours. Big guy. Drives a dark sedan with campaign bumper stickers."

The clerk gave me a sly smile. His nametag said Timothy. "You mean His Honor, our mayor?"

Well, that was easy.

"A police detective has already been here. I told him all about the mayor."

Marty and I exchanged glances. I'm sure my face looked as surprised as hers did.

"Carlos Martinez?" she asked.

Timothy riffled through messy stacks of papers and empty take-out containers on the counter. Extracting a business card, he held it at arm's length and squinted to read it in the dim light. "One and the same," he said. "I'll tell you what I told him. I almost had a maid quit after the last time the mayor rented a room here with a lady friend."

"Was his friend Camilla Law, the woman who was murdered?" I asked.

"Couldn't tell. When I saw the lady, she was carrying a whip and wearing nothing but black stockings with garters and some kind of hood. I couldn't see her face, not that I was looking there."

He leered, showing a mouthful of decayed and broken teeth. Must be all that soda.

"How did you come to see her?" Marty asked.

"Another guest complained to the maid about the racket they were making in that room."

"Do you get many complaints like that?" she asked.

"Not usually. Our guests tend to be ... uhmm ... tolerant." He took a long swallow from his bucket o' beverage. "That night, though, there was the sound of screaming and furniture banging. I think the other guest was scared someone was getting murdered."

That word seemed to jolt both Marty and me. The clerk clarified. "Nobody was. They were into role-playing, not bloodshed." He sucked on his straw; drew in air. Pulling a two-liter bottle of Mountain Dew from under his counter, he refilled the empty plastic cup. Now that my eyes had adjusted to the lack of light, I saw the superhero was the Hulk.

"Anyway, the maid went up and knocked at the door. His Honor yelled 'C'mon in.' She did, and got an eyeful. There he was, spread eagled on the bed. He was naked as a baby, except for a dog collar around his neck. Black fur handcuffs held his wrists at the headboard. His ankles were trussed up with black leather straps, tied to the footboard."

Timothy's cell phone rang. He looked at the caller ID, and sent it straight to voice mail.

"The maid said he wiggled his tongue at her like a snake, pumped his pelvis up and down, and begged her to join their little party."

"Ewww," Marty said.

"Exactly!" He chuckled, his laughter trailing off to a smoker's wheeze. "The maid came running into the office in tears. I don't have too many rules here, but nobody harasses my staff. Especially the ones who aren't eighteen yet."

"So," I said, "chivalry isn't dead after all."

"Absolutely. When I marched over to their room, the woman answered the door. Like I told you, she was wearing this hood deal. She said they were sorry; things had gotten a little out of hand."

"Did the mayor say anything?" I asked.

"Not a peep. His head was turned to the wall. When he left, he asked me to apologize to the maid for him, and left her an envelope with fifty bucks. He slipped me a Benjamin…"

Marty cocked her head in a question.

"A hundred-dollar bill," I said. "Ben Franklin."

"Right. He gave me the dough, and said he'd appreciate my discretion."

"Misspent money, huh?" I said.

"I told you, I don't like people messing with my staff. I don't owe him a thing. Besides, I voted for the other guy."

"Me too," Marty said.

"All that sanctimonious stuff he was spouting during the campaign about family values? It really turned me off. Turns out it was all bullshit anyway. Typical hypocritical politician."

He inhaled more soda. "Hey, would you girls like to join me for dinner? I get off in about twenty minutes."

"Naw, but thanks," I said. "My sister has to get home to her husband and I'm engaged." I held up my left hand, remembering too late I'd removed the ring after Carlos and I argued. The lack of lobby light worked in my favor. Timothy didn't seem to notice my finger was bare.

While we said our goodbyes, I dug into my pocket, my fingers touching the ring. It felt hot, somehow, like it was going to burn my skin. Why hadn't Carlos said anything about the mayor while he was lambasting me for withholding information about Kenny? Who didn't trust whom?

Marty and I were almost to the door when I stopped and turned around.

"What did the woman in the mayor's room sound like?"

Timothy thought for a moment. "Classy. Like the ladies on public TV."

"Like Masterpiece Thea-tuh?" Marty asked, doing her best Downton Abbey impression.

"Exactly." He drained the Hulk cup; wiped his mouth with the back of his hand. "She had an English accent."

FORTY-SEVEN

The Friday morning air smelled of bacon frying and coffee brewing. Marty and I stood outside Maddie's door, waiting for her to let us in.

"Maybe she's feeling better," Marty said, sniffing at the cooking smells. "I wonder if she'll have pancakes, too?"

That would be the old Maddie. She placed pancakes at the very apex of her food pyramid.

Mama parked, and hurried up the walkway to wait with us at the closed door. The kitten heels on her persimmon-colored sandals *click-clicked* all the way.

"Poor Maddie. She's probably not even able to drag herself out of bed. Hang on, girls. I think I've got one of her front door keys in here somewhere."

She'd barely begun pawing through her purse, in a matching persimmon, when the door swung open. A smiling Maddie stood on the other side—hair done up neatly in a French twist; lips colored a becoming shade of pink. She quickly waved us in.

"Bacon's about to burn. Help yourselves to some coffee."

She surely did look better. She was wearing her doing-battle-as-principal clothes—a dark, knee-length skirt paired with a powder-blue blouse in polished cotton. On her feet: No-nonsense pumps. Over her shoulder, Maddie spoke to Marty: "I haven't forgotten you, sister. Instead of bacon, I'm making you eggs for protein. The pancakes are just because we like them."

In the kitchen, Marty and I filled our favorite coffee mugs and took our seats. Mama flitted about behind Maddie, peering first over one shoulder and then the next.

"Hadn't you better turn that flapjack now, honey?" *Flutter, flit.* "Don't scramble the eggs so hard." *Flit, flutter.* "They'll be as tough as an old saddle."

Maddie glanced at Marty and me and rolled her eyes. "I think I've got it covered, Mama. Why don't you put out some plates and have a seat?" She turned again to the stove.

"You seem pretty chipper this morning," I said to her back.

I didn't add that this good mood was the last thing I expected. Maybe she hadn't seen the late news last night, which led off with her cheating husband's perp walk through shouting protestors. Maybe she hadn't talked to Henry, who'd told me Kenny had spent the night at the Himmarshee County jail. Mama, Marty and I had schemed to meet at Maddie's first thing in the morning. I'd expected us to be propping up an emotionally devastated woman. At the very least, I thought we'd be providing her with the support of her loving family.

Instead, she calmly poured batter onto a flat griddle to start another pancake. It sizzled when it met the hot pan.

"You seem surprised I seem chipper." She flattened one of the flapjacks with a spatula. "Did you expect to find me with my head in the oven?"

Mama stirred her coffee, spoon pinging against the cup.

Marty removed and re-straightened the napkins in a holder.

I contributed to the silence, my hands clasped on my lap under the table.

"Well?" Maddie prodded. "Did you think I'd keep moping around here forever? I talked to Henry last night. I know y'all are trying to prove Kenny had nothing to do with this awful murder."

She slid the scrambled eggs into a serving bowl and covered it so they wouldn't get cold. The plated bacon went into a toaster oven. Maddie turned the temperature dial to warm. When we still hadn't spoken, she cleared her throat.

"I want everybody to stop tiptoeing around me. I'm not dying of some terrible disease. I'm a wife who's been cheated on. I wasn't the first; I won't be the last. I know in my bones my husband is no murderer. He's only guilty of one thing, and that's thinking with the wrong head."

Mama nodded. "Been there, got the T-shirt. Kenny can get in line with all the other husbands guilty of that."

"I appreciate everything you've already done to find another suspect. I'm ready to pitch in, too." Maddie pointed to the answering machine on the counter. "We can start right here, right now. Listen to this."

She pressed play.

Beep. *How does it feel to be married to a killer?*

Beep. *No Mercy for Murderers!*

"Not that nonsense," she said. "This next one."

After the beep, there was a long pause. Then a muffled voice spoke: *The police have the wrong person in jail. Your husband didn't kill Camilla Law. I might know who did.*

Mama started to interrupt. Maddie held up a single finger, like a teacher warning an over-eager kindergartner.

The message continued.

I'm afraid to come forward. If I speak out, I could be a victim next. Tell your sister to keep hunting for the real killer. The swingers' club holds the key.

The message ended. "Did you punch in star-69 to see the number that called you?" I asked.

"Of course I did: 'Unknown.' It was probably one of those disposable cell phones like the criminals use on TV."

"It sounded like they were talking through a mouthful of cotton. I couldn't tell if it was a man or a woman, could you?" Marty raised her eyebrows at us.

We all shook our heads.

"Play it again," Mama said.

Maddie skipped ahead to the right call.

"Wait!" I said, listening closely. "That's definitely the sound of music; maybe some glasses clinking in the background."

"Could be a bar," Maddie said.

"Great," Mama said. "There are almost as many bars in this county as there are churches."

"Could you hear what song was playing?" Marty asked me.

I shook my head.

"You need to tell Carlos about this, Mace. The police will be able to figure out a lot more than we can from the phone message," Mama said. "When are you going to see him next?"

I took a sip of coffee. Blew on it, and then sipped again.

"Oh, no!" Mama grabbed my left hand and dragged it out from under the table, where I was hiding it in my lap. She waved the ring-free digit at my sisters. "I knew it!"

I didn't want my sorry romantic saga to distract us from helping Maddie. "We have not broken up, Mama. Things are just a little tense between us. It might be better if Sal tells Carlos about the phone call."

Mama dug in her heels, looked like she was ready to argue. "But—"

"—Enough!" Maddie slapped the table between us, startling Mama and me. "As fascinated as we are by Mace's on-again-off-again engagement, my husband is being slandered as a murderer. Is it too much to ask that we focus on finding out who really killed Camilla, so we can clear Kenny's name and bring him home?"

Marty raised her coffee cup in a salute. "Hear, hear."

Maddie rested her hand on her belly for an instant. I doubted that Marty or Mama caught the protective gesture. They didn't know her secret yet. She got out syrup and butter for the table; and served our pancakes from the griddle.

"By the way," Maddie said, "the party is still on for tomorrow night. I'm going to hold my head high and call it 'Free Kenny Wilson Night.' Maybe we can force the real murderer to show his hand."

She doused her pancake with syrup, scooped up a mess of eggs, and passed the bowl to me.

As I helped myself, the pieces of a plan to unmask Camilla's killer began to take shape.

FORTY-EIGHT

"Have you spotted anybody yet? Tell me what you see, Mace."

"Thanks for the spit shower." I dried the inside of my ear, and returned Mama's whisper. "And, no, I haven't spotted anybody. It's the middle of the night, and cloudy. I can barely see."

"Are you sure this is the right spot for the swingers' soiree?" She spritzed my ear with each shushed *S*.

"You can speak up. It's clear we're all alone."

We'd driven to a secret location at the country club, stashed her car behind the closed restaurant, and took cover in the shadows of the golf cart barn. Jason had called while I was at work to invite me to the gathering.

I'd groaned into the phone. "You start at three o'clock in the morning? Are your pals vampires as well as swingers?"

"You asked me to let you know when the next party was. Well, this is it. I'm sure you'll find it worth your while."

He'd revealed the closely guarded details: On arrival, guests were to knock four times, pause, and knock once more. The code word for the night was *Dandelion*. The group would meet in a large apartment kept for visiting golf pros, located beside the shed where electric carts were charged and stored.

"We have to make sure we're not accidentally discovered. As you can imagine, these kind of parties call for absolute discretion."

"As discreet as you can be stark naked," I said. "By the way, if I do come, I won't be taking off my clothes. I'll only be there as an observer."

He laughed. "That's what they all say."

My Jeep was still being processed by the cops. It hadn't taken much effort to persuade Mama to drive me to the golf course, especially after the message on Maddie's machine implied the swingers were the key to everything. I wanted to find out more about them, especially the mayor. I had a hunch he was involved in Camilla's murder. I needed to know how.

I stood now at the front of the cart shed, watching the entrance to the vacant parking lot. Mama was half-concealed behind a boxy silver machine that dispensed practice balls for the driving range. I had no intention of showing my hand—or anything else—until we'd staked out the situation.

Mama reminded me—again—of her ground rules for our reconnaissance mission: "I am *not* taking part in any of that funny business."

"And you think I am?" I said.

"I don't know what you're up to now that you've broken things off with Carlos. Maybe you're in the market for a little excitement."

"First of all, I haven't broken it off. I told you we're taking a rest. And second, I'm not interested in that kind of excitement."

"Don't knock it until you've tried it, Mace."

Once I finished sputtering, I planned to pursue that line of inquiry with Mama. Just then, though, I heard a car approach. I raised my hand to signal her to hush. "Head's up. Here's our first guest."

Stepping out from behind the ball dispenser, she craned her neck to peek around me.

A second car followed close behind the first. In the flash of its headlights, I saw the mayor's shapely "aide" climb from the front seat of the first car. Another young woman, the one who'd been interviewing for a job in his office, got out of the back. When the driver exited, I was not surprised to see it was Angel. She caressed the cheek of the mayor's aide, and gave the job-seeker's bottom a friendly pat. The aide—Ruby? Diamond?—adjusted a halter top, hefting first one breast, and then the other. Her already considerable cleavage was now pumped up to its most flattering display. Licking her lips, Angel grazed her fingers across the aide's chest.

"I knew there was something fishy about that barmaid!" Mama hissed.

The trio teetered toward the apartment in tight tops, micro-minis, and impossibly high heels. Angel unlocked the door and stepped in first. Light flooded out through the windows.

Five guys piled out of the second vehicle, a red SUV. The smell of men's cologne and cigar smoke wafted our way as they made their way to the apartment. The SUV was familiar. I'd bet it was the same one that terrorized us and several other drivers along the stretch of highway near Hair Today Dyed Tomorrow. I also recognized the tallest man in the group as the developer with the gold watch who had visited Himmarshee Park with the mayor. I'd wondered that day about his smirking innuendoes about threesomes and foursomes. Now they made sense.

I scanned the cluster of men, recognizing a couple more from the day at the park. The mayor was not with them. Jason hadn't shown yet, either. The tallest man counted out the requisite five knocks. "Dandelion," he said, and the door opened.

Next, a convertible sports car roared up. I thought it might have been a Porsche; a car not often seen among the pickups and dilapidated beaters driving the local roads. A well-preserved, silver-haired couple extricated themselves from the low-slung seats. The man's ample stomach made me wonder how he could fit behind the wheel to drive. The woman wore something short, tight, and golden. It shimmered in the light from the windows as they approached the porch.

"Do you know them?" I asked in a low voice.

Mama shook her head. "Probably drove up from Palm Beach. With that hair, she'd look better in silver sequins than gold."

"I'm sure she'd appreciate the fashion tip. Maybe you can write a column for the newspaper: What to wear to a sex party."

A sharp poke on the arm made me shut my mouth.

The man from the sports car rapped five times, and whispered the code word. Angel answered the door. She draped a hand over each of their shoulders, welcoming them. Her fingers slid down their chests, giving each what looked like a nipple tweak. The woman tittered; her date returned Angel's pinch, goosing her in the rear end.

"How many are in there now?" Mama asked.

I tallied up the swingers: the mayor's gals, Angel, and the granny from the Porsche made four women. The old broad's beau and the five guys from the SUV made six men. I held up both hands, ten fingers outstretched.

"Quite a get-together," Mama said.

"No Mr. or Mrs. Mayor, though. I expected to see them."

She stepped around me, her eyes searching the dark parking lot. "Maybe they're still on their way."

I glanced at my watch: Three-twenty-five.

"I think everybody's here. I'm going a little closer. They might talk about Kenny, or the murder. I want to be able to see, or at least hear, what's going on inside."

From what I'd seen so far, Camilla's murder seemed to be the last thing on the party guests' minds.

"Are you sure you want to do that, Mace?" Mama grabbed my wrist.

"Don't you want to find out what they do?" I asked.

"I can guess," she said. "I know where all the parts go."

After a bit of arguing, I finally left Mama hiding in the cart barn. I crept to the apartment, trying to skirt the light shining from the windows. Stealthily, I mounted the steps to the porch. I stopped in my tracks when the bottom stair creaked behind me. A ripple of fear rolled down my spine. My breath caught in my throat. Slowly, I turned ...

... and saw Mama, her hands over her mouth and her eyes as wide as saucers. "Sorry," she whispered through her fingers. "I changed my mind."

The creak may have given me a scare, but I doubted if anyone inside heard it. The music was loud, and so was the chatter. A male voice boomed, "Take it off!" Shrill, girlish laughter followed.

I pulled Mama onto the porch. Holding tight to her elbow, I propelled her to the darkest corner. We both inched along the side of the wall to a spot by a window. I pointed at my eye, then at the window, motioning her to look inside. At the same time, we both peeked through the glass from our respective corners. Mama gasped. I may have, too.

The two girls from the mayor's office were naked from the waist up, writhing in an erotic embrace. The silver-haired fox from the Porsche was the male filling in the middle of their female sandwich. Mrs. Silver-Hair watched from a couch, fiddling with what looked like metal clamps on her bare breasts.

One of the suits tossed off his tie. He'd just begun to unbutton his dress shirt when I felt something jab into my lower back. "Stop it, Mama."

"Stop what?"

I felt the pressure again, more insistent this time.

"No sense in standing outside looking in. Why don't you and your mum come in and join the party?"

The voice was clipped and ice-cold. The accent was English.

FORTY-NINE

Prudence Law glared at Mama and me. She repeatedly slapped the palm of her hand with what looked like a horse-riding crop. She was dressed in a getup very similar to what her murdered sister wore when we found her body at the dump: leather bustier with laces and studs, black stiletto heels, and fishnet hose. Instead of the spiky dog collar, though, Prudence wore a severely symmetrical wig, in neon blue. Black fur handcuffs hung from one of the many silver buckles on her bustier.

It looked like the conservative dark suit and the white blouse with the Peter Pan collar had been moth-balled for the evening.

"Well?" She traced the swell of my breasts with the tip of her leather crop. "Are you interested in *coming* inside?"

She lowered the crop, stroking at my groin. "You can take the meaning of that verb either way you want."

"Not tonight." I stepped back, crossing my arms over my private parts to block the crop. "Not ever."

"Not so fast, honey." Mama took a quick peek through the window. "I'm not saying you should go inside, but that tall one with the gold watch is kind of cute. Just keep him in mind as a Plan B man if you and Carlos don't get back together."

"Sure. He's a developer *and* a sexual deviant. We sound like a match made in heaven." I folded both arms over my chest and looked at Prudence. "I'm not interested in your little party or my mother's notion of Mr. Plan B."

She raised an eyebrow at Mama. "What about you? Interested?"

Mama smoothed her hair. "I don't need to get my kicks with this kind of thing. My husband, Sal, is *very* satisfying in the sex department, thank you very much. I've always loved a man who isn't afraid to—"

"—I think we've got enough information, Mama." I turned to Prudence. "Nice outfit. Did you find that in your sister's closet?"

A flicker of sadness crossed her face. Tears welled in her darkly shadowed, heavily made-up eyes. I felt like I'd just kicked a kitten. A dominatrix kitten, but still.

"Sorry. I'm just surprised to see you here. I thought you told us at dinner that dangerous sex was Camilla's deal, not yours."

An image of Prudence making herself at home so quickly in Camilla's house flashed into my mind. I suddenly knew what had been nagging at me. "In fact, you seem to act a lot like Camilla. You know a lot about her, too, considering you were so estranged."

She and Mama looked equally perplexed.

"What are you driving at?" Prudence said.

"You told me you'd never been to Camilla's house, yet you knew exactly where to look for her booze. That hidden bottle opener, too."

"Our parents always kept their liquor on the top closet shelf. It seemed likely Camilla would, too. As for the other, my sister and I lived together when we were younger. I constantly misplaced the bottle opener until she thought of putting it out-of-the-way, on the wall side of the fridge."

As I stared at her, something about her costume tugged at my brain. Exactly what remained just out of reach. I gestured at her sexy garb, and asked a general question instead. "What about those clothes, and being here tonight? You were very clear Camilla was the one with dark tastes."

Mama nodded. "Mace is right. When you came to dinner, you said you disapproved. 'For such a clever girl, Camilla could be quite stupid.' That's what you said about your sister."

Now, both of us stared at Prudence. She wouldn't meet our eyes. Her head was down, and that bright blue wig cloaked her face. She traced a figure eight against her thigh with the leather crop.

Suddenly, I had an epiphany. "Did you want to *be* Camilla, the golden-girl sister?" Mama gasped as I blurted out the question. "You're going to live in her house. You've asked for her job at the library. Did you kill your sister to take over her life?"

Prudence's head snapped up. "So I'm the evil twin? You can't be serious."

The incredulous look on her face and her derisive tone made me feel less sure of my theory than I'd felt a moment before. Mama's sharp pinch didn't help my confidence, either.

"I think you've internalized a plot from some insipid show on your American telly."

A long sigh escaped Prudence's lips. They were colored blood-red, and outlined in an even darker shade. "The truth is my sister's murder has reminded me of thoughts—desires—I thought I had extinguished."

Quietly, she knuckled away tears. They left streaks of ultra-black mascara under her eyes. We waited for her to continue. Not even Mama uttered a word.

"Camilla and I did things like this regularly when we were young. We dressed alike." She waved the crop up and down, indicating her leather garb. "We role-played. Sometimes I was the dominant one; sometimes she was. Sometimes, we both were. We liked that best. Being subjugated by identical twins excited men...us, too, to be honest."

"I've always heard English men have a thing for being spanked. Is that true?" Mama asked.

"Where in the world did you hear that?" I said.

"Around," she answered, with unsatisfying vagueness.

"It is true," Prudence said, "but it's not just English men."

Mama's eyes got wide. "Well, who else—"

I cut her off before she could begin inquiring into the sexual practices of all the member states of the United Nations. "How can you party with these people?" I asked Prudence. "One of them might have killed your sister."

She narrowed her eyes. "From what I hear, your brother-in-law killed my sister. I expect he got carried away. Some people aren't capable of knowing when to stop." The chilly tone had returned. "Not that it will bring back Camilla, but I take some comfort in knowing he'll be punished. I understand Florida employs an electric chair."

"Not anymore," Mama said. "They retired Ol' Sparky from Death Row after a couple of condemned men caught fire during their executions."

"How barbaric." Prudence shuddered.

"We give them the needle now," Mama added.

"Kenny is not getting the needle, because he didn't do it," I said. "If one of my sisters had been murdered, I'd be out trying to find out who killed her. I wouldn't be dressed up like Halloween for a swingers' session."

Prudence glared at me, crop hitting leather-clad thigh.

"Now, girls…"

Prudence interrupted Mama, words exploding from her mouth. "The point is your sister was *not* murdered. Mine was. I needed a distraction from my grief. A release, if you will. When Angel asked me to come tonight, I leapt at the chance to lose myself for a few hours."

Mama nodded agreeably. "That's certainly understandable."

"Whose side are you on?" I asked her.

Ignoring me, Mama lowered her voice and nudged Prudence in the ribs. "So, what will y'all do in there?"

"Wouldn't you like to know? There's only one sure way to find out." She pointed to the door with the riding crop.

I sneaked a peek through the window. The granny was kneeling in front of one of the suits. He wasn't wearing his suit.

If I were alone, I might have considered going inside, partly out of curiosity and partly to see what I could find out about this crowd. But with my Sunday-school-teaching mother in tow? No way. Before Mama could barge through the door, I answered for both of us.

"We'll take a rain check. Would you do me a favor, though? Ask Angel to call me as soon as she can. I'd like to know a little bit more about tonight's invitees."

"Angel's the one with all the answers." Prudence struck a mysterious tone.

"Not Jason?" I asked. "He's the one who told me to come tonight."

She snorted. "Jason is a pretty boy-toy, nothing more. Angel calls the shots."

She placed the crop under Mama's chin, lifting her face. "So you're curious about spanking, are you?" She stared into Mama's eyes, affecting a strict headmistress voice. "Have you been a bad girl, Rosalee?"

"Never!" Mama said.

Prudence smiled, switched to her normal voice. "You're supposed to say yes."

"Okay, yes."

The muscles flexed in Prudence's slender arm, as taut as steel cords. The crop made a *swish* as it cut through the air. She brought it down, hard, against Mama's bottom.

"Ouch!" Mama's hand flew to her rear end. "That's not sexy. It stung like a nest of wasps."

"Pain is pleasure, Rosalee. Remember that." Prudence tucked the crop under one arm and lit a cigarette. A curl of smoke rose.

"That was not pleasure; it was pure pain." Mama rubbed her butt. "I can tell you one thing. If Sal spanked me that hard, I'd knock him out with a frying pan. That man never even leaves a mark."

I put my hands over my ears. "Have you never heard the phrase, 'Too Much Information,' Mama?"

———

Jason did not show, and neither did the Grafs. We stayed on the porch until the party inside moved to a more intense phase. I heard the slap of Prudence's crop against naked flesh. There were muffled shrieks and moans of pleasure. The music switched from loud rock to seductive rhythm and blues. "Let's Get it On," indeed. When the light through the windows dimmed, I took that as our exit cue.

Crossing to the parking lot, I slid a small penlight from my pocket. "Got anything to write with?" I whispered.

Mama dug in her purse, pulling out a pen and a bank withdrawal slip. I shone the light on the Porsche, reading off the license numbers as she wrote them down. Sure enough, the tag holder advertised a luxury car dealer in Palm Beach County. We moved around to the other vehicles, recording each tag number. I may have come to look for the mayor, but I found several other people who shared his kinky tastes. Registered owners of vehicles are public records in Florida. I had no intention of relying solely on Angel to reveal the invitees on her party list.

I needed their names for my suspect list.

FIFTY

"I'm as full as a tick on a fat dog. Why'd you let me have that second piece of butterscotch pie, Mace?"

"I didn't put a gun to your head. I told you it wasn't a good idea to follow a big breakfast with a double serving of pie at four-thirty in the morning."

"I just want to climb into my nice soft bed and go to sleep." Mama yawned.

We'd been wound up after our excursion to the swingers' soiree. I suggested a trip to the twenty-four-hour truck stop in Sebring for ham, eggs, and hashed browns. I'd taken over driving halfway back to Himmarshee. As I looked across the front seat of Mama's big convertible, I saw her eyelids fluttering, and her head dropping down toward her chest.

Now, the radio was turned up and the windows were rolled down. I told her she had to stay awake and talk to me until I got us to my house. I already regretted that, and we weren't even halfway there.

"What do you think you'll do about Carlos? Is it over for good? Do you think you'd be in this situation if you'd taken my advice?"

"Hmm?" I said, acting distracted. "This mess with Kenny is really on my mind. I thought we could go over who we think are likely suspects to have killed Camilla."

Mama took up the challenge. "My money's on the mayor. He's as sleazy as they come, playing around with all those different girls."

I told her what Marty and I had discovered about his S & M encounter at the NoTell Motel with a woman with an English accent.

"That seals it," she said. "His partner had to be Camilla. They were involved in some kind of sexual game. It got out of hand. He accidentally killed her, but he couldn't report it. Not with him spouting off all during his campaign about family values. So, he dumped her body to get rid of the problem."

I knew she could be right. Still, I felt there was more to the story of the mayor and Camilla than we knew.

"Who else had a good reason to want her dead?"

"You mean besides Kenny?" Mama asked.

I cut my eyes at her. "Obviously."

"I'm just trying to think like your former fiancé would. And speaking of that, I have some ideas about how you could win Carlos back."

"Could we attend to the matter at hand?"

She slid across the bench seat and placed her finger with the giant wedding ring over my left hand. "This is the matter at hand. Your *ring-less* hand."

"Mama, could you please focus on your other daughter? Her marriage is on life-support. If we let Kenny go to prison, it's like pulling the plug. They won't survive that."

I thought about Maddie's unborn child, and his or her absent father. I thought about that child, growing up with a convicted murderer for a daddy. I would not let that happen.

"Suspects," I said. "That's what we need to concentrate on."

"Okay, what about the swinging barmaid, Miss Hotsy Totsy what's-her-name?"

"Angel."

"Never was a name more inappropriate."

"You just don't like her. Admit it."

"True. But consider this: Angel was queen bee of the swinger set when Camilla moved in and started taking over. Camilla was younger and prettier. Plus, she had all those moves she learned with her twin sister. Angel was jealous. She killed Camilla so she could get back her power again."

I scanned the oncoming lane. Seeing no traffic, I pulled around a pokey tractor. "Hmmm, that scenario has potential. But Angel seems more like a manipulator than a murderer. If she wanted somebody to disappear, she'd design an elaborate plan or trick someone else into doing the dirty work. She's smart that way."

The country station on the radio started playing Hunter Hayes' song, "Wanted." I was quiet for a couple of moments, thinking. "Let's go to the other end of the intelligence scale. What about Jason, the golf pro? He invited me to party with the swingers tonight, and then never showed up. Why?"

Mama punched the radio to find another station. "Who knows? Maybe he fell asleep and slept right through it. We would have too, if I hadn't set three alarms to wake us. Who starts a party at three o'clock in the morning? I've never heard of such a thing."

I was about to say she'd never heard of a swingers' party, either. Then I remembered her comments about spanking and Brazilian waxes, and I kept my mouth shut. If it turned out Mama knew more about swinging than I did, I didn't want to know why.

"There's more to Jason than meets the eye," I said. "I got the impression he has some real feelings for the mayor's wife."

"No way!"

I nodded. "If nothing else, that shows he's more complicated than some golf course gigolo, out for a good time and a few extra dollars."

The sky outside was still dark. I tuned the radio away from talk and back to country music. Mama aimed the rear-view toward her so she could check her lipstick.

"What about Mrs. Mayor?" She pursed her apricot lips. "Maybe Jason had a thing with Camilla and Beatrice was jealous. She certainly looks strong enough to strangle a little bitty thing like Camilla."

"Yeah, she's a big'un all right. But she's out of shape, and flabby in the arms and shoulders. Moving the body by herself would be a challenge. She would have needed help."

Mama tapped her cheek, considering. "Didn't Elaine do all that research and find out Beatrice's family was in waste hauling up north? She'd know how things work at the dump."

"What's to know? At our dinky dump, you pretty much drive up and dump. It's not one of those state-of-the-art 'solid waste landfills.' "

Drumming my fingers on the steering wheel, I kept time with Carrie Underwood's "Good Girl." We were all alone on the lonesome road. An image came to mind of me fleeing in my Jeep, pursued and under fire.

I thought of the mayor's wife, talking about shooting skeet. I remembered the receptionist saying the hunting trophies in His Honor's office had actually been bagged by Mrs. Graf.

"You know," I said, "Beatrice Graf is an excellent markswoman. It could have been her shooting at me, trying to scare me away from looking into the murder. If the mayor was fooling around with Camilla, Beatrice could have killed her because she was jealous. Or, she might have been afraid he'd compromise his political standing. No political standing for him, no high profile for her as the First Lady of Himmarshee. That'd be a reason for her to want Camilla out of the way."

"I don't see that," Mama said.

"Why not?"

"First of all, she's fooling around herself, with that fine-looking Jason. Being jealous about the mayor would be like craving hamburger after you've filled up on filet mignon. Second, didn't she say she'd been out of town when we found the body?"

"That's what *she* said; the mayor acted like he didn't agree. I didn't confirm the alibi."

"Let's hope Carlos has. Before you broke up, he might have told you that kind of information."

I looked at her sideways. "On what planet? Bizarro world? Carlos never shares any information with me. Besides, we are not broken up."

I tried to sound more certain about that than I felt.

We were both quiet for a time. The re-tuned engine of Mama's vintage car purred. The tires thrummed on the highway. The fresh scent of a sudden rain shower blew in through the open windows. The rain passed so quickly, I didn't bother to close them.

"What was that crazy thing you said, accusing Prudence of killing her sister? That was rude, Mace. Even for you."

"Prudence would be even ruder, if she did murder her sister." In my mind, I saw her sitting in Camilla's home, waiting for the bank to call. "She stands to inherit her sister's estate. Money has always been a powerful motivator."

I slapped the steering wheel. "Dammit! I just remembered another thing that bothered me about her. Remember dinner at your house, when we were talking about her sister? When Prudence mentioned the collar Camilla was wearing when she was killed, she said 'complete with O ring.' The police report never described it so specifically. How'd she know?"

Mama waved a dismissive hand: "A fetish collar is a fetish collar."

I wasn't so sure about that, but I didn't want to pursue my mother's familiarity with fetishes. I summed up instead: "How much do we know about Prudence anyway?"

"We know she was in Atlanta when Camilla was killed."

"Right." I rubbed my eyes. "I'm so tired, I'm not thinking straight about anything."

Suddenly, I smelled the dump more than I smelled the damp air of dawn. I knew we were getting close to the county line. My little cottage wasn't far beyond that. Maybe I'd be able to grab a couple of hours of sleep before I had to be at work at ten o'clock.

I flew past a garbage truck, idling on the shoulder of the road.

"That truck's out early," I said.

Mama yawned.

"Crap! Did I forget to put out my cans? No, wait. This is Saturday."

A bigger yawn.

We passed the next couple of miles in silence. In my periphery, I caught Mama nodding and blinking, trying to stay awake. My own eyeballs felt like somebody had scuffed them with sandpaper. Slowing as I neared the turnoff to my house, I maneuvered the convertible onto my oak-lined drive. That brought her back to life.

"I-I-I wi-wi-wish yo-yo-you'd ge-ge-get th-th-this dr-dr-drive-way pa-pa-paved."

"Stop being such a baby," I said.

Easing Mama's car into my front yard, I killed the engine. She immediately pulled her smart phone from her pantsuit pocket. "I'll just be a minute," she said. "My phone's almost out of juice, but I want to text Sal. I'm going to tell him I'll be on my way just as soon as I stop at your house to tinkle."

"WTMI, Mama. Waaaaay Too Much Information. Why didn't you go before we left the truck stop?"

"Did you see those toilets? I decided to hold it. I don't have to go too bad now, but I sure will by the time I drive home. You live out in the boonies, Mace."

"Yes, by design. I'm exactly thirteen miles from you. My lucky number."

She stuck out her tongue. I stood there waiting for her, until I realized she was still typing.

"You know, you could have used the bathroom already and been on your way if you didn't have to tweet your every movement."

"I'm not tweeting. I'm texting."

"Whatever. I'm going to bed." I tossed the keys I was holding through the window and onto the floorboard.

She waved me off. "Sal's up. He's texting me back. You go ahead. I'll be right in."

As I left, she was still in the car. Head buried in her phone, she was texting like mad.

The sun hid below the horizon, but a pink and yellow glow began to color the sky. An early-rising mockingbird sang a welcoming tune. I whistled a few notes in return, letting Florida's feathered symbol know I appreciated the cheerful greeting.

I was just about to open my front door when a shot blasted out from the woods. Everything that unfolded next happened really fast.

I heard a hiss, and smelled propane gas.

Mama yelled, "Take cover, Mace!"

My eyes flicked toward her. An instant later, they took in the sight of an above-ground propane tank in the side yard. I barely registered the sound of a second shot, before I saw a flash of light sparking through the air. Mama hit the ground, next to her car. I screamed her name.

I heard nothing in reply except the boom of the propane tank exploding.

FIFTY-ONE

ARE THERE ROCKS IN heaven?

I hoped not, because several sharp stones jabbed into my back and butt. The ground beneath me was hard, and damp with morning dew. Smoke billowed in the air. Fire popped and crackled, burning a small outdoor shed next to the propane tank. The tank itself was gone: Blown to bits.

I raised myself to my elbows, checking to see which body parts hurt. They all did. The joints still moved, though. Familiar images began to form in blurry focus. There was my purse on the ground, twenty feet away. Had I tossed it there, or did the explosion send it flying? I saw Mama's car, seemingly intact. The passenger door stood ajar.

Mama!

She'd dropped to the ground when the shooting started. Was she hit? Where was she now?

I struggled to my knees and blinked, trying to clear my vision. Something warm and wet coursed down from above my eyebrows.

I rubbed my hand across my eyes. Even in the dimness of dawn's light I could see blood coating my palm. A jagged hunk of white metal, now scorched black, lay near where I landed. It looked like a shard from the propane tank. Was that what hit me?

Pulling a bandana from the pocket of my jeans, I pressed it to my scalp. It came away moist, but not soaked. Gingerly, I worked my fingers from one side of my head to the other. Nothing poked back at me. No obvious fragments were embedded there.

I began crawling on all fours toward Mama's car. Halfway there, I felt strong enough to try to stand. My legs wobbled. A wave of dizziness washed over me. I stood there swaying, as I squinted to see through the smoke and hazy light. Haltingly, I walked to the convertible, where I hung onto the door for support.

Mama was not where I'd seen her last, flat on the ground beside her car.

Wide tire tracks criss-crossed the yard. Whatever had made them was heavy enough to sink deep into wet grass. Black mud oozed up, filling the tread marks. As the smoke from the shed fire began to disperse, I noticed another smell. Familiar... stinky... garbage. Several small piles and black plastic bags dotted the ground like odoriferous ant mounds. Images started connecting in my brain: The too-early garbage truck, out-of-place as it idled near my home. The dump, where Mama and I had found Camilla's body. Beatrice Graf's family business.

Someone had taken Mama, and I thought I knew where. I prayed I wasn't too late.

———

The convertible swallowed the road. I was grateful for all eight cylinders. Mama's keys had been on the floorboard, right where I dropped them. Her cell phone was under the car, near where she'd hit the ground. Had she consciously hidden it? Or, did the phone land there because she'd been shot?

I pressed my boot against the accelerator, urging an ounce more speed from the old Bonneville. I wasn't sure how long I'd been unconscious, but I didn't think it was long. The sun was still low on the horizon; the sky only dimly lit.

I grabbed Mama's phone: The battery indicator was in the red zone, for almost-out-of-juice. I started to call Carlos … when my mind blanked. I'd phoned him by name on my speed dial for so long, I couldn't recall the digits. My fingers scrabbled across Mama's key pad to find the names of her favorite contacts. There was Sal, at the top. I felt a tug at my heart when I saw that I was second on the list. If Mama was safe, I vowed never to avoid her calls again.

I pressed to dial Sal, and the call went straight to voice mail. I fought to keep the panic from my voice. "Listen carefully. The phone's nearly dead. I'm northbound on State Road 98, on my way to the Himmarshee dump. Whoever killed Camilla ambushed us at my house. They've got Mama, probably in a garbage truck. Call nine-one-one. Call Carlos, and tell him to meet me there … and Sal? Please tell Carlos I'm sorry, and that I love him."

I rang off before he could hear the lump in my throat squeezing my words.

Barely slowing, I swung a sharp left onto the road that led to the dump. Everything on Mama's front seat went flying: cell phone; tissue box; bottled water. Some loose golf clubs in the back clattered to the floorboard. Sal had been trying to teach Mama a few basics of the game.

I saw taillights just ahead. Gears ground. Air brakes hissed. The noisy truck was stopping, silhouetted by a mountain of trash beyond. I cut Mama's engine and pulled off the road, coasting to a stop behind a stand of cypress trees. It immediately occurred to me I had no weapon and no strategy beyond the element of surprise. I jumped from the car, and my eyes lit on the golf clubs. Choosing the one with the widest, heaviest metal head, I sprinted along a line of trees toward the truck.

————

Creeping up from behind, I could see a heavy tarp thrown across the open hopper at the truck's rear. It was a gaping metal bin, where the contents of household cans were tossed in by the garbage guy who normally rode on the back. On this morning, I saw just one person with the truck: the driver, who had opened the door and was about to climb from the cab. The reflection in the truck's side mirror revealed a dark baseball cap, pulled low over the driver's face. In sunglasses, baggy slacks, and a loose, long-sleeved shirt, it could have been anyone.

Even when the driver stepped to the ground and shut the door, I still couldn't tell who it was. The clothes were shapeless, and his—or her—hair was tucked up under the cap.

At the back of the truck, no movement disturbed the tarp. My heart pounded. Was Mama hurt under there? Worse, was she dead?

As the driver crossed in front of the cab, I raced to the truck's left side. My breath rasped out in gasps. I hoped they didn't sound as loud as they did in my own ears. Peering under the truck, I watched booted feet moving on the other side, from front to right rear. I situated myself alongside the huge tires, careful to hide my own legs there in case the driver happened to glance underneath.

The boots stopped at the right rear corner of the truck.

In that instant, I knew my mother's fate. The controls for the compactor were on the right rear. The driver planned to crush Mama like ninety-eight pounds of household garbage. I placed my hand against the truck's fender and said a silent prayer. "Hang on," I added, hoping Mama would sense my presence. "I will not let you get trashed."

I bolted around the back of the truck. The driver's hand was within inches of the control lever. Raising the club overhead, I swung with all my might. The sweet spot struck solidly. Howling with pain, the driver staggered backward. The hat fell off, revealing a full head of blonde hair, kissed daily by the sun on the golf course.

Jason.

"The cops are right behind me," I said. "You won't get away. Don't make it any worse by hurting someone else."

He reached with his left hand to pull the lever. I wound up and swung again. The club slammed his wrist with a sickening thud. Jason squealed like a pig caught under a gate. Keeping one eye on him, I pounded the side of the truck. "Can you hear me, Mama? Give me a sign you're okay."

Only silence came from inside. That bastard Jason managed to smirk at me, even through his pain. I aimed the club straight at his head. "Don't think I won't knock you into a coma," I said. "Now, get down on the ground and stay down."

With Jason seated on the roadway, and my club within reach, I pulled off the tarp. The hopper brimmed with loose garbage and lumpy plastic bags. I poked my hand in, searching for anything that felt human.

A muffled *mmmppfff, mmmppfff* issued from the trashy depths. I dug frantically, tossing out trash bags as I went. My hand encountered the familiar shape of a kitten-heeled sandal. Empty. Somewhere in there was its matching persimmon mate, hopefully attached to the intact foot of my unharmed mama.

Casting out pizza boxes, clumped kitty litter, and the spoiled, slimy remains of what seemed like an entire salad bar, I unearthed a rolled-up carpet. A hank of platinum hair stuck out of the top. Panting with effort, I hauled it out. I was thankful for Mama's petite build and my years of lifting hay bales and feed bags. As gently as I could, I lowered the rug to the ground and unrolled it.

"*Mmmppfff! Mmmppfff!*"

Duct tape covered her mouth, and bound her hands behind her back. Crushed taco shells and wet clumps of something unnaturally orange clung to her hair. A crab claw hung over one ear.

"This will hurt," I warned, as I ripped the tape from her face.

She gulped in a couple of deep breaths and then shouted, "It was Prudence! She and Jason were in on it together. She's the one who blew up your propane tank!"

So it *was* the evil twin. I knew it.

FIFTY-TWO

I poked Jason in the leg with the golf club. When he wouldn't look at me, I poked him harder. "Where's your girlfriend, Miss Fragile English Rose, now?"

He shrugged.

"Guess this means you're not going steady with Beatrice Graf."

His face was hard, absent of all traces of the flirtatious, good-time guy. "I want a lawyer."

With my pocketknife, I sliced the duct tape from Mama's wrists and ankles. We found the rest of the roll in the garbage truck. I taped Jason's feet together to make sure he wouldn't run. His club-pummeled hands were blowing up like balloons, so I didn't bother taping them.

I detected sirens, wailing faintly in the distance. Thank God, Sal had gotten the message. The cavalry was on its way. Jason heard the sirens, too. He leaned back against the truck's tire and dropped his head to his knees.

I turned my attention to Mama. "How'd you end up in the truck?"

"Right after the explosion, I was still under my car. I saw Prudence come running, carrying a rifle in one hand and a bright red flare gun in the other. About the same time, this big ol' garbage truck rumbled into your yard. She crouched over you, real calm, and checked you out. Then she shouted to the truck, 'She's alive.' My own heart started beating again once I heard those words."

Mama's gaze focused on the rug on the ground. She waited a beat, and then continued.

"I heard Jason's voice call out, 'What about the old lady? Where is she?' Prudence looked surprised. She probably thought you'd dropped me off and were coming home alone."

"'Old lady?'" I repeated. "I should have let *you* hit Jason with the golf club, Mama."

She gave me a weak smile. "It didn't take long for them to find me under my car. In that haughty tone, she told Jason to 'take care of the witness.' That was me, Mace!"

Breathing through my mouth, I pulled her close for a hug. I plucked the crab shell from behind her ear, and finger combed a chunk of what looked like rotten pork from her hair.

"When he rolled me up and tossed me in that truck, I saw my whole life flash by. Buried in trash was not the way I'd planned to meet my maker."

"It was your mother's fault for being there, you know."

I glared at the newly verbal Jason.

"We only planned on scaring you by making the propane tank go boom. It was supposed to be a warning to keep away from the murder investigation, just like the note on your sister's door. But I noticed there were two of you in the car when you passed my truck on the highway. We couldn't leave your mother behind to tell the cops."

The sirens sounded closer.

"It won't be long before Mama and I both get to do that," I said. "I've got it all figured out. You and Prudence conspired together to get rid of her sister. She probably had some kind of serious grudge against Camilla, who was better than her at everything. Plus, Prudence stood to inherit. You like women with money, so the two of you were a match made in heaven."

"What about the garbage truck?" Mama asked.

"Jason had Beatrice Graf wrapped around his finger," I said. "He must have convinced her to pull some strings and let him use the truck." I could hear the certainty in my own voice.

He smirked at me again. "You think you're so smart, but you don't know shit."

"Language, son," said Mama, ever the Sunday school teacher.

Tires screeched on the highway. Sirens screamed. The first of several cop cars sailed onto the turnoff to the dump. Carlos's car was the second one in line. Prudence sat in the back seat, her face impassive. Sal's gold Cadillac brought up the rear of the police parade.

I pointed with the golf club at Prudence. "Looks like your girlfriend didn't get far. She was probably trying to run when Carlos caught her. He's good at getting people to confess. By now, she's probably given you up, too."

Jason's mouth was set in a grim line. Where were his adorable dimples now?

FIFTY-THREE

CARLOS SLAMMED ON HIS brakes. Prudence stared out the opposite window, as if bored by the scene in front of her. She seemed to be dressed for a morning hunting pheasants on the English moors, sporting a ladies' tweed shooting vest over a crisp white blouse.

With a glance at his suspect in the back, Carlos got out and strode toward Mama and me.

"Are you two okay?"

Worry clouded his eyes. The touch of his hand, stroking my face, was warm. But his voice was colder than I thought it would be. Had Sal delivered the last part of my phone message?

When I didn't answer immediately, Mama jumped in: "We're fine. Though I think you should check Mace for injuries, slowly and thoroughly."

I felt my face flush. Was Mama really trying to promote some hanky-panky with her would-be murderer waiting to be arrested? I was encouraged, though, to see the hint of a smile cracking through the granite of my ex-fiancé's jaw.

"I'm okay." I gestured toward Jason, who ducked when he saw me point the club. "He might need some medical attention, though. I whacked at both his hands to stop him from compacting Mama into a trash cube."

Sal had arrived. He hugged Mama tight, and then bent to look at Jason. "That left wrist might be broken. Remind me not to stand too close when you're swinging your way out of a sand trap, Mace."

I must have looked at him blankly, because Mama translated: "This club's called a sand wedge, honey." She touched the broad head. "You use it to try to get the ball out of a sand trap, a shot that has become unfortunately familiar to me."

I'd had enough golf for one day. I jerked a thumb at Carlos's back seat. "Did the evil twin confess?"

"No. She says she knows her rights. She asked me for a 'barrister.'"

"Her boyfriend said the same, except he wants a lawyer," Mama said.

Carlos crossed his arms over his chest and focused on me, unsmiling. "You know this carelessness of yours is almost criminal. It's a pattern. You had no business putting yourself and your mother into danger."

The lid that kept my temper from boiling over began to rattle. After what Mama and I had just been through, I expected him to wrap me in his arms and comfort me. I hadn't expected to be berated.

"They're the ones who came after *us*," I said. "We were minding our own business, returning home after a nice breakfast at the truck stop."

"Yes, after you showed up at a sex party to 'investigate.' Camilla clearly thought you were getting too close, which set this morning's events into motion. That much I learned before she quit talking."

"Prudence." I corrected him.

"No." He shook his head. "I said it right the first time. The murder victim was Prudence, the out-of-town sister. The killer was Camilla, the librarian."

I stared at the woman in his car. She looked back, eyes cold as stones.

"Say what?" Mama tilted her head sideways and shook it. "I must have gotten some garbage juice in my ear. I thought I heard you say the murdered sister was Prudence. Wasn't she still in Atlanta when Mace and I found Camilla dead at the dump?"

"Not according to data from Prudence's cell phone." He held up his own phone as a visual aid. "That showed she arrived in Himmarshee two days before you discovered the body. Prudence was likely strangled by Mace's pal, Jason, aided and abetted by her own sister, Camilla."

I thought of the days of anguish we'd been through, when it looked like Maddie's husband might have killed Camilla. Now, it turned out Camilla wasn't even dead? Steam started rocking the lid on my temper pot.

"How long have you known this?"

Carlos shrugged. "Suspecting something and getting the information I need to prove it are two different things."

"How long?"

"A couple of days after you found the body. Neighbors in Atlanta saw Prudence packed and leaving for Florida last week, well before the call went out to her cell phone as Camilla's emergency contact."

His gaze shifted briefly to the back of his car. His suspect stared back coldly.

"I contacted some of the twins' old friends in England, who revealed how deep their rift really was. Camilla hated Prudence. Prudence was their parents' favorite, and more accomplished at everything than Camilla was. She'd been jealous of her sister her whole life."

"And knowing all this, you allowed Kenny's name to be dragged through the mud, despite how fragile my sister's marriage is right now?" My voice had gotten louder.

Sal put a hand on my arm. "That's police work, Mace. Sometimes you have to keep a false impression about guilt and innocence hanging out there to lure in the bad guy. Or girl, in this case."

I whirled to confront Sal. "Did you know, too?"

He shook his head. Mama said, "You can't expect Carlos to share everything about his investigations with you, Mace. People's lives could be at stake."

"So you're on his side?"

Mama gave me the same sad look I'd seen when she had to tell me my childhood dog was dead, fatally kicked by a horse. "Honey, this is Carlos's job. There shouldn't be a 'his side' and 'your side' to this. If you keep seeing things that way, maybe you're right. Maybe you aren't ready to be married."

Carlos cleared his throat. "Speaking of my job, I need to get these two processed."

Mama, Sal, and I watched as he read Jason his rights. He called over two more officers to help load him into the back of a squad car, since he couldn't properly walk with duct tape around his ankles. When they were done, Carlos returned to his own car. Without a goodbye, he drove away with Camilla.

Did I want to question Sal? Did I want to know? I decided I did, even if it was humiliating or painful.

"Thanks for getting the message to Carlos," I said. "Did you tell him everything I asked you to?"

Pulling at his collar, Sal aimed his gaze on the ground. "I told him everything, Mace. Including that you were sorry and you loved him."

"And what did he say?"

Sal mumbled something, his eyes avoiding mine. Mama nudged him to repeat it. I was sorry when he did.

"He said he wished he could believe you."

FIFTY-FOUR

A HAPPY BIRTHDAY BANNER flapped over the entrance to the VFW hall. A cake in the shape of a monster truck dominated the room, minus the words Maddie once planned for the top—*To the World's Best Husband*. A disc jockey spun some of the birthday boy's favorite country tunes: "Bubba Shot the Jukebox"; "Mud on the Tires"; and "Lifestyles of the Not So Rich and Famous."

Marty had pulled the DJ aside earlier, asking that his playlist not include "Whose Bed Have Your Boots Been Under?" or "Your Cheatin' Heart."

Maddie looked resplendent, yellow dress and all. She sipped a soda as she welcomed the party guests. Her husband had been sprung from his holding cell after the true suspects were arrested. Carlos told the reporter for the *Himmarshee Times* Kenny had been kept overnight at the jail "for his own protection." The newspaper didn't publish over the weekend, but word of Kenny's innocence had already spread over the unofficial hotline.

Some of the same people who'd wanted to hang Kenny for murder showed up to see if my sister would kill him for cheating instead.

He sat in a chair against the wall, accepting birthday wishes and half-truths from friends who claimed they knew all along he didn't do it. Every few minutes, his eyes shifted toward the wife he'd wronged. Maddie had on her game face, but I knew she'd need time before she'd trust him again, completely. Camilla had manipulated Kenny, pushing all the right buttons for male pride and ego to lure him into her plan. Still, the fact he'd made any progress on the road to forgiveness was probably due to Maddie's condition.

Before the party started, she revealed to Mama and Marty that she was pregnant.

"I knew it!" said Mama, after hugs and congratulations were exchanged. "A mother can always tell."

"Get real," I said to her. "You had no idea. You were blaming some bad Brunswick stew for Maddie's nausea."

"That's not how I remember it," Mama said airily before rushing to fetch Maddie a ginger ale.

D'Vora arrived an hour late with the infamous Darryl. She looked lovely in a glittery red dress. He, on the other hand, sported a wrinkled Western shirt, jeans with a can of dippin' tobacco in the rear pocket, and boots so crusty they looked like he'd been out stomping cow patties. When he headed straight for the bar, I cornered D'Vora: "Glad you could make it."

Her eyes were glued to the pointed toes of her red high heels. When she finally looked up, a tear spilled onto her cheek. "The whole thing was so confusing, between what I saw in Kenny's truck, and what everybody was saying. Then, his mug shot was on TV. He looked awful guilty."

I waited to see if she was done.

"I'm sorry. I should have listened to you, Mace." She sniffled, and wiped her eyes. "I'm going to apologize to Kenny, too. He was never anything but nice, and I was quick to jump to conclusions, like everybody else."

I was ashamed to admit that same tendency applied to me.

We both looked across the room at Maddie and Kenny. She'd walked over to join him, and he leaped up to settle her into a chair. Maddie didn't look wedding-day happy, but she didn't look thunderstorm angry, either. As she sat, Kenny put a hand on her shoulder. She gave it a brief pat, instead of knocking it off.

D'Vora sighed. "I wish just once Darryl would act sweet to me. I better go find him before he gets drunk and falls into a food platter."

After D'Vora left, I studied the scene around me. Elaine Naiman made an appearance, shaking hands and introducing herself to party-goers. I could definitely see her running for mayor. Big Bill Graf and his wife may not have committed murder, but they were up to their naked asses in the swingers' circle. That kind of sinfulness would go over during a campaign like a stripper at a church supper. Elaine would be a shoo-in.

Mama regaled a group of guests with her garbage-truck adventure.

"I'll never be able to wear my persimmon pantsuit again. It's completely ruined."

Mercifully, my phone rang so I didn't have to re-hear the already familiar story. My heart sank when I saw it was an unfamiliar number. Not Carlos. He hadn't returned any of the messages I'd left.

I moved away so as not to disturb the crowd, and then clicked on the call. Glasses clinked and music played on the other end. Suddenly, I knew who'd called Maddie's answering machine to say Kenny did not commit the murder.

"Hey, Angel."

"How'd you know it was me?" She seemed surprised.

"Sounds like the 19th Hole. Are y'all busy?"

"Slammed. I just called to tell you I'm glad the real culprits were arrested. Camilla played me like she did everyone else."

The scene with the picture album at Camilla's house ran through my mind. She'd paged through the photos, describing the more accomplished twin. Everything she said applied to Prudence—the sister she'd envied, hated, and finally murdered.

"Did you know Camilla was pretending to be Prudence?"

"I suspected, but I wasn't sure until she came to the swingers' party. Camilla had a scar ... well, let's just say it was in an intimate spot. I saw it that night. Even before that, I tried to tell you to keep looking for the killer."

"I appreciate that."

"I would have said more, but I was afraid. Camilla could be vicious."

"Obviously."

"I've got to get back to the bar. I hope you come in sometime to visit. I'll buy you a beer."

"Sure," I said, though both of us knew I was lying.

As I hung up, I saw Mama was coming to the conclusion of her story. Clasping her hands behind her back, she spun two or three times, apparently acting out being rolled up in the rug. She gave a couple of short hops, her feet together as if bound.

"What in the world is she doing?" Marty had sidled up next to me.

"Performing the tale of the day she almost got trashed," I said. "Either that, or dancing the most unfortunate bunny hop ever."

Marty gave a soft chuckle, before her expression shifted to something more serious. "I'm sorry about you and Carlos, Mace. Mama told me things aren't so great between you."

She gently lifted my hand, looking in vain for the engagement ring. I patted my blazer pocket with my right hand. Foolishly, I was still carrying around the ring.

"Is Carlos coming to the party?"

I shrugged. "I think I've really screwed things up. I left messages, telling him I'm sorry and I don't want to lose him. But I haven't talked to him since this morning, when he sped off with Prudence … I mean Camilla … handcuffed in the back of his car."

"Well, at least she's used to handcuffs," Marty said. "How do you suppose the murder happened?"

Mama stopped beside us to butt in: "This is how some of the swingers say it went down. Camilla had the whole thing planned. She talked her sister into a visit so they could reconcile."

"Maybe she gave Prudence the diamond bracelet as a peace offering," I said.

"Then she got her to dress up as a submissive for old time's sake. She hooked her up with Jason, saying he liked to role-play being dominant," Mama added.

"That set Prudence up to be strangled," I said. "She picked Kenny as a convenient suspect, jumping his bones in a public place so someone would be sure to notice."

Mama said, "Camilla told Jason to make the rough sex serious—and fatal."

Marty's eyes had begun to widen at "some of the swingers." By the time Mama said "rough sex," my little sister was sputtering: "How in the world do you know so much about this kind of thing, Mama?"

"Honestly Marty," I said, "that's a part of the mystery you may not want solved."

George Strait's "I Cross My Heart" started playing. Sal came and whisked Mama onto the floor for a slow dance. Marty went to find her husband, Sam, to do the same. To my surprise, Kenny and Maddie were also on their feet, swaying to the love song. George had just gotten to the part about making all the dreams come true, when I smelled sandalwood and spices.

Carlos must have rushed to get to the party before it ended, because his hair was still damp. A dab of shaving cream nestled near his ear. I wiped it off. He straightened my collar, which had bunched at the neck of my blazer. His touch made my breath catch in my throat.

"*Buenas noches, niña.*"

"Good evening to you too," I managed to say. "Did you get my messages?"

"All of them." He smiled. "You're very determined."

"What can I say? I'm in love."

Side by side, we watched the dancers. Maddie and Kenny had inched imperceptibly closer. When the song ended, Kenny's fingertips rested for just a moment on Maddie's belly. I couldn't begin to imagine the emotions each read in the other's eyes.

Carlos leaned toward me. His breath against my cheek was warm. It smelled sweet and delicious, like *flan* and Cuban coffee. "Looks like Kenny is forgiven."

"Not yet," I said.

"Do you think they'll get there?"

I nodded. "I do, eventually. I guess that's how people in love are. They may argue. They may even disappoint each other. But they don't give up, even if it takes some time."

"Kenny loves her. He'll give her all the time she needs."

I turned to face him. "Are we still talking about Maddie and Kenny?"

He traced the outline of my lips, his fingers as light as butterfly wings. I felt a shiver from my mouth to my toes.

"We're talking of whatever you want to talk about." His voice was husky.

"You mentioned time…" I let the word trail off as I took the ring from my pocket. As he watched, I slipped it back onto my finger.

"What about time?" He whispered, his lips brushing my ear.

"It's the right time." I ached to be with him; to finally be one with him. "Reverend Delilah is here tonight. What do you say we choose a date and ask her if she'll marry us?"

His eyes searched mine. He must have found what he was looking for, because he pulled my face to his for a kiss that made my feet feel like they were floating high above my head.

"What are we waiting for?" he said.

He put his arm around my waist. Together, we walked toward the minister who would unite us forever as husband and wife.

THE END

Charles Trainor, Jr.

ABOUT THE AUTHOR

Like the characters in her Mace Bauer Mysteries, Deborah Sharp's roots were set in Florida long before Disney or South Beach came to define the state. She does some writing at a getaway in the wild region north of Okeechobee, and some at the Fort Lauderdale home she shares with her husband, Kerry Sanders. A former *USA Today* reporter and native Floridian, she knows every back road and burg, including some not found on any state maps. The little town of Himmarshee may be fictional, but the rodeo-and-ranches slice of Florida that inspires it is both authentic and endangered.

www.MidnightInkBooks.com

From the gritty streets of New York City to sacred tombs in the Middle East, it's always midnight somewhere. Join us online at any hour for fresh new voices in mystery fiction.

At midnightinkbooks.com you'll also find our author blog, new and upcoming books, events, book club questions, excerpts, mystery resources, and more.

Midnight Ink Ordering Information

Order Online:
- Visit our website www.midnightinkbooks.com, select your books, and order them on our secure server.

Order by Phone:
- Call toll-free within the U.S. and Canada at 1-888-NITE-INK (1-888-648-3465)
- We accept VISA, MasterCard, and American Express

Order by Mail:
Send the full price of your order (MN residents add 6.975% sales tax) in U.S. funds, plus postage & handling to:

> Midnight Ink
> 2143 Wooddale Drive
> Woodbury, MN 55125-2989

Postage & Handling:

Standard (U.S. & Canada). If your order is:
> $24.99 and under, add $3.00
> $25.00 and over, FREE STANDARD SHIPPING

AK, HI, PR: $15.00 for one book plus $1.00 for each additional book.

International Orders (airmail only):
> $16.00 for one book plus $3.00 for each additional book

Orders are processed within 12 business days. Please allow for normal shipping time. Postage and handling rates subject to change.

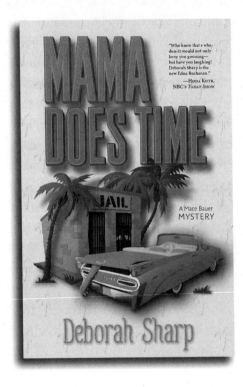

"Who knew that a who-dun-it would not only keep you guessing—but have you laughing! Deborah Sharp is the new Edna Buchanan."
—HODA KOTB,
NBC's *Today Show*

A *Mace Bauer*
MYSTERY

Deborah Sharp

Mama Does Time
Deborah Sharp

Meet Mama: a true Southern woman with impeccable manners, sherbet-colored pantsuits, and four prior husbands, able to serve sweet tea and sidestep alligator attacks with equal aplomb. Mama's antics—especially her penchant for finding trouble—drive her daughters Mace, Maddie, and Marty to distraction.

One night, while settling in to look for ex-beaus on *COPS*, Mace gets a frantic call from her mother. This time, the trouble is real: Mama found a body in the trunk of her turquoise convertible and the police think she's the killer. It doesn't help that the handsome detective assigned to the case seems determined to prove Mama's guilt or that the cowboy who broke Mace's heart shows up at the local Booze 'n' Breeze in the midst of the investigation. Before their mama lands in prison—just like an embarrassing lyric from a country-western song—Mace and her sisters must find the real culprit.

978-0-7387-1329-8, 336 pp., 5³⁄₁₆ x 8   **$13.95**

Mama Rides Shotgun
Deborah Sharp

Mama's fixin' to marry husband number five. But before she does, she convinces daughter Mace to saddle up for some country-gal bonding on the Florida Cracker Trail. The six-day ride is going fine until wealthy rancher Lawton Bramble keels over in his Cow Hunter Chili.

A one-time beau of Mama's, Lawton Bramble had a bad ticker and tons of enemies. Mace has her doubts about natural causes, along with a long list of suspects who might have "spiced" the cattleman's chili. Mace's worried sisters Maddie and Marty join the ride, as does her sexy ex-beau, Detective Carlos Martinez. With—or despite—their help, Mace is determined to corral this killer.

978-0-7387-1330-4, 336 pp., 5³⁄₁₆ x 8   **$14.95**

Mama Gets Hitched
DEBORAH SHARP

According to Mama, a *Gone with the Wind*-themed wedding—including a ring-bearing Pomeranian—is just fine for her fifth trip down the aisle. But what's a bridezilla to do when the caterer is murdered? Thanks to the nonstop gossip train in their small Florida town, Mama's gator-wrestling daughter Mace is getting the dirt on who did it. Prime suspects are two East Coast Yankees: the bridegroom's cousin, C'ndee, who's sorely lacking in Southern charm and her gorgeous nephew, Christopher, whose family may be linked to the Mafia.

978-0-7387-1922-1, 336 pp., 5³⁄₁₆ x 8   **$14.95**

NOV -- 2013